The Secret Book
of Frida Kahlo

The Secret Book of Frida Kahlo

A Novel

F. G. Haghenbeck

Translated by Achy Obejas

ATRIA PAPERBACK

New York • London • Toronto • Sydney • New Delhi

ATRIA PAPERBACK
A Division of Simon & Schuster, Inc.
1230 Avenue of the Americas
New York, NY 10020

Copyright © 2009 by F. G. Haghenbeck

English translation by Achy Obejas

English language translation © 2012 by Simon & Schuster

Originally published in the Spanish language in 2009 by Editorial Planeta Mexicana, S.A. DE C.V.

Illustrations provided by Editorial Planeta Mexicana, S.A. DE C.V.

First Atria Paperback edition September 2012

ATRIA PAPERBACK and colophon are trademarks of Simon & Schuster, Inc.

Note to readers: The recipes included in the main body of this book are meant to add flavor to the story, not to be made. If you are interested in cooking some dishes inspired by Frida Kahlo, please refer to the recipes at the back of the book.

For information about special discounts for bulk purchases, please contact Simon & Schuster Special Sales at 1-866-506-1949 or business@simonandschuster.com.

The Simon & Schuster Speakers Bureau can bring authors to your live event. For more information or to book an event, contact the Simon & Schuster Speakers Bureau at 1-866-248-3049 or visit our website at www.simonspeakers.com.

Manufactured in the United States of America

10 9 8 7 6 5

Library of Congress Cataloging-in-Publication Data

Haghenbeck, F. G. (Francisco Gerardo)
[Libro secreto de Frida Kahlo. English]
 The secret book of Frida Kahlo : a novel / Francisco Haghenbeck.—1st Atria Books trade paperback ed.
  p. cm.
  I. Title.
PQ7298.418.A34L5313 2012
863'.7—dc 23   2012045561

ISBN 978-1-4516-3283-5
ISBN 978-1-4516-3284-2 (ebook)

For Luis and Susy with love
Because they know how to delight in life's pleasures

FRIDA'S SECRET BOOK

Among Frida Kahlo's personal effects, there was a little black book called "The Hierba Santa Book." It contained a recipe collection for offerings on the Day of the Dead. According to tradition, on November 2 the departed have divine permission to return to Earth, and they must be received with altars filled with Aztec marigolds, sweet pastries, photographs from long ago, religious postcards, mystically scented incense, playful sugar skulls, and votive candles to illuminate their path to the next life. The altars must also be strewn with the departed's favorite dishes. When the little black book was found in the museum on Londres Street in the beautiful Coyoacán neighborhood, it was instantly a cherished treasure. It was to be exhibited for the first time in a monumental exhibition at the Palacio de Bellas

Artes on the anniversary of Frida's birth. Its mere existence confirmed her passion for building her famous altars to the dead.

But the day the exhibition opened to the public, it was discovered that the notebook had vanished.

CHAPTER I

That night in July wasn't like any other; the rains had gone, leaving a starry sky free of careless clouds weeping tears on the city's residents. Occasionally, a slight breeze whistled like a mischievous child playing in the trees surrounding the imposing blue house slumbering in the warm summer night.

It was precisely on this quiet summer eve that a constant drumming rolled through every corner of the Coyoacán neighborhood. A horse's hooves clip-clopped against the cobblestone streets. The echo of its steps rang out on every corner and in front of the tall tile-roofed homes to warn residents of the visiting stranger.

Curious, because Mexico City was already a modern metropolis far removed from its archaic fables and provincial legends, the residents of Coyoacán interrupted their suppers to peek at the mysterious rider who came in on a cool summer breeze more appropriate to the dead or to apparitions. A mad dog barked at the stranger, which didn't bother the beautiful white steed, much less its driver: a sullen horseman dressed in brown with holsters bearing loaded guns crisscrossing his chest. His large straw hat was like a church dome, completely obscuring his face. The only things visible through the shadows were his startling bright eyes and a thick mustache that extended beyond the sides of his face. As he rode by, the elders double-locked, bolted, and barred their doors; they still had fearful memories of the Revolution, when strangers brought ruin and desolation.

The horseman came to a stop at the corner of Londres Street, in front of an indigo house whose all-cobalt façade made it stand out in the neighborhood. The windows looked like giant eyelids on either side of the door. The horse was a bit nervous but calmed down when the man dismounted and tenderly petted its neck. After adjusting his hat and holsters, the stranger swaggered toward the door and pulled the cord to ring the bell. An electric light flicked on and the entire entryway was immediately lit up, revealing an army of moths humming desperately about the spotlight. When Chucho, the houseboy indispensable to any respectable home, stuck his head out and saw the visitor, the man stared straight at him and took a step. Trembling, the houseboy let him in after crossing himself several times and murmuring a few Hail Marys. Without a word, the visitor crossed the hall with giant strides until he reached a marvelous courtyard decorated with artisanal furniture, exotic plants, and pre-Columbian idols. The house was full of contrasts. Objects reminiscent of painful and happy memories, of past dreams and current nightmares, all managed to coexist. Everything spoke of the private world of the owner who waited for the caller in her room.

The newly arrived guest walked through each room with the confidence of someone who knew them by heart. On his way, he ran into a huge cardboard Judas with a thick baker's mustache, which would not be revered on an Easter Sunday but would serve instead as a model for one of the owner's paintings; he strolled past grinning sugar skulls; he passed Aztec mortuary figures and a book collection cloying with revolutionary ideas; he crossed the living room that had sheltered artists who had changed a nation and leaders who had transformed the world, but he never looked at the old and familiar photographs of previous tenants, or at the paintings with colors that leapt like rainbows drunk on filmy mescal, until he reached the wooden dining room table, feeling nostalgic for the easy laughs and the noisy get-togethers of yesteryear.

La Casa Azul was a place to welcome friends and acquaintances with pleasure. And the horseman was an old friend of the owner's, which is why when Eulalia the cook, saw him, she ran to the kitchen lined with shiny Talavera mosaics to get him a drink and prepare some snacks. Of all the rooms in the house, the kitchen was where its heart beat, where the inert edifice came to life. Much more than a simple abode, La Casa Azul was its owner's sanctuary, refuge, and shrine.

La Casa Azul was Frida herself. It housed all her life's memories. It was where portraits of Lenin, Stalin, and

Mao Tse-tung serenely shared space with rustic altar pieces for the Virgin of Guadalupe. Her collection of porcelain dolls (survivors of various wars), naïve crimson carts, cubist hand-shaped earrings, and miraculous silver pieces—to bless favors granted by saints—flanked Frida's brass bed. Everything gave testimony to the forgotten wishes of the woman sentenced to live nailed to a bed. Frida: patron saint of melancholia, woman of passion, painter of agonies, who remained in her bed, her gaze on the mirrors that silently struggled to reflect back her best image: the artist, dressed as an indigenous woman from Oaxaca, a Zapotec, or in an array of all the different cultures of Mexico. The harshest of all the mirrors was the one above her bed, which insisted on displaying the theme of her entire body of work: herself.

When the stranger found the bedroom, Frida turned her anguished face, and their eyes met. She looked extremely thin and tired. She seemed much older than her half century of life. She had a faraway look in her coffee-colored eyes, aimless because of the many drugs she was shooting up to keep the pain away—and because of the tequila in which she marinated her lovesickness. Those eyes like dying embers, which had once been fiery flames when Frida spoke of art, politics, and love, were now distant, sad, and—more than anything—weary. She could barely move; an orthopedic corset held her prisoner, restricting her freedom. Her only leg moved nervously in search of its companion—the one that had been amputated months before. Frida stared at her visitor, recalling their previous encounters, each

4

one tied to a misfortune. She had been desperately waiting for this meeting, and when the room filled with the smell of the countryside and wet earth, she knew that the Messenger had at last responded to her call. The Messenger continued to simply stand by, letting his gleaming gaze rest upon her delicate and broken body. They didn't greet each other; old acquaintances can be forgiven for dispensing with useless niceties. Frida merely lifted her head as if to ask how things were going in his part of the world, and he responded with a slight tug on his hat that indicated everything was just fine. Then, irritated, Frida called for Eulalia to attend to her guest. Her screams were rude and vulgar. Her old humor, flirty and quick, had been buried with her amputated leg; that part of her had died after all the surgeries and the distress of her illness. She was now a bitter lemon when it came to others.

The servant appeared with a tray adorned with flowers and a place mat embroidered with birds that read "Hers" in white rose petals. She placed it on the little nightstand next to the bed. The treats for the visitor included tequila and appetizers.

Nervous because of the man's presence, Eulalia served the liquor in two blown-glass cups the same blue as the house and accompanied each with respective sangritas. She brought over fresh pico de gallo, a thick oven-baked cheese loaf, and quartered lemons, then vanished.

Eulalia couldn't avoid the shivers provoked by the stranger's presence in the house at that hour of the night;

he gave her goose bumps. As soon as she could, she explained to the rest of the staff that she'd never seen his body cast a shadow. Like Chucho, she recited the necessary Hail Marys and Our Fathers to keep away the evil eye and funereal airs.

Frida lifted her cup of tequila. With that particular way she had of raising her single brow, she brought the cup to her mouth, in part to mitigate the sharp flashes of pain, and in part to accompany her guest. The Messenger performed his part with the cup but did not drink the sangrita. It was a shame that he slighted it, because it was prepared with one of the recipes that Lupe, Diego's ex-wife, had taught her. Frida served herself another cup. It was not her first that day, but it would be her very last. The alcohol slipped down her throat, awakening her sleepy head.

"I called you because I need you to take a message to my Godmother. I need to change our appointment on the Day of the Dead. There won't be an offering this year. I need her to come tomorrow. Tell her I hope the journey will be a joyous one and that I don't want to come back this time."

Frida then kept quiet to let the Messenger answer, but, as always, there was no response. Even though she'd never heard his voice, she insisted on talking to him. His eyes, hungry for earth and freedom, stayed upon her. He drank his last tequila like an act of solidarity, put down the cup, turned to leave the room, his spurs jangling, and left the artist a wreck, like her body. He walked across the courtyard like a ranch foreman, passing the patio, where the parrots, dogs, and monkeys all screeched when they saw him. He reached the door, which was held open by Chucho, and bid a dry farewell with a nod, while the terrified houseboy crossed himself more times than a widow on Sunday. The man mounted his white steed anew and disappeared down the street into the blue-black night.

As soon as she heard the hoofs grow faint in the cold wind, Frida wrapped her hand around a brush dripping black ink. She scribbled a phrase in her personal diary and adorned it with vignettes of black angels. She finished the drawing with tears in her eyes. She closed the diary and called the cook again. Then she took a faded notebook from her desk, a gift from days gone by, when she could still dream of living. It had been given to her by her friend Tina a few months before she married Diego. Besides being a keepsake, it was the only wedding gift she'd kept. She opened it to the first page and read with an imperceptible movement of her lips: "Have the courage to live, because anyone can die." Slowly and carefully, she began to turn the pages, like a librarian before a Bible written on ancient scrolls. There were treasures hidden on each page, pieces of herself scribbled out in recipes she'd spiced up, a delicious stew of poems and commentary about everyone in her life. She called it "The Hierba Santa Book" as a kind of joke. It was there that she kept the recipes she used to build the altars for the Day of the Dead to keep a promise she'd made long ago. She searched through the pages scented with cinnamon, pepper, and small bundles of hierba santa for the recipe she'd give to Eulalia.

"I'm going to entrust you with a very important task, Eulalia. You'll prepare this dish tomorrow, exactly as I have written it out. You'll go to the market early to get everything you need. I want it to be sublime." She pointed to the recipe. She paused to let the anguish pass, knowing life was slipping by, then continued giving orders. "After the rooster crows, get him and slaughter him for the stew."

"Fridita, you're going to kill poor Mr. Cock-A-Doodle-Do?" Eulalia asked, astonished. "But he's your favorite. You spoil him as if he were your own child."

Frida didn't bother to respond but simply turned her face and closed her eyes to see if she could get some sleep. Eulalia left the room, the notebook held against her heart.

On the bed that was her prison, Frida dreamt about banquets, sugar skulls, and paintings at an exhibition. When she awoke, she did not see Eulalia. The house was still. She began to question whether the Messenger's visit, and in fact her whole life, including her first death, had not been a trick played on her by the drugs she'd been prescribed to contend with the pain that so tortured her. After considerable thought, she realized everything was true. And she broke down crying, in rage and in agony, until sleep lulled her away again, far from reality.

Hours later, Diego arrived from his studio in San Ángel.

When he came into the bedroom to see Frida, he

found her asleep, wearing a pained expression. He thought it odd that there was a bottle and two half-filled cups of tequila on the nightstand. He was even more intrigued when the servants told him the lady of the house had not had any visitors. He pulled the rocking chair next to his wife's bed and sat down. He took her hand with great care, as if it were a piece of fine porcelain, and caressed it as if he feared he could hurt her. All the while, his memory journeyed through their shared past: he conjured the fire he still felt for that tiny body he loved with ardor as well as with a child's devotion to his mother. He savored their nights of sex, of Frida's white breasts, small as peaches, and recalled the roundness of her ass. He remembered how, when he mentioned it to her, she gave a saucy response: "My ass is like hierba santa?" Then she explained that the herb grew in the shape of a heart. He cried for a while at her side, realizing the source of his rapture was now a withered form. "My Frida, mi querida Fridita," he murmured as sleep overtook him.

The next morning, after Frida's favorite rooster announced the new day, just like he had done so marvelously for more than twenty-two years, they twisted his neck and boiled him into a stew. But Frida never brought it to her lips.

The medical report said her death was due to pulmonary complications. With the complicity of the authorities, Diego managed to avoid having her autopsied. Since then, the theory that she committed suicide has spread like the aroma of morning coffee over a slow fire. The last heartrending words Frida wrote in her diary were:

"I hope it's a joyous march, and that I don't come back this time."

THE MESSENGER

"Whoever wants to be an eagle should fly; whoever wants to be a worm should crawl and not scream when he's stepped on," he once said. He didn't say it to me. I don't really know who he said it to, but there's no doubt he said it. He needs to be offered tequila, sangrita, and something to eat, because he's surely exhausted from his long journey. I'd be dead on my feet, too, riding around like that.

PICO DE GALLO

Once, when she was in a good mood, Lupe told me that tequila and pico de gallo were indispensable to the pre-dinner ritual in Jalisco. Back in her hometown, when the workers returned home from the fields, they'd sit in leather chairs in the shade of the corridor and eat spicy fruit and cheese loaves between sips of tequila.

2 freshly peeled jicamas
4 large juicy oranges
3 peeled cucumbers
1/2 peeled pineapple
3 unripe mangoes
1 xoconostle (prickly pear) cactus
1 handful green onions
Pomegranate seeds (optional)
6 lemons
4 green chiles
Coarse salt
Ground chile (optional)

✱ The jicamas, oranges, cucumbers, pine-apple, mangoes, cactus, and green onions must be chopped uniformly and in equal quantities. If pomegranates are added to the dish, the seeds can be arranged like the Mexican flag. The dish must be dressed with juice from the lemons, the chiles, and 1 tablespoon of salt. Or it can be seasoned with the lemons and powdered chile.

CHEESE LOAF

QUESO PANELA HORNEADO

This loaf, from the land of tequila, is made with a very delicious and fresh cheese, different from what I usually buy. You can get it in the markets and little stores. Lupe would bring some from her travels sometimes.

1 queso panela (cheese)
1 large garlic clove
1/4 cup chopped cilantro
1/4 cup chopped parsley
1/4 cup chopped basil
1 tablespoon fresh oregano
1/2 cup olive oil
Salt and freshly ground black pepper

❋ The fresh cheese must be placed in a clay pot and covered with a salsa that's

prepared by chopping the garlic clove together with the rest of the ingredients.
It's seasoned with salt and pepper and
left to marinate for 6 hours in the open air,
either in the courtyard or on the windowsill,
careful to make sure the monkeys don't
eat it. Later, it's oven-baked at 350°F for
about 20 minutes or until it begins to melt.
It's served hot. This dish is particularly
good as an appetizer accompanied by tostadas or slices of bread.

SANGRITA

I devised this recipe while traveling with Muray.
That's when he taught me that I needed to
drink my tequila alongside something bitter-
sweet. I take my tequila straight, like a man,
and it has always served me to impress the
gringos when they come to see Diego.

2 ancho chiles
2 tablespoons diced onion
2 cups orange juice

1/2 cup lime juice
Salt
Tomato juice (optional)

✳ Roast the chiles, and discard the seeds and veins. Boil the chiles for 2 minutes, then let them rest for 10 minutes. In a blender or molcajete (a Mexican mortar and pestle), bring together the onion, orange juice, lime juice, and ancho chiles. Mix well; add salt. More orange juice, lime juice, or tomato juice may be added.

The sangrita is a woman. She's redolent of spices and onions. She's who adds color and fire to the macho tequila. The two of them, together, are a perfect idyll.

How I'd love to be that way with my Dieguito. He can be my friend, my son, my lover, my colleague, but never my husband. After the crash on the bus, he's the worst accident I've ever had.

CHAPTER II

She—the woman who painted the themes she knew best; the one with the deep eyes and thick eyebrows arching like wings about to take flight, the hard mouth, the quick glance, and infinite pain—she was not always this way. Although there were constants: the absence of God—she'd become an atheist on principle—a passion for the day to day, and a lust for tomorrow. In the same way that the monumental ahuehuete trees that silently contemplate history were once seeds, Frida was once a girl.

Frida had learned to sew, to mend, to embroider, to do everything that a good girl should to be married, but she refused to learn to cook. Her palate was limited to an occasional treat from the family dinner table, but, to be frank, that reed of a girl didn't have much of an appetite.

Not that there was ever a lack of delicious home-made food. Following the deeply rooted traditions of her Spanish and Oaxacan indigenous heritage, her mother was as skilled at preparing the most succulent dishes as she was at having girls. In fact, in the Kahlo household there was an excess of females. Frida was the third of four daughters and, to her imperious mother's shame, the least feminine. But her father, Guillermo, a German immigrant descended from Jews and Hungarians, thought differently: "Frida is my most intelligent daughter, and the one most like me," he liked to say.

The child grew up believing she was unique and special, like a four-leaf clover hidden in a field. Nothing else could have been expected of Frida; her roots were so exotic, and her family history—like Mexico's—so full of pain and earth.

But the Kahlo marriage was strange from the start and ended badly; they were incredibly unhappy. When he was nineteen, Frida's father emigrated to Mexico, where he exchanged the Teutonic Wilhelm for the more poetic Guillermo; the name agreed more with his new country. He came from a family of artisans who'd passed down a delicate view on life that made him one of the best photographers of his time. But that great talent would not save him from suffering tears and snubs.

As soon as he arrived in Mexico, Guillermo began to work at a jewelry store owned by German immigrants. For this hard young man, the customs in his adopted country contrasted greatly with his obtuse, European way of life. The heat bothered him, as did the zeal with which Mexicans engaged in all their activities. He was amazed by the plunging necklines worn by the girls selling fruit on the streets, their ample breasts on view while they flirted openly with the mule skinners, who took off their shirts without pretext at the first sign of warmth in the spring. But little by little, Mexico's sounds and smells invaded his nose, his mouth— all of his senses. Soon he felt a great fire in his heart and fell in love with a beautiful local girl named María. The minute he acquired a modicum of financial stability, he married her, and they had their first daughter together.

That's when pain and misfortune sealed his fate. Death would haunt him just like the epileptic fits he suffered all his life. The second girl born to Guillermo Kahlo died within days of her birth. His wife, determined to give him a son, got pregnant again. With the third pregnancy came a healthy baby girl, but destiny cast a loaded die and left Guillermo a widower with two little girls.

Guillermo's was a frigid soul, capable of understanding the complex laws of physics, but capable, too, of ignoring the need for a hug from the person he loved the most. The same day his wife died, he began looking for a new partner: he sent the two girls off to a convent and proposed marriage to Matilde, a girl from Oaxaca who worked with him at the jewelry store.

Matilde never loved him, and if she accepted his proposal it was only because he reminded her of her first lover, also a German, who had possessed her in such a way she was sure she'd seen the face of God. To Matilde's misfortune, that blond angel had killed himself and left her with a fiery passion that Guillermo's austere soul would never be able to extinguish. From that moment on, religion would be the only succor for this woman's tormented spirit.

His new father-in-law, Antonio Calderón, taught Guillermo the art of photography. Between the penetrating chemical smells of his trade and hard work every single day, he soon acquired the skills to be a portrait photographer and even learned to paint landscapes, to which he dedicated his sleepy weekends. He became so famous that Porfirio Díaz himself commissioned various pieces from him.

The Kahlos had a marriage of convenience. Matilde gave Guillermo four daughters: Matilde, Adriana, Frida, and Cristina. And Guillermo gave her money, status, and a house in the village of Coyoacán. But the combination of the two of them left a bitter taste unworthy of being savored. His much-awaited heir never came, and so Guillermo educated his third daughter like a boy. The women in Coyoacán said that the day Frida was born they could smell change in the air. Those were difficult days, when the future hung by a thread and hope was scarce. People remembered the slaughter of the striking workers in Río Blanco and talked about a little man from up north named Madero who preached like Jesus about a new future in which the government would be democratically elected. Those whispers and rumors mingled at the market with the news of the Kahlo family's newest arrival.

Frida had the misfortune of not being cared for by her mother. Matilde refused even to feed her, so Guillermo contracted an indigenous nursemaid who took care of the girl from the moment she was born. She lovingly fed her delicious traditional dishes and entertained her with songs from the countryside.

As the years passed, the gentle breezes became a windstorm, and, beyond the great walls surrounding the big house in Coyoacán, Death began to circle, icy winds carrying anguish and fear. The country became a slaughterhouse during the Revolution. And when, up at the governing palace, President Madero was betrayed by General Victoriano Huerta, who ordered that he be shot in cold blood, Death knocked on the Kahlos' door. That February day, a strange northern wind began to blow between the trees around the big house. Leafy branches swung from side to side like giant hands reaching for the Kahlo home. The streets were swept by a devastating dust storm that forced everyone to take refuge wherever they could. The tempest worsened and, like an angry ogre, brought down trees and lampposts. The town's washerwomen and gossips said that a gale like that carried the screams of a woman in labor. No one imagined that those icy currents were a call to a worried Guillermo, who observed it all while protected behind his window. His little Frida was sick in bed. When the doctor left, Guillermo slammed shut the front door to make sure that evil wind did not sneak inside their home.

"Doctor, what's wrong with my daughter?" he'd asked as the doctor gathered his hat.

"She's very sick, Guillermo. She has polio. If it's not brought under control, it will affect her nervous system, and that could leave her paralyzed or even kill her," the physician explained.

Guillermo and Matilde each responded in their own way: she sighed deeply; he closed his eyes and lowered his head. Neither shed a single tear. But Frida's nanny, who'd been listening behind the door, shed enough for the girl's parents and her sisters, too. Her lamentations crept past the locks on the door and windows, swirling with the mysterious wind that roiled the streets, drawing it near, just as an injured prey draws a predator with the scent of its own blood.

Before going to bed, Guillermo Kahlo visited the room where the tiny six-year-old rested in a huge bed flanked by wooden columns standing guard at each corner. Even though he tended to be dry and distant, sometimes barely turning his head toward his daughters, that night he gazed sweetly at his favorite child. In his hands was a hardcover book covered with gold letters and pictures of elves, fairies, and princesses.

"What do you have under your arm, Papá?" Frida asked with a big smile.

Her father sat by her side and, with a rare tenderness, held the book out to her.

"It's a gift. I bought it for your birthday, but I thought maybe you'd like to read it now," he said as he caressed her obsidian hair.

"What's it about, Papá?" Frida asked, curious.

"They're stories about my country, about Germany. Two brothers collected them so they wouldn't be forgotten. They're the Grimm Brothers' tales."

The girl eyed the book and became immediately fascinated by its many bright colors. Her smile grew when she discovered a story about a young man who meets a mysterious being in the middle of the road. The creature wears a long black cape and carries an enormous scythe. Frida was astounded to see it was a skull looking down on the young man. She looked for the story's title: "The Dead Godmother."

"Who is the dead godmother?" she asked.

Unlike her mother, her father was a freethinker, an atheist who hated talking about religion, faith, and death. But he was a bit taken aback by the question because, all morning long, that story had been haunting him.

"That's my favorite story. It tells how Death wanders the Earth, trying to put out the candles that represent human life. One day, Death agrees to become a boy's godmother and gives him the gift of knowing who will live and who will die. But she warns him that he can't oppose her decisions, because Death can't be deceived or contradicted. When the boy grows up, he becomes a famous healer who saves his patients or kindly helps them deal with their upcoming demise. One day, he falls in love with a princess and, when he sees that his godmother wants to take her to her domain, he offers himself instead."

"Does he do it? Can a common man cheat Death, Papá?"

"He doesn't cheat her, he makes a deal with her. If you're smart, sometimes you can cut a deal with Death, but you have to be very careful what you ask for," he explained when he saw how much his daughter was enjoying the story.

"Do you think Death wants to be my Godmother and save me from this illness?"

The question upset poor Guillermo. Although he was an atheist, he preferred not to tempt fate by invoking death in such a banal fashion, especially since his daughter's life was in danger at that very moment. He decided not to respond and chose instead to read her the story of a boy who leaves home so he can experience fear.

While Guillermo and Frida continued reading fantastic stories about singing donkeys, sleeping princesses, and generous fairies, the Kahlos' doorbell rang. Frida's nanny half opened the door, unsure of who might visit during such a storm. A tall, slender woman dressed in fine silk, with a stole that looked like a feathered snake, a broad-rimmed hat with flowers, and a veil that covered her face, stood on the other side of the door. But, convinced that cold breezes never bring good things, the nanny refused to let the elegant woman enter.

"Good evening, young lady. I've come to visit family but I'm lost. I can hear shots in the distance and I'm frightened. Could I please take refuge in your home?" she asked with utter poise.

The nanny hitched up her shawl, rearranged her apron, and slammed the door in her face. But the woman didn't move or lose her composure.

"¡Largate! Get out of here! Frida will get well, you'll see!" the nanny growled.

"It's bad manners to not invite company in; it's even worse to send them on their way without offering them something to eat or drink," the woman said from the other side of the door.

Quickly, the nanny rushed to the kitchen and packed up tamales, a hot drink, bread, and sweets. She rushed back to the door and opened it only enough to push the food through.

"Here you go, fill your bones with that and be gone!" she snarled, again closing the door in the woman's face.

When she didn't hear anything more, the nanny opened the window a crack so narrow that a mouse could barely get through and quietly looked around. There wasn't a soul in sight. Still frightened, she turned to find little Frida standing behind her.

"Who was that?" she asked.

"Off to bed, young lady, if your mother sees you she's going to be very, very mad," she answered.

The ominous wind that had been blowing since morning finally subsided. The nanny took Frida back to bed and, smiling, gave her tamales and a hot maize drink. Now she knew for sure that the child would get well.

Frida survived polio but it left her with one leg shorter than the other. From then on they called her Pata de Palo—Peg Leg—at school, confirming that it's possible to escape Death but not the cruelty of children.

MY NANNY'S RECIPES

My nanny was from Oaxaca and loved to sing "La Zandunga" as she prepared a meal for me and my sister, Cristi, while we played with our dolls under her enormous petticoats.

She would tell us stories about apparitions. "The dead only come for Mass, to show where gold is buried, or to annoy. That's why you always have to give them something to eat, so they'll go away," she'd say with a big smile. What I remember best about her were her lace blouses. I've managed to find a few like them on my travels with Diego. But I'll never forget her tamales: they could certainly wake the dead.

PUMPKIN TAMALES

TAMALES DE CALABAZA

Diego told me that indigenous people consider a really good tamale, the kind eaten in the pueblos, a gift from the gods. Tamales were part of the Miccailhuitontli, the Feast of the Dead. And the Indians were absolutely right: When you see the tamales warm and dressed in corn leaves, they look like dear little dead children, dressed for their own funerals. When the priests arrived in the New World, they changed the feast date to All Saints' Day. It's always the imperialists who screw over the Indians, while they quietly eat their masa.

2 1/4 pounds small pumpkins
3 red cuaresmeño or jalapeño chiles
2 Oaxaca string cheeses
1 big handful epazote leaves (just the
   leaves)
Salt
Baking soda
1/4 cup lard
2 1/4 pounds corn masa
1 handful green corn husks

❋ Everything must be chopped very finely: pumpkins, chiles, cheese, and the epazote leaves. Dissolve the salt in a little bit of water with the baking soda, then mix into the lard for softness. Mix the lard with the masa. Pour 1 spoonful of the mixture into each corn husk, pat it down to extend it, and add a spoonful of the chopped pumpkin and other ingredients. Fold the husks and steam them for 1 1/2 hours. You know they're cooked when the husk can be peeled off. A coin is usually added to the steamer so that it will vibrate if the water boils off.

PINEAPPLE CORN DRINK

ATOLE DE PIÑA

4 cups water
Corn masa
1 very ripe pineapple
Sugar to taste
3 quarts milk
A pinch of baking soda

✳ Stir the water and masa together, letting the mixture rest for 15 minutes. Then strain the mixture and set the water aside. Peel and chop the pineapple, then liquefy it in a blender. Strain it, then heat it until it boils. Blend in the masa and sugar. Lower the heat and continue to cook for 15 minutes. Add the milk and baking soda. Leave it on the heat without stirring until it's cooked through and through. Do not let it boil again.

FRITTERS AND BROWN SUGAR SAUCE

Buñuelos y miel de piloncillo

4 cups sifted flour
4 ounces lard
1/2 teaspoon anise dissolved in 1 cup water
Corn oil for frying
1 pound curds

✳ Knead the flour and lard. Add the anise water until the mixture is soft and manageable. Let it rest for 1 hour. Then make little balls that are rolled out over a floured surface, keeping them round and long. Heat the oil and fry the fritters. Remove the fritters and let them rest on a papered surface to absorb the excess grease. To make the sauce, boil 3 cups brown sugar, 4 cups of water, 1 big cinnamon stick, 4 guavas, and 3 apples until the sauce thickens. To serve, put the fritters on a big plate, sprinkle crumbled curds over them, then cover with the sauce.

CHAPTER III

Frida's childhood, like that of everyone who grew up in the twentieth century, was anchored in a difficult and hypocritical society. The bonds of Family were particularly tight in the Kahlo home. The Rules were enforced to the letter of the law. Whoever chose to break them was subject to harsh punishment and Mamá Matilde's ponderous sermons. Matilde was a beautiful woman but very arrogant and self-righteous. Her husband captured her defiant chin—as well as the kind of pride that can only be allowed in a Zapotec queen with rich lips and enormous black eyes—in silver and gelatin prints. Oh, what a combination for Frida! A father who possessed Germanic cool and a mother with the haughtiness of indigenous nobility.

One of the family's inviolable rules was that they must attend Sunday Mass. Impeccably dressed, the girls went to the parish of St. John the Baptist, which was just a few blocks from home. They had a private pew where their mother, the girls, and their staff listened to the Sunday sermon. Afterward, Frida was allowed to stroll the town's main plaza, from which she'd occasionally escape in cahoots with Cristina, her younger sister, to the Coyoacán fish farms, a jungle-like park crisscrossed by an elusive river that wound between rocks and trees. The aftereffects of polio were no obstacle to Frida's tree climbing and whirlwind play. In fact, her doctor recommended she be allowed to indulge her taste for adventure. Thanks to her father's support, Frida became quite good at a number of sports, including swimming, soccer, boxing, skating, and biking. She competed with boys, not caring that the town gossips whispered that such activities were not appropriate for a respectable young woman. To disguise her thinner polio leg, she'd layer sock upon sock until it looked as thick. But even so, she wasn't able to avoid the cruelty of neighborhood boys who, jealous of her talents, called her Birdie Peg Leg because when she ran, she appeared to be trying to take flight.

One sleepy morning when the early dew still covered the forests, Frida was playing with her sister Cristina under her nanny's watchful eye when a foreboding wind began to blow, lifting their starched skirts. For the girls it was all fun, but their nanny recognized the earthly signs sent to warn of impending strife. Her fears were realized when a horseman galloped by, announcing the arrival of revolutionaries. She immediately called out to the girls, who had disappeared among the thick tree trunks and forest scrub and refused to answer. Her frightened screams were heard amid the distant cacophony of rebel gunshots when the poor woman, in her harried search, finally found the girls squatting under a fallen tree as they watched, in awe, a skirmish between the Zapatista rebels and government soldiers. She immediately tugged them by the arms to drag them home, but Frida resisted, not wanting to leave behind the brave spectacle of those men in rags taking on the much-better-equipped soldiers. Frida finally relented, and they ran as fast as they could down the cobblestone streets until they reached the house, but found the door locked to keep out the commotion. Luckily, their sister Matilde saw them through the window and rushed to tell their mother who, with pistol in hand, opened a window to let them in. Just a few steps behind them, the soldiers and rebels were killing each other.

Bullets ripped through the rebels, and it looked like victory was tipping toward the government soldiers. Frida was amazed to hear her mother shout to the Zapatista contingent to take refuge in their house. Her mother and nanny opened the heavy door that protected them and the men rushed in, carrying their injured comrades. And it was right then, as the two women closed the door while they continued to pray aloud—so as to avoid a stray tragic bullet—that Frida saw for the first time the strange presence that would follow her for the rest of her life: the Messenger. Through the crack in the door as it closed, Frida's eyes lighted upon a dark man with a thick mustache and hungry eyes who, while astride his beautiful white steed, emptied his pistol in rapid succession into a government soldier. The girl remained lost in her vision, sure that she'd never forget those eyes in which she recognized a cold-blooded man who carried Death with every bullet. The thud of the door brought her back from her trance.

"In this house, we respect freedom, and so we ask you, gentlemen, to also show some respect," Mamá Matilde told the Zapatistas who were lying about the living room.

Servants attended to the injured men, who didn't seem so dangerous anymore. They looked hungry and were so filthy that their features seemed distorted to the girls.

"There's not much to eat, so you'll have to make do with what little we have until things calm down. Then you'll have to go, because I don't need any trouble from the government," Frida's mother warned them. Later she ordered her four daughters to take additional food to the men.

Saved from the terrible concert of gunshots, the whinnying of horses, and screams of pain out in the streets, the men devoured corn gorditas, shortbread, and aguas frescas. By nightfall, the only sound outside was the aimless trotting of a riderless horse.

Frida and Matilde, her older sister, were charged with keeping watch; they had to make sure everything was calm enough on the streets so that the injured rebels could return to their camp. Before heading out, Frida grabbed a fistful of orange shortbreads like the ones they'd fed to the wounded, taking little mousy bites to allay her nerves.

When they opened the door, all they found outside was desolation and darkness; there wasn't a single sentry who dared to light the streetlamps, which were splattered with the blood of men and horses from both sides. The girls scanned the area. Curious by nature, Frida walked ahead of her sister to inspect the holes the bullets had made in the now-lifeless bodies and the large red ovals that had pooled beneath them. She walked along the cobblestones, letting the echo of her footsteps bounce off the walls. Without realizing it, she left her sister behind and was swallowed by the night. The same wind that had blown in that morning to warn them about the battle now made her shudder. A sudden gust stopped her dead in her tracks and fear nailed her feet to the ground. She found herself face-to-face again with the revolutionary she'd seen that morning. The man was astride his horse but not moving. Both creatures gazed at her with incandescent eyes. She thought about running for help, but that heavy wind, like a blanket of earth over a tomb, struck her as strangely familiar.

"Your men are at the house. My mother took them in, cared for them, and gave them food to eat," Frida said with false aplomb, because though she'd always been brave, that towering horse scared her.

The man didn't respond, but the pawing horse snapped the tiles on a nearby bench with his hooves.

"I have orange shortbreads. Do you want some?" She stretched her arm out to offer them to him.

He reached down and took one, and chewed it slowly, his mustache moving like a razor over the silence.

When he finished, he did something that scared the little girl even more: he offered her a huge, satisfied smile, revealing shiny white teeth that sparkled in the dark. Still smiling, he spurred his steed and turned away at a slow and peaceful trot. The blackness of night engulfed him until he vanished from Frida's sight. She remained anchored there until her sister found her.

"Let's go home! Mamá is looking for us!" Matilde whispered, anxious at being separated.

Matilde grabbed her sister by the shoulder and took her home. Behind Frida, the injured soldiers filed out of her house, following the same path as the mysterious horseman, helping each other or using walking sticks. Guillermo had been in the city throughout it all, and never knew what had happened.

The Revolution changed the country and proved a misfortune for the Kahlos: they no longer received generous government commissions, their economic privileges vanished, and Mamá Matilde could not help but nurture her bitterness. The disgrace that followed her husband's joblessness forced her to scrimp and save. Not only did she have to mortgage their home, but she had to sell part of her collection of fine European furniture and even rent rooms to make extra money. Frida and her sisters suffered their mother's increasingly frequent and angry fits as she saw her comfortable life dissolve like salt in water. Frida and Cristina would spy on her at night as she counted her money. Since she didn't know how to read or write, that was her only distraction. For stubborn Mamá Matilde, the few coins that trickled in like drops of water on a parched tongue provided her daughters with a traditional education and a religious one, too. She considered education the most valuable of all treasures.

But Frida's rebellious nature clashed with her mother's impositions. She threw religion aside because she found it useless and too heavy to carry around in her easy day-to-day life. Guilt, forgiveness, and prayer were not for Frida; she knew she'd find something else to hold onto in her life. She began to make fun of the prayers before meals, making her sister Cristina crack up in the middle of a Hail Mary; she'd skip catechism classes to play ball with the neighborhood boys; she'd even throw rotten oranges from the roof at the seminarians. Frida so tried and exasperated her mother that one day her mother disdainfully declared that Frida was no daughter of hers. Wounded, Frida decided to take revenge by helping her sister Matilde run away from home.

Matilde was the oldest and had just turned fifteen. She was a big girl, with ample breasts that she'd reveal coquettishly under lace; her hips were round like an apple, and she had a mature face. She'd decided that the young man who was courting her was the love of her life, but he was not looked upon with favor by her family. Frida mischievously proposed that Matilde escape down the balcony while she devilishly distracted their mother. Matilde's plan was to flee to Veracruz with her boyfriend. Incredibly, everything worked out so well that after she was punished for the fake tantrum that allowed Matilde to escape, Frida closed the door to the balcony as if nothing at all had happened and peacefully went to sleep. The next day, when their mother discovered her favorite daughter gone, she became hysterical, screaming and pleading with the saints to keep her daughter safe. In a typically contrasting reaction, Guillermo Kahlo merely collected all of his daughter's things in a suitcase and ordered that they be sold. Afterward, he locked himself in his studio and didn't say a word.

Matilde's fate was a mystery for many years. Family life continued painfully, silently. The Kahlos kept up appearances, exactly as any honorable household would do: feelings were smothered and a false peace was carefully tended. Frida continued to have confrontations with her mother, and so, to escape the daily arguments, she began to help her father in his photography studio.

One day while they were riding the train, she heard him sigh. "How I'd love to see your sister again, but we'll never find her."

Frida consoled him and, feeling sorry for her involvement, tried to make up for it by telling him she had a friend who had told her there was a Matilde Kahlo living in the Doctores neighborhood.

"But how do you know it's Matilde?"

"Because everyone says she looks just like me," Frida responded.

Without giving her father further explanation, she led him to Doctores. At the far end of a patio they found

Matilde watering her vegetable garden and feeding birds she kept in a large cage. That's where she lived with the boyfriend she had eloped with, and with whom she enjoyed a comfortable economic position. Her father smiled, his eyes teary, but he refused to speak to his daughter. Frida ran to her and hugged her. The sisters kissed and laughed together. But when they turned to Guillermo, he was gone.

Of course, Mamá Matilde wouldn't let her daughter Matilde back into the house, even when she came bearing enormous baskets of fruits and exquisite delicacies. Matilde felt obliged to leave them at the door, where her mother would pick them up later and serve them for dinner. As the festivities for the Day of the Dead neared, Matilde's culinary creations became even more sublime. Aside from fresh-baked breads, there were sugar skulls with the names of each member of the family. In one of the baskets she left a note for Frida, who read it and smiled: "I made you some shortbreads, because you gave yours to that rebel."

Twelve years after she left, Matilde was finally welcomed back into her home.

When he saw her, her father had only one question: "How are you, my daughter?"

MAMÁ MATILDE

A Day of the Dead offering for Mamá Matilde must include that photo Guillermo took, the one in which she looks so pretty and devout. I know she loved that one just as she liked that dark silk dress. We never have to place tequila or any other kind of liquor by the photo, because she never really cared for alcohol. But, a really fine, delicious rice water like the kind she gave the rebels when they arrived in Coyoacán, made the accompanying pork rinds sing. Not even General Villa would have argued with my mother about that.

HORCHATA

Because Mamá Matilde was from Oaxaca, she made horchata with milk instead of water. Guillermo was always asking for her horchata.

7 cups water
12 ounces (1 3/4 cups) rice
2 cinnamon sticks

2 cups milk
Sugar

✳ In a pot, blend 3 cups of water with the rice and let stand for 2 hours. Chop and toast the cinnamon sticks in a pan. Drain the rice and mash it with the cinnamon and milk. Then run it through a sieve, mix with 4 cups of water in a pitcher, and sweeten with sugar.

CORN GORDITAS

GORDITAS DE MAÍZ

Mamá Matilde would buy these gorditas after church. We would always find a vendor mashing a ball of masa to stuff into a tortilla. Cristina could eat three packs of these in one sitting.

1 cup flour for tamales or cornmeal
1 tablespoon lard
1/2 teaspoon gelatin
1/4 cup sugar
Water

❋ Mix the flour and lard; add the gelatin, sugar, and water as needed in order to make a manageable dough. From this, make small balls, about the size of a walnut, which can be flattened and made into the shape of gorditas. They're cooked on a griddle or on a grill at medium heat, turning them over once in a while.

ORANGE SHORTBREADS (MY FAVORITES)

POLVORONES DE NARANJA

4 ounces vegetable shortening
1/2 cup sugar
1 egg yolk
1 orange (juice and zest)
1/2 cup flour
1/4 teaspoon baking soda
Sugar for decorating

❋ Beat the shortening with the sugar until it's spongelike, then immediately add the egg yolk, orange juice, and zest. Then add, very slowly, the flour already mixed with the baking soda. Continue kneading and rolling, extending the dough until it's 1/4 inch thick. Cut into 2-inch circles and place them on a greased pan. Bake at 400°F until they're golden. Let them cool. Sprinkle with sugar.

CHAPTER IV

Frida spent the rest of her life haunted by two things: the memory of the man she'd call the Messenger and the spindly leg polio bequeathed to her. Nonetheless, she grew into a pretty girl with a gleaming halo of vitality. To fully renounce conventionalism and proclaim her youthful emancipation, she cropped her hair. It was a boyish cut that sensuously showed off the dimple in her chin. As soon as she was accepted to the National Preparatory School, where the cream of the crop of Mexican youth studied, a great passion awakened inside her, a thirst for knowledge, for partying, and for love—pleasures that would enthrall her for years to come. It was a privilege to attend the Preparatory: she was one of the first thirty-five women ever accepted in a class with two thousand men. But for her, everything was about getting away from Mamá Matilde, who was opposed to her daughter going away to school. Guillermo, who saw in Frida the son he never had, managed to convince his wife that their daughter's aspirations were proper and made Frida promise to ignore the boys in her class. Of course, it was a promise Frida could never keep. She was soon involved with a gang of intellectual boys who called themselves the Dictators. Because Frida always had the ability to be the center of attention, the group's leader, Alejandro Gómez Arias, fell hopelessly in love with this wild girl, and they soon began an affair.

In the beginning, their relationship was simply a pure and youthful courtship. They strolled the streets hand in hand with sweaty palms and starry eyes. But little by little the flame of their passion grew, and innocent kisses gave way to daring caresses. She was the instigator, the one who found hiding places in the park where they could explore each other's body in the shadows of the trees, amid the smell of fresh-baked meringues and ice cream. Before her fifteenth birthday, Frida already knew carnal pleasure with a man.

While her parents believed she was at school with the rest of the girls under the prefect's watchful eye, she was in fact with Alejandro when he attended his meetings, went to sports events, or was out misbehaving with his gang.

One of their favorite pastimes was harassing the artists whom José Vasconcelos, the secretary of education, had commissioned to paint murals. Sometimes they even set the artists' canvases on fire. As a result, it was perfectly normal for artists to show up at the school armed to the teeth. Among the pistol-packing bunch was a master who'd lived in Russia and France and painted alongside the geniuses of his time: Diego Rivera.

He wasn't an easy man to domesticate, and not just because of his cocksure attitude. He had no qualms about pulling the .45 caliber pistol he carried to protect his artwork. That only left room to joke that he was fat and ugly, but how could they do even that when he was constantly surrounded by a harem of beautiful women who made him seem like an earthly god? Though not a particularly graceful god: he had a big belly, big froggy eyes, and hands as big as his appetites, knowledge, and fantasies. Everything about Diego was big.

He was an ogre who could make the girls sigh as if he were a famous movie star. Frida fell under that spell; she liked to hide in the courtyard and watch him work, and would even warn him, when he was with his mistress, that his wife was on the way.

"Careful, Diego, Lupe's coming!" she'd shout.

Frida liked the painter so much that one day, as Diego lunched with Lupe on the delights Lupe had brought him in a basket, Frida summoned the courage to talk to him.

"Would you mind if I watched you paint?"

Rivera smiled at the girl; she didn't seem older than twelve. He shrugged gamely and continued working after he finished his lunch. Lupe fixed her sharp gaze on the insolent brat who refused to leave and began firing insults.

"Please, ma'am, be quiet. You're distracting the maestro," Frida said seriously, without ever taking her eyes off Diego's brush.

Lupe roared like a lioness and stormed off in a rage. Frida stayed, watching awhile longer, and later innocently bade Diego good-bye. She wouldn't see him again for several years, when her own passion for art would be in full bloom.

Frida's innocent little face helped her get away with quite a bit of mischief, including shooting off a handmade rocket during a speech given on a national holiday by a professor whose dissertations were as long as they were soporific. Using her delicate features to good effect, Frida concealed the explosive package under the professor's lectern, then casually walked away. When the firecracker went off like a machine gun, she was already gone. No one could have imagined she was responsible for an explosion that shattered glass and splintered furniture. But her jealous schoolmates, who hated her, turned her in to the Preparatory's director. Furious, the director sent the case over to José Vasconcelos.

Because of his political duties, it took Vasconcelos a full week to visit the Preparatory. In the waiting room, Frida sat terribly nervous, while in the director's office the respected intellectual listened to the director's accusations against the girl who was as dangerous, he declared, as a full-fledged revolutionary. After listening patiently to the whole boring speech, Vasconcelos asked that Frida be reinstated immediately.

"If you can't control a girl like this, you're not fit to run the Preparatory," he said sharply.

As he was leaving, the famous secretary of education stopped and looked at Frida, who gazed up at him with her full, puppy-dog eyes. He smiled, ruffled her hair and went off in pursuit of the presidency of Mexico.

Alejandro, watching the whole thing unfold through a window, laughed and began to sing his alma mater's fight song. *"Shi . . . ts . . . pum . . . Gooya, gooya, cachún, ra, ra, cachún, cachún, ra, ra, gooya, gooya— Preparatory!"*

Frida leapt out into the hall and gave him a kiss. The rest of the gang carried her out to the courtyard on their shoulders, which set off a long celebration that ended off-campus at an eatery where they enjoyed a bowl of pozole between stories and jokes. When the party was over, the lovers felt an intense heat that made them nervous as they sat in their chairs, holding hands. The landscape turned to warm colors and the world began to melt in front of them.

"Let's go to my house; there's no one there. Mamá and my sisters are at church," Frida proposed.

Giggling, they left their friends behind and boarded a bus to Coyoacán. But Frida felt cold air passing over her as if she were the only one who could feel what was coming, the only one who could see the strings of fate attached to the two of them like marionettes.

"We should go back to the school," she suddenly told her boyfriend, trying to pull herself away from such dark forces, and got off the bus. "I forgot my umbrella."

Alejandro didn't understand that his girlfriend was seeing something beyond this world and insisted they catch the next bus. Frida relented, hoping to push down the eerie sensation, because, in fact, she didn't believe in mysticism or ghosts.

Once inside the old wood and metal bus, the young couple made their way among the crowded passengers. In the back, a painter carrying large jars of gold paint kindly offered them his seats.

"Sit, sit. I'm getting off at Tlalpan," he said as he got up.

From her seat, Frida looked out at the streets, wet from the morning's downpour, and felt the same uncomfortable sensation as before. She couldn't seem to push away the uneasy feeling of foreboding. A shiver went up her spine when she saw through the window the rebel from her childhood, mounted on a white horse in front of the San Lucas market.

People passed him without so much as a glance. But when their eyes met, she thought she might drown in his white pupils. He greeted her with a slight tip of his hat, and she felt an icy tingle from her heel to her head. Alejandro didn't seem to notice the horseman. Was he real, or merely a specter conjured by her deepest fears? The question died in her throat, drowned by a deafening crash.

The bus was torn to pieces, bending as if it'd been buffeted by an unseen hand. An intense heat shot through Frida's body, which lay compressed between metal tubes and other bodies in the wreckage caused by a head-on collision with a train. Her left knee hit someone's back and she felt the cold on her naked skin. The crash tore the clothes from her body, but her nakedness was nothing compared to the realization that all around her, others were shrouded in death. In the midst of the chaos, she heard anguished voices crying out: "The dancer! The dancer!"

She saw Alejandro's face in the crowd, and his expression confirmed the worst of her fears. She lay surrounded by the bus's debris, completely naked, covered in blood and gold dust from that kind painter. Her body seemed to have been outlandishly decorated and imprisoned by metal tubing. The handrail had impaled her pelvis. The strange combination of crimson and gold painting her body made others think Frida was some kind of exotic dancer, and they kept calling out: "The dancer! The dancer!"

"That tube has to come out!" cried a man who moved a speechless Alejandro aside. The man grabbed the tube and pulled.

A scarlet rush pooled on the ground in the shape of a heart. That was the first time Frida Kahlo died. . . .

THE DICTATORS' FAVORITE SNACKS

Back when I was with the Dictators, we were obsessed with sneaking away from that Preparatory and instead, eating the fast food that was served downtown. A dog named Pachezco, who limped like me, was always asleep at the entrance to February Fifth Street and served as a kind of sentry. Alex would say to me, "Pachezco and I will see you there." It was a good place and the flies were free... but, oh, what a pozole they served! That corn gave us our nationalism. And the dish was so Mexican: red, white, and green.

RED POZOLE

POZOLE ROJO

2 1/4 pounds cacahuazintle corn (hominy)
1 tablespoon lime (calcium hydroxide)
Salt
1 pound pork bones
1 pound pork head
2 1/4 pounds pork leg
3 guajillo chiles
1 onion
1 head garlic

To accompany the pozole:

1 onion, chopped
1 head lettuce, chopped
Lemons
Chile powder
1 handful radishes, chopped
Tostadas

✱ A day ahead of time, cook the caca-huazintle corn in 2 quarts of water with the lime, stirring constantly with a wooden spoon. As soon as it boils, turn off the heat, cover, and let sit overnight. The next day, drain the corn and rub it together until its kernels have all fallen off the cob. Wash the corn repeatedly under a stream of water. Put the corn in a large pot with 3 quarts of water and salt; boil over medium heat until the kernels burst. Add the pork bones, pork head, and pork leg, chopped in pieces. In the meantime, soak the guajillo chiles and, in a blender, mix them with the onion and garlic. Drain the mixture and add it to the broth.

Continue cooking until the meats are tender. Serve with chopped onion, lettuce, lemon, chile powder, radishes, and tostadas.

CHICKEN TOSTADAS

TOSTADAS DE POLLO

Oil for frying

12 corn tortillas

1 1/2 cups refried beans

3 cups finely chopped lettuce

1 chicken breast, cooked and shredded

1 onion, sliced

2 tomatoes, sliced

1 avocado, peeled and sliced

1/2 cup crema

Shredded cheese

Salt

✳ Heat the oil in a pan over medium heat and cook the tortillas until they're golden. Remove them from the heat and drain the oil.

The tortillas may be prepared beforehand, but it's important that they be crispy. Heat the refried beans and spread them on each toasted tortilla. Cover them with lettuce, shredded chicken, a slice of onion, a slice of tomato, and a slice of avocado. Add crema, a bit of cheese, and salt. If more flavor is desired, add red sauce.

RED SAUCE

SALSA ROJA

Large tomatoes
6 cuaresmeño (jalapeño) chiles
1 garlic clove
1 onion, chopped
1 bunch cilantro, chopped
Salt

✳ Toast the tomatoes, chiles, and garlic, then pound them together in the molcajete (mortar). Add onion, cilantro, and salt to taste.

CHAPTER V

"The dancer! The dancer!"

The children's screams echoed and ricocheted in Frida's head. She opened her eyes to find herself in an electric-blue sky rolling along with cotton candy clouds, all of which reminded her of a great boiling pot of soup. She then noticed the words were coming from a giant avocado tree with leaves as big as bedsheets. A pair of spider monkeys jumped about on a branch, wisecracking, which inevitably ended in loud laughter punctuated by aromatic bursts of mint. Frida responded but with caution, because they'd made her the butt of their jokes.

"I'm not a dancer, I had polio . . ." she groaned as she lifted her skirt up to her knee so they could see her cinnamon stick of a leg.

The monkeys carefully checked out the leg. One of them pretended to be a doctor and put on a pair of eyeglasses. They examined Frida for a minute. They looked seriously at one another, then let loose with a burst of laughter that smelled like fresh apple.

"She's lame! She's lame!" they sang off tune.

Frida got up from the floor, irritated and confused once she realized she'd awakened in a strange new place. She surveyed her surroundings to see if there was something she could throw at the monkeys to crack their skulls and silence their cruelty.

"And who are *you*? I bet you're just a couple of jerks who spend your days wandering aimlessly, entertaining yourselves at the expense of any woman crossing the street."

"Hey, we have names! And if you don't like them, we have several others to choose from. My friends and family call me the Honorable Sir Chon Lu, but since you're neither, you may call me sir."

Irritated, Frida kicked at the ground, which only made them laugh over and over like a needle skipping on a vinyl record. As soon as she realized it was impossible to reason with them, she let loose a string of unfathomable words that made the smart-ass monkeys seek shelter behind the trees. Satisfied, she decided to take a look around: she was in the middle of a great open space bracketed by a line of houses. She was probably close to Coyoacán, because she recognized the arch from the park and also La Rosita, a pub close to her home. In the distance she could see the church's cupola and all three towers, and she even thought she could smell corn steaming. The entire place was lit by thousands of candles, their flames dancing in rhythm as they consumed their wax. There were large, robust ones and smaller ones, too, that were almost burned through. Each one as different as people in real life. In the midst of the candle-light, Frida's shadow reached for an elegantly set table that was adorned with flowers and tropical fruits reveal-ing their meaty insides, like lustful exhibitionists. There were huge plates with soursops, pomegranates, and red melons alongside an enormous bread-for-the-dead, with its perfectly sculpted bones coated with sparkling sugar.

"Welcome! We invited everyone to the celebration," a guest told her. This was a papier-mâché skeleton sipping delightedly from a cup of chocolate in which it dipped a slice of bread-for-the-dead. As soon as it saw Frida, its eye sockets grew large and its teeth gleamed like an ear of corn. At its side, a cardboard Judas laughed, twitching his huge mustache. He was covered with bottle rockets that looked like thorns. In the corner, there was a pre-Columbian statue of a pregnant woman who showed off her swollen belly while she talked on and on in Nahuatl; her fetus played like a mouse in a cheese wheel.

"What are you celebrating? It's still a long time till the Day of the Dead," said Frida, taking note that she was no longer naked or injured. She now wore a long strawberry-colored skirt with gaudy lace that frolicked with the flowers on her blouse like puppies, curling around fabrics from Oaxaca and needlework from the Tarahumara. Seeing herself dressed up that way, and now also wearing a complicated braid in her hair, she de-cided to join the unique cast of characters.

"Every day is a Day of the Dead here," said the skeleton while cutting a slice of bread that, on contact with the knife, gave off a delicious air of lemon blossom.

"She gets the bread bones! The Skeleton and the Skinny One have her now!" the two spider monkeys cried from their hiding place between hiccuping laughter.

Frida simply stuck out her tongue at them—not a particularly gracious move on her part, but certainly a comforting one. Just then, her reasoning kicked in and she realized the party was taking place in a cemetery. The tombstones looked on with their long faces and the mausoleums stood guard as if they were faraway castles.

"We have to wait for the boss before we start," said the skeleton.

"For Her Majesty," added the Judas, laughing the whole time.

"Until the lady arrives," proclaimed the stone statue.

It was such a lovely party that Frida didn't mind waiting for their host, and she killed time watching the fruits twirl in a mating dance while merrily singing "La Llorona":

> *Everyone calls me the black one, Llorona,*
> *black but lovable.*
> *I'm like the green chile, Llorona,*
> *spicy and tasty.*

They were so very merry. Those coconuts, chiles, and peaches sure knew how to dance. Their song brought a pair of dolls to the dance floor, one made of cardboard and the other dressed as a bride; she blushed at the melon's flirty smiles. During the musical number, a pair of curtains opened as if on a stage and revealed a thin figure wearing a guava-pink skirt sprinkled with knitted seeds and decorated with nervous flowers jiggling their petals. The blouse was like a crazy swirl, with the chile's colors battling to outshine the black mole tint of the fabric.

The woman was breathtaking, dressed like an empress, but Frida was frustrated because she couldn't see the face behind the veil. The fruits went on with their song, harmonizing sublimely for their newest guest.

The pain and absence of pain, Llorona,
everything is pain to me.
Yesterday I cried from wanting to see you, oh Llorona!
And today I cry because I finally did.

The woman raised her left hand, in which she held her heart, beating to the rhythm of the song.

"The lady will speak now," the skull said, very solemnly.

"Go ahead, boss," said the Judas as it groped the pregnant statue.

The woman in the veil turned to the recently arrived Frida. She used a pair of forceps in her right hand to yank out a vein from the heart, which caused a rush of blood to spatter her dress. Then, with a tender voice she began to recite a poem:

The silent life
Giver of worlds
Injured deer
Traditional Oaxaca dresses
Death backs off
Lines, shapes, nests
Hands create
Eyes open
Diego feelings
Whole tears
All very clear
Cosmic truths
Tree of Hope
Stay strong.

Applause erupted and more guests arrived: a very nervous little deer, a naked dog that looked like a pig, and a couple of black-pepper-colored parakeets.

"I know that voice," Frida said. "I heard it for the first time when I was six years old and had a very intense friendship with an imaginary girl my age."

The woman moved her hand, gesturing for her to continue her story.

"It all happened through the window in my room in the house on Allende Street. I breathed steam on the glass and drew a door with my finger. I went flying through that door, quickly, happily. I crossed a plain and went deep into the earth, where my friend was always waiting for me. She was a sweet and agile dancer who moved as if she were weightless. I imitated all her moves and told her all my secrets while we danced. I'm sure now that friend was you."

"I remember it as if it were yesterday, Frida, my lovely goddaughter. Welcome to my home, where you belong," the woman said.

The heart in her hand bowed, kindly greeting the guest.

"If you're the one who stops hearts and takes lives, then am I dead?" a frightened Frida thought aloud.

The skull offered a smile in response like two ears of corn with their kernels dropping.

"I called and you came: Let's celebrate your arrival!"

Frida shot up and threw her bread. That insolence, so rude and vulgar, scared the pumpkins, who ran and hid behind the papayas, which growled and showed their seeds.

"Godmother, I don't want to argue with you. I know I can't win, but I think you tricked me, and in a really bad way."

"Are you questioning what destiny has in store, little girl?"

"Oh, Godmother, I'd barely begun to enjoy life's pleasures, and now you tell me the party's over. Don't you know that I want to marry Alejandro and have children? Besides, I'm ready to be something special, a fine lady. Why would you take that opportunity away from me? No matter how you look at it, it's not fair."

"No one said life's fair. It's just life."

"But you tricked me. And you know I'm not a stupid girl. I demand, in the name of freedom, which is everyone's natural right, that you take me back home. Alex and my family must be terribly worried about me."

"You're making demands? You? Fridita, is your vision so pedestrian that you can't understand that I'm the most communist of all beings? As far as I'm concerned, there are no rich or poor, no big or small. Everyone—without exception—winds up here, with me."

Frida could feel passion overflowing every aspect of her being. Pumping herself up with courage, she said, "I should continue living. I'm asking you: please."

"I can't keep your place in my kingdom empty. Order is indispensable, and if destiny has determined you belong to me, then you need to be here," the lady said in a motherly tone.

"You could put my portrait in my place, a painting that looks so much like me that everyone who saw it would say, 'It's her!' "

Her Godmother didn't answer. The music stopped and everyone was quiet for several minutes. The papier-mâché skeleton continued to chew its bread in silence and the monkeys looked on, no longer laughing, waiting to hear the Godmother's response.

"It's possible that a painting could take your place, but I warn you: as the years go by, you'll get closer and closer to me and I'll rip that life you yearn for to shreds. There are things humans can't undo, but I'll grant what you've asked because you've livened up my party. Before we say farewell, however, I'll exercise the privilege of being your Godmother to give you something to think about: Frida, be careful what you wish for. Sometimes those wishes come true."

"I won't disappoint you, Godmother. I promise to never forget your kindness."

"Frida, if what you want is to show your respect, then you should make me an offering every year. I'll gladly delight in the foods, flowers, and gifts you bring me. But I'm warning you now: you will always wish you'd died today. And I will remind you of this every day of your life."

"An offering on the Day of the Dead—that's all you want?" Frida asked, too rushed to pay heed to her Godmother's warning.

Suddenly Frida awoke in the Red Cross Hospital.

The lady from Oaxaca decked out in the colors of nature had disappeared. In her place was a dowdy, chubby-cheeked nurse.

"Are you awake now, dear? This is a good sign," she said with joy when she saw Frida was conscious. "Stay calm so you can rest a little."

Unfortunately, Frida spent a month in the hospital and three more recuperating at home. Her spinal column had been fractured into three pieces. Her clavicle, ribs, and hips were also broken. And her right leg was fractured in eleven different places. The doctor considered it a miracle she was alive.

THE DAY OF THE DEAD CELEBRATION

We Mexicans laugh at death. Birth and death are the most important moments in life. And any excuse is a good one for a party. Death is both mourning and joy. Tragedy and comedy. To make peace with our final hour, we make a bread of sugar-covered bone shapes, and round, like the cycle of life. In the center we set a sugar skull. Sweet, but macabre. That's me, I guess.

BREAD FOR THE DEAD

PAN DE MUERTO

8 cups flour

7 ounces (1 3/4 sticks) butter

3 1/2 ounces shortening

A little more than 1 cup sugar

11 eggs

2 tablespoons baking powder

1 teaspoon salt
1 tablespoon orange flower water
Extra egg for brushing the bread before
   baking
Extra butter and sugar for decorating

❋ Amass the flour into a mound. Form a well
in the center. Place the butter and shortening in the center and, using your hands,
knead everything together. Add the sugar
and then the eggs, one at a time. Dissolve
the baking powder in 1/4 cup of water and
add. Then, slowly, add the rest of the ingredients. Knead until the dough comes off
the table and your hands. Then be patient
and let the dough breathe for approximately
1 hour, until it gets spongy. Knead again
and form the dough into the shape of the
Bread for the Dead. Remember to set some
of the dough aside to make the bones later.
Then let the dough sit again, covered with
a towel and away from any drafts, until
it rises to twice its size. To make the bones,

roll the dough with your fingers until it's thin, then place it over the bread, like ribs. Brush the bread with a lightly beaten egg. Preheat the oven to 400°F, then bake for 20 to 30 minutes. Once baked, brush the bread with butter and sprinkle with sugar.

CHAPTER VI

As soon as Frida awoke from the operation in which she'd died for several minutes, she asked to see her parents. But she fell into a deep depression when a series of extraordinary events kept them apart for several weeks. Upon hearing the news of the accident, her father had fallen terribly ill and was confined to bed for weeks. Mamá Matilde slipped into a catatonic state while in her rocking chair. They had to yank her embroidery from her grip; it took the servants more than an hour to set her hands on her lap. She remained completely silent. As she improved, her daughters tried in vain to get her to eat, cooking all kinds of healthy soups that she barely deigned to taste.

While Frida was in the hospital, everyone at La Casa Azul wore black. True, Frida had survived, but a veil of mourning fell over her parents, sisters, and servants, who went to Mass every afternoon to pray for the girl's soul. In time, Mamá Matilde got her voice back and affirmed that Frida's destiny had been to die that day, but a miracle had saved her.

The only person to visit Frida in the hospital during her convalescence was her sister Mati, who lived nearby. She decided to care for Frida, probably as a way of thanking her sister for having helped her escape. Mati focused her emotions in this way, now more maternal than sisterly. She'd come every day with a basket full of snacks and sweets wrapped meticulously in little embroidered tea towels.

Frida happily looked forward to her arrival, especially on Fridays, when she brought tlalpeño soup made of chicken and vegetables, a salve that made her feel at home. Matilde's homemade goodies were as comforting as her raunchy sense of humor, which had developed since she'd managed to get away from their mother. Her jokes and wry comments helped Frida endure the long convalescence.

Alejandro and the Dictators also visited; she'd anxiously count the minutes that separated her from her lover. But as the days went by, her boyfriend's visits became increasingly infrequent. Frida began to feel frustrated and decided to calm her nerves by writing him long love letters in which she also told him about the terror that overwhelmed her at night when her eyes betrayed her in the dark. On one occasion, while she writhed in pain from her injuries, she was awakened by cold fingers playing with her hair. She was startled to see her Godmother, the woman in the veil, floating toward the door. Two days later, wrestling with dreams near dawn, when the moans from the sick were particularly anguished, she made out the figure of the Messenger about halfway down the hall. The next morning, when Alejandro came to visit, she told him about her bizarre dream and confided that Death danced around her hospital bed at night. He tried to calm her, telling her she was talking crazy—something the doctors blamed on the pain medication. For her part, Frida was sure that the queen of the End of Days expected her to keep her part of the bargain. To avoid being called mad, she kept absolute silence for the rest of her life about the hallucination she'd had when she stopped breathing. Fear, however, wouldn't let her be. She confessed to her sister Matilde that dying wasn't her concern, rather the fear that once she went back home, they'd treat her as if she were already dead.

"I'm starting to get used to suffering," Frida confessed.

When she left the hospital to continue convalescing at home, her fears became reality. Although her mother had recovered her ability to speak, she was becoming increasingly irritable. Her father would lock himself in his room for long periods of time, shut off from reality. Her friends from school stopped visiting because she lived so far away. Frida thought her home was the saddest place on Earth. She wanted to flee the house in Coyoacán but also felt great relief to be back home.

What affected her most was when her beloved Alejandro discovered that his girlfriend was not the innocent she claimed to be in her love letters, and that the sexual beast within her had already awakened to kiss his friends' lips, boys and girls alike. When he asked her about it, Frida responded nonchalantly: it was to quell the lust burning inside her. For Alejandro, this meant the end: this was betrayal. And after a huge fight, he put distance between them. Maybe he had simply refused to recognize that, since the accident, their lives were headed in very different directions: while a very successful professional career awaited him abroad, Frida still had many months of recovery ahead of her. Alejandro viewed his girlfriend as a burden, an obstacle in his path. And though she tried to regain her lover's trust through an infinite number of love letters, she wasn't able to hold on to him. He broke the promise they'd made to stay together, and she was cast adrift. In one of her letters, she desperately apologized for her affairs.

"Though I've told many I loved them, and even kissed them, you know that deep down I only love you."

On one of the many nights in which she fell asleep thinking she would have preferred to die than have to endure Alejandro's indifference, she had another dream about the woman in the veil.

"I know you're doing this to stay close to the love of your life," the woman told her, "and I admire your decision, my dear."

When she woke up, lying on her bed in a plaster cast, Frida decided to keep her promise to her Godmother. It was a decision that would change the course of her life. She asked her father for her bag of oil paints, a few brushes and canvases, and she began to paint. Hopeful that painting would be distracting enough to help her forget her suffering, Mamá Matilde had a special easel built for her so she could paint while lying on her back. Drawing wasn't new to Frida. She was constantly illustrating her school notebooks with faces, landscapes, and funny scenes. In fact, she'd helped her father retouch negatives, using very delicate brushstrokes to render perfect shadows. But this was the first time she'd taken painting seriously.

As soon as she picked up a brush, she felt her pain lighten. With her eyes wet from tears from the loss of her lover, she brushed a dab of bloody red on her tablet, followed by black and ochre, colors that reminded her of the accident and the shouts of "The dancer!" She breathed in the singular smell of the pigments and, placing the brush on the paper like a powerful phallus penetrating a woman, sank it into the picture and sighed with pleasure and pain. In this way, she gave birth to a work of art. When the brush carried the wedded colors to the canvas, she stopped crying and her soul felt a comforting calm. Then came the smell of mangoes, lips like strawberries, cheeks like peaches, and chocolate hair. For the first time in her life, Frida felt something that set her apart from the world, which offered her the succulence of sex, the pleasure of good food, and the composure of a woman. She felt free.

She finished the piece, a self-portrait. It was her, immortalized for her Godmother. This was her way of surrendering a piece of her life, of her heart, of her emotions. The proud girl in the picture fearlessly displayed each of her virtues and each of her faults.

As Frida finished the promised portrait, she wrote letters to Alejandro, who'd left for Europe without saying good-bye.

Alex,

How I'd love to tell you about my suffering, every minute of it. . . . I can't forget you for a single moment. I see your face everywhere.

I do nothing but think of you all day long since you left me. Everything I ever did was for you, so you'd be happy. But now I don't feel like doing anything at all.

Write me.

And more important, love me.

Frida

There was no response. In the meantime, the work on her portrait neared its end and the weight that had pinned her to the bed seemed to lift little by little as her health improved.

That night she again dreamed of her Godmother, and how she would take the painting to her as an offering. Her lovesickness and the suffering caused by the accident poured into the painting. When she awoke, she finally understood what her Godmother had told her, that her destiny was to survive but that there would be crosses to bear. She accepted that her life hung by a precarious thread that could snap at any time. From this moment on, she would live life on borrowed time.

MY SISTER MATILDE'S RECIPES

Every time I see my sister Matilde, I wonder how she got to be this fun and crazy woman, given how uptight our parents were. Seeing her rosy cheeks and infectious laugh, I think maybe Mamá Matilde found her in the park or something. I told her that one day—I was just kidding around, though later I felt guilty about it—but she laughed just the same. "They found me and took me home with them because they wanted a pretty baby, not a skinny, hairy baby like you." That's when I understood that Matilde had her own way of getting over suffering, of transforming it into joy. I envy her that because, in contrast, I'm pretty stormy . . . I also envy her soups, because they're strong enough to raise the dead.

TLALPEÑO SOUP
CALDO TLALPEÑO

This is my favorite soup. Mati wheedled it out of a village woman from Tlalpan, where they invented it. Every time I make it, there's not a drop left over.

1 pound chicken breast
6 cups water
Salt
1 cup chickpeas
2 garlic cloves
1 tablespoon oil
1 cup chopped carrots
1 cup chopped onions
2 pickled chipotle chiles, cut into strips
1 fresh epazote leaf
1 avocado, peeled and cubed
2 tablespoons chopped cilantro
1 thinly sliced serrano chile
1 chopped tomato
Lemon slices
1 cup cooked white rice

✳ In a good soup pot, put the chicken breast, water, salt, chickpeas, and garlic. Cover and cook until the chicken is tender. Remove the breast and let it cool for shredding later. Heat the oil in a pan, add the carrots and onions, and cook for 3 minutes. Add to the soup pot. Then add the chipotles and epazote. Cook for 30 minutes, adding salt to taste. Put the shredded chicken and the avocado cubes into the bowls in which the soup will be served. Add the soup and serve the cilantro, serrano chile, tomato, lemon, and rice separately so everyone can add to their bowls according to their taste.

MEXICAN CHICKEN SOUP

CALDO MEXICANO DE POLLO

One day, one of Diego's guests—one of those know-it-all gringas—asked me why all Mexican food included chicken. I'd never thought about it. Chicken is fundamental to our cuisine. That's why I have no doubt that chicken soup is Mexican, even if it was invented by the French—surely they bought it at the Merced market.

8 cups water
1 medium chicken, about 3 1/3 pounds
1/4 onion
2 garlic cloves
2 big peppers
1 celery stalk
Salt
2 potatoes
4 carrots
1/2 cup rice
Chopped cilantro
Tortilla chips and chopped onion for serving
2 lemons
1 finely chopped serrano chile

✳ In a pot with the water, cook the chicken (in pieces), onion, garlic, peppers, and celery. Add salt and bring everything to a boil. After the chicken has been boiling a good while, add the potatoes (cut in quarters), carrots (cut into pieces), and rice. To serve, add the cilantro, the chopped onion, and the tortilla chips. Serve the cut lemons and the serrano chile on the side.

CHAPTER VII

Frida had turned twenty and had recently learned to walk again, slowly, like a tightrope artist. It was then that she met her soul mate: Assunta Adelaide Luigia Modotti Mondini. She had an unquestionably devilish name, her photographer friend, and so everyone called her Tina. She was as captivatingly beautiful as she was impulsive, like a hurricane transforming everything as it made its way across the Earth. She'd had as many men as she'd had jobs: seamstress, designer, stage actor, Hollywood movie actor. After meeting her, all the women Frida had ever known seemed like simple peasant girls trying to pass for modern women. Tina was as hard as a rock, smiled like a man, had eyes like a cat, a voice like a teenager, and the hands of a medieval duchess. She was capable not only of awakening a zest for life in anyone but also of provoking any man or woman's hidden carnal passions. Part goddess, part desire, Tina was life itself.

After they had become fast friends, the two girls shared a great intimacy forged by the same passion: the struggle for social justice. They were committed to world revolution and were active militants in the Mexican Communist Party.

"Honestly, sometimes I get confused and I don't know what I love more, the man who's making love to me or his dream of revolution," Tina confessed to Frida one day.

"But which do you find more satisfying, the man or the revolution?" Frida asked, goading her. If it was a contest of truth-telling, Frida wouldn't be left behind.

She'd always been interested in politics, and as soon as she got well, she dedicated herself completely to militancy, embracing communism as a way to drown her lovesickness. Meeting Tina, Frida clung to her.

"The revolution, of course. And certain women," Tina responded, ending the game so she could kiss Frida, who listened avidly to her political dissertations and romantic adventures.

It was because of Tina and her conviction that communism was the wave of the future for Mexico and the world that Frida became a party member. In her she also found the lover who would help her forget Alejandro. It wasn't hard at all to fall in love with the stunning Italian. Other women, jealous, called Tina a poseur, not a rebel. And how could they not be jealous? Tina was the very heart of the artistic and intellectual get-togethers she hosted in her apartment in the Roma neighborhood. Orozco, Siqueiros, Rivera, Montenegro, Charlot, Covarrubias, and the beautiful Nahui Olin were all there. Tina introduced Frida to a bohemian world where they drank tequila, sang corridos, and, most important, talked politics. What had started as a friendship soon blossomed into attraction. They'd lie in Tina's bed, waiting for her famous guests to arrive. That was how they protected themselves, listened to each other, and comforted each other, because even though they put on a tough exterior, every woman is fragile until she can find a true love to hold onto.

"I'm going to teach you to make pasta the way the women do in Venice," Tina said as they put away the groceries. They'd already opened a bottle of wine and were waiting for the warmth in their throats to help rid them of their inhibitions.

"And are those women as pretty as you?" Frida asked as she snatched a bunch of basil leaves out of Tina's hands. Later she would steal a fevered kiss from Tina's lips.

"As pretty as Mexican women," Tina responded, then stole a kiss of her own.

Their eyes were bright from the kind of complicity shared by two girls on the verge of mischief.

There was a language of caresses between the two of them, smiles and sweet nothings that carried more weight than any of the corny poems men sometimes wrote to clumsily court them.

Tina began to look for something among the papers in her kitchen and didn't stop until she came up with a beautiful black book closed shut with a rubber band. It was a gift from her new boyfriend, the journalist Julio Antonio Mella.

"This is for you, so you won't forget me."

"How could I forget you?"

"Friducha, because nothing is forever. You need a man to protect you, to love you . . . a communist, of course," Tina said.

Frida seemed happy enough, intoxicated with her new life, but she was struck by loneliness now and again. It's possible she'd already forgotten the woman in the veil and the painting that had served to replace her, but love was scarce and she was inclined toward excess.

"Introduce me to Diego," Frida dared to ask, remembering her student days when she'd been hypnotized by watching him paint.

Tina had just finished posing nude for Diego's murals in Chapingo, and of course she'd ended up sleeping with him.

"Diego's bad for you, Friducha. He'll chew you up and spit you out like an ogre."

"When I was a kid, I said I'd have Diego's baby, but all my girlfriends said he was a dirty fat man. But I didn't care. I figured I'd bathe him before I slept with him."

They burst out laughing shamelessly. Tina kissed Frida's hands with the tenderness of an older sister giving her blessing to the younger who is about to be wed. It was her way of saying their affair was over but that their lives would go on, more comfortably now because they knew each other so well. They hugged for a long time, recalling the hours they'd embraced in the nude, their gaze fixed on the bare light bulb above them while they told their life stories, joking around in ways that only they understood. They loosened their embrace and continued cooking; their friends would soon arrive. The guests were devoutly communist but wouldn't forgive them if there were no tacos or tequila to accompany their worldly discussions.

"Sooner or later, you'll be sorry," Tina said as she mashed vegetables for the pasta.

She knew Diego had an uncommon appetite for food and for the bodies of young women. And Tina also knew that Frida was fragile and wanted to protect her. Even so, that night she kept her promise and introduced her former lovers. Diego was already drunk when he arrived and pulled out his gun at the slightest provocation, shooting at anything that reeked of imperialism. The party ended when he put two bullets into the phonograph. Frida was a little frightened by his violent behavior, but she was simultaneously fascinated by the dangerous air surrounding the ogre with the froggy eyes.

A few days later they had their first rendezvous. It was a rainy afternoon, one of those when Mexico City's skies weep like a melancholy widow. Diego was up on a scaffold, painting a mural at the Ministry of Education building. He heard a feminine voice echoing through the building, like a siren calling to him from below.

"Diego, please come down. I have something important to tell you."

He studied his interlocutor with his amphibian eyes.

She smelled of fresh meat to be deliciously and vigorously devoured. She had a beautiful face, with deep eyes and charcoal hair. He noticed that her thick eyebrows met in the middle and crowned her delicate nose. He imagined them as wings of a blackbird struggling to fly.

Diego slowly made his way down the scaffolding. When he reached her, he realized how very tiny she was. Tina had already dubbed them the beauty and the beast.

"I didn't come here to play," Frida told him. "I have to work to earn a living. I have some paintings that I want you to see, but I'd appreciate it if you didn't treat this as a joke or try to blow smoke up my ass, because you're not going to get me into bed. I want your professional opinion. I don't need my ego fed, so if you don't think I can be a good artist, then I'll just burn them and be done with it. So, do you want to see them?"

As she showed him her work, she leaned the canvases against the wall where he was painting, creating a charming metaphor for the two of them as a couple: her diminutive oils against his overwhelming mural. Diego was impressed. His reaction was clear and honest. In each work he saw an unusual burst of energy, with lines that blurred between severe and delicate. He was accustomed to seeing neophytes use gimmicks to get noticed, but Diego could find nothing contrived in her work. Every brush stroke was true, exuding her sensuality and screaming her pain.

Frida immediately noticed Diego's excitement. She

could see the enthusiasm on his face. She put her hands on her hips and, like a little girl reprimanding her dolls, wagged her finger at Diego and hammered on about what she wanted.

"Don't hold back. . . . I want your real unvarnished opinion."

"Listen, little girl . . . if you have so little faith in what I'm going to say, then why the fuck do you even bother to ask me?" Diego shot back.

Frida was taken aback at first but regained her composure.

"Your friends told me that if a girl asks your advice and she's not totally horrible, you'll say whatever it takes to get in her pants," Frida grumbled as she gathered her paintings.

Diego watched but didn't stop her; he was amused by this interruption to his monotonous hard work. With paintings in hand, Frida turned and looked straight at the muralist. A long and awkward silence ensued. Suddenly, the sound of heels clicking on the floor brought them out of their dream state. It was Lupe, Diego's wife, with a huge basket of provisions and some hot soup.

"Who's this kid?" she asked. Lupe looked like a Renaissance painting: tall, with generous breasts and curvy hips atop a pair of shapely legs.

Without acknowledging Lupe, Diego turned to Frida. "You should keep painting. You should get to work on some new pieces. I can come see them on Sunday, when I'm not working."

"I live in Coyoacán, Londres 126," Frida said, and

started on her way without greeting Lupe, who looked on, burning with jealousy.

"That's the same little bitch who used to go see you work on the mural at the Preparatory," she spit at her husband.

With the satisfaction of a lion who's just swallowed his prey, Diego confirmed it: "The very one."

Diego arrived at Frida's to find a hacienda-style house, elegant and sober. He adjusted his large cowboy hat and knocked with aplomb on the wooden door. As he waited, he heard someone whistling the Internacionale. As if falling from the sky, the song rained down from a socialist paradise. As soon as Diego entered the hacienda, he found Frida in a pair of overalls, up a tree, picking lemons.

When she saw him, she bounded down from the tree, laughing the whole time. She took him by the hand as if she were a little girl leading an adult to see her toys, and took him to her room, where she had laid out the rest of her paintings. The frog king didn't know whether to delight more in the work or the woman. He kept all his words to himself, in his heart, because he was completely taken with her. Frida knew she'd put a spell on him, and she let herself be courted.

After various visits, Diego finally kissed her under a streetlamp near her house as if she were his first girl-friend. There was such electricity in that kiss that every streetlamp down the block went out. When Frida left him that night—a man eighteen years her senior—she was certain something extraordinary was happening.

Out of the corner of her eye, she caught a glimpse of the woman in the veil turning the street corner, as ephemeral as a streaking black fly.

Their surprised friends, including Tina, didn't know whether to laugh or cry when they heard Diego planned to marry Frida. And Mamá Matilde wasn't exactly thrilled that her daughter was going to marry a religion-bashing, divorced womanizer. In contrast, Guillermo put aside his German reserve.

"I see that you're interested in my daughter," he said to Diego.

"Of course. Otherwise I wouldn't be making the trek from Mexico City to Coyoacán to see her," he responded, as if it were obvious.

"She's a handful, a real devil," Guillermo cautioned him.

"I know."

"Fine. But don't say I didn't warn you." With that, Guillermo ended the conversation with his daughter's intended and left to read in his studio. The proposal had been accepted.

TINA'S RECIPES

When all the ass kissers came to Tina's apartment, she'd serve up tacos and they'd provide drinks and smokes. It was quite a challenge to cook for everybody. We'd set up a giant pot of pasta with various sauces on the side. Our art dealer would get us smoked Cotija cheese from the deli on the corner, the one next to the Condesa building, to substitute for the Parmesan. It was cheaper, and besides, a drunken painter can't tell the difference.

SAUCE FOR PASTA WITH MUSSELS, ORANGES AND TOMATOES

SALSA PARA PASTA CON MEJILLONES, NARANJA Y TOMATE

1 pound tomatoes, peeled and seeded

2 teaspoons olive oil

1 large onion, finely chopped

1 crushed garlic clove

1/2 teaspoon minced chile

3/4 cup dry white wine

3 teaspoons oregano

1/2 teaspoon sugar

3 tablespoons orange juice

Salt and pepper

20 cleaned mussels

2 teaspoons orange zest
2 teaspoons chopped parsley

✳ Mash the tomatoes with a mallet. Heat the oil in a pan and fry the onion, garlic, and chile for 5 minutes. Then add the tomatoes, some of the wine, the oregano, sugar, and orange juice. Season to taste with salt and pepper and let it boil for a while. Lower the heat and let it simmer until the sauce thickens. In the meantime, pour the rest of the wine over the mussels and heat in the oven until the mussels open. Mix the mussels and their juices with the sauce. To serve, sprinkle orange zest and parsley over the sauce.

ANCHOVY AND OLIVE SAUCE

SALSA DE ANCHOAS Y ACEITUNAS

7 ounces sliced green olives
1 teaspoon anchovy filets, cut into fine strips
1/4 cup grated Parmesan cheese
1/2 cup crushed nuts

1 teaspoon oregano
3 teaspoons chopped fresh basil
1 teaspoon chopped parsley
1/2 cup extra virgin olive oil
Salt and pepper

✳ Mix the olives, anchovies, Parmesan, nuts, oregano, basil, and parsley. Then, slowly, pour in the olive oil, stirring until it thickens into a paste. Let it sit for 2 hours so the flavors blend well. Season with salt and pepper and serve with pasta.

TIRAMISÚ

Tina once told me that the name of this cake came from the expression "It's so fresh, let me at it." Who knows whether she was lying. I liked it and made a mental note, but later I heard it really means "pull me up." You can never trust an Italian, unless they're saying "I love you."

1 cup sweet cream
8 ounces ricotta cheese or mascarpone

1 package cream cheese, 8 ounces
1 cup confectioners' sugar
1 cup espresso coffee
3 tablespoons coffee liqueur
3 tablespoons brandy
1 pound ladyfingers
Cocoa powder as needed

❋ Beat the sweet cream with the cheeses and sugar. In a separate bowl, mix the espresso, coffee liqueur, and brandy; soak the ladyfingers in this. Line a pan with the soaked ladyfingers, then add a layer of the cheese mixture and sprinkle with cocoa. Repeat the layers and finish with a final sprinkling of cocoa. Refrigerate for no less than 2 hours.

CHAPTER VIII

Frida fell in love with Diego in that way that women surrender to men who will only bring them pain. From the moment she decided Diego would be her new reason for living, Frida threw her heart, eyes, and instincts away into a river of passion. She'd realized her dream of having Mexico's most important intellectual enthralled with *her*—a delicate dove, a limping dove—and not only did her ego swell but her head filled with impossible dreams as she was elevated to the Olympus where the Frog King reigned, making her his goddess as well.

It had been difficult for her to fall in love again after the break from Alejandro. Her fleeting sexual relationships with other men and women had merely eased the fire that had been burning since the accident. No matter how she surrendered her body to her lovers, she couldn't put out the fire. Everything was different with Diego. She'd finally found someone with whom she had an intellectual affinity, with whom her agile and unconventional mind would never be bored. She knew it when she heard Diego say, "Frida, I'd rather have one hundred intelligent enemies than an idiot for a friend." It seemed that they would never tire of each other. They engaged every evening in talks about an endless number of interests they had in common. She would sit under the scaffold as he painted and they'd discuss socialist realism, the proletarian struggle, art, and naughty gossip about their friends.

One day, Lupe, Diego's ex, came by to discuss their two daughters. During the visit she realized Frida was no longer wearing black skirts and elegant white blouses with low necklines. She was slowly transforming herself, as if she'd entered a butterfly's cocoon. She was wearing a simple red blouse with a shiny brooch bearing the hammer and sickle, denim pants, and a leather jacket. She was freeing herself from the symbolic banality of the bourgeoisie.

"And this child? Have her parents given her permission to stay up past her bedtime?" Lupe asked. Her voice dripped with venom, her looks meant to kill.

"Lupe, I'm going to marry Frida. I've asked for her hand!" Diego yelled down to her, jovially, from the scaffold.

Frida arched her thick single brow and made a triumphant face.

"He asked me yesterday evening," she confirmed.

Lupe kicked the scaffold. As she turned to leave, she offered Diego's new bride some advice: "His love turns just like a weather vane."

Frida didn't give it credence. She knew she'd won. Having crowned themselves the artistic gods of the proletariat, they decided to consummate their union in a style worthy of two Communist Party militants: very simply, very sparingly, very merrily, and with plenty of alcohol.

The festivities took place on August 21 of the last year of the 1920s. Frida gave a lot of thought to preparing the party; she was the last single daughter in the family and, in keeping with tradition, she wanted to shock everyone. She asked to borrow one of her servant's long caramel-colored skirts. Then she looked among the other clothes belonging to the same girl, who was from Oaxaca, and found a blouse still redolent of the kitchen where mole, bread, and pastries were made. For a final touch, she borrowed a rebozo, the symbol of Mexican motherhood but also of the revolutionaries, strong and robust women who weren't afraid to fight to save their men. She made a braid in the back of her head, with her hair parted in the middle, thinking that her Godmother would surely approve of the style. Then she perched her rickety leg atop a worn but shiny shoe.

That's how she went to the Coyoacán city hall with the only kin that accompanied her: her father, Guillermo, who took her proudly by the arm down the town's cobblestone streets. He would nod as a greeting at any acquaintance they saw on the way. The Spaniard from the bar complimented the beauty of the bride, the corner storekeeper gave her a rose, and the local police officer whistled with all his might in celebration.

In an austere bureaucratic office in which the only decoration was a portrait of the president of the republic, the mayor of Coyoacán waited, with an elaborate hairdo, a tie as wide as a tablecloth, and alcohol on his breath. Turned out he ran a pulque business on the side. Proud witnesses rolled their hats in their hands, all salt of the earth: a barber, a homeopathic doctor, and a local judge. Waiting for the bride was the greatest living Mexican painter, wearing a pair of miner's boots that were screaming for a good polishing, a pair of too-short pants tied above the waist to keep them from falling from his great belly, a shirt that had been pressed once upon a time, a wool coat, a huge tie, and a hat that couldn't contain the orgy of curls on his head. Next to him, so lovely that looking at her was like staring at the sun, was their friend Tina, dressed to play the part of maid of honor.

"We are gathered here to celebrate the marriage of Mr. Diego Rivera and Miss Frida Kahlo," recited the mayor, using the same tone he would for a speech to end a political campaign. Then he went on, quoting Melchor Ocampo's poetry, underscoring all the macho elements that so amused Frida and made her turn smilingly to Diego, searching out his complicity. After the whole hullabaloo was over, the mayor invited the couple to kiss, and everyone applauded. The congratulations and shaking of hands went on and on. Guillermo approached

Diego and offered him his hand like a gentleman; the two men shook cordially.

"Be aware that my daughter is sickly and that she'll be that way all her life. She's smart but not pretty. Think about it; you still have time to run."

Diego gave his father-in-law such an intense bear hug that he lifted him off the ground. They both burst out laughing until Diego let him go and, drunk, decided to toast with one of the mayor's brews.

"Gentlemen, isn't it true that we're performing a bit of theater?"

The party continued on the roof of Tina's apartment. Between the neighbors' laundry lines there were hundreds of colorful little paper flags with doves carrying messages of love, hearts, and reminders that the union of two souls is the end stage of our time on Earth. The colors danced in the breeze, competing for the guests' attention with the gaily decorated tables. Plates were already set out on contrasting colored tablecloths, waiting for the succulent dishes that would be served. The plates themselves were simple, appropriate to a town wedding: made of clay, glazed, and with different animals painted in green.

The bride and groom eventually arrived at the folkloric scene. The mayor of Coyoacán presented them with various liters of his brews, including celery and pear juices, followed by tequila, all of which made for an explosive party. When all the guests were present—they were many and very diverse—the food was warmed and ready to serve. Delicious dishes competed with each other for the guests' palates, some prepared by Lupe, others bought at the market. Everything looked so delectable. It was hard to decide what to eat first. There was authentic Oaxaca mole with the usual turkey and bean tamales on the side. The rice, sprinkled red and green, had a central place at the table. There were chiles rellenos in tomato sauce, and chiles huazontles filled with cheese. To top it all off, an uninvited cloud of bees was attracted to a collection of exquisite desserts: buñuelos, dulce de leche, glazed fruits, puddings, pastries, and Zamora buns.

The ones responsible for this culinary carnival of temptations were Tina, who was in charge of ordering from the merchants at the Puebla Street market, and, incredibly, Lupe, who maintained a strange love-hate relationship with her ex-husband. She'd prepared various dishes herself, surprising Frida by being so accommodating.

Dishes and friends danced before Frida's gleeful eyes. Everyone followed the town tradition by skipping the silverware. They ate from their plates using tortillas, with beer and tequila to drink; only in Mexico is the tortilla a spoon, a plate, and an accompaniment.

At dusk, when the mariachis were playing songs about revenge to the inebriated crowd, they lit a series a paper lanterns and the place became covered in colorful twinkling lights. Diego could barely stand by then, and it seemed like whatever he was saying through his alcohol-infused breath was being dragged on the floor.

Frida left his side as he sang his sad version of a revolutionary corrido. She went to sit on the edge of the roof of the beautiful Victorian to look out at the avenue. There were a few night owls in their cars out in the green Roma neighborhood. The magpies' murmurs while looking for a place to spend the night had stopped. Now it was just her and her future. With that, she gulped down the shot of tequila she'd been carrying and toasted the woman she knew was accompanying her out there somewhere. It was at that very moment that she thought of a phrase she wrote in the notebook Tina had given her: "Have the courage to live, because anyone can die."

She sighed with satisfaction, feeling lucky about her life. Unfortunately, her feelings were misleading, and like all tragedies disguised as celebrations, the night ended badly. Lupe, with tequila in hand and envy in her heart, had her eye on Frida. She took advantage of a break by the mariachis to shout out to the gathered crowd. Everyone turned to her, eyes and ears on alert. She stood in front of Frida, who never saw it coming: Lupe lifted Frida's skirt all the way to her undies.

"Look at these two fucking sticks Diego got for himself now, and how embarrassing they are compared to my beautiful legs!"

And as if it were a real contest, she uncovered her own legs so everyone could admire how shapely they were.

Without a doubt, Frida's were little competition.

Lupe growled, spit out a "Fuck you," and dramatically stomped out of the party. The mariachis began again, trying to cover up everyone's embarrassment. As if all that wasn't enough to make Frida cry, her own husband spoiled the wedding for her: Lupe's spectacle was still fresh when Diego, enraged and plastered out of his mind, pulled out his pistol amid an argument with a guest.

Frida fled, her tears dampening her rebozo. Her father took her home to Coyoacán, where she locked herself in her room and drowned her anguish in her pillow. No one realized she'd left until the end of the fight, but it didn't stop Diego from continuing to drink.

It would be several days before Diego took her to live with him. If Frida had been able to interpret the events, she would have known what embarrassments and shame lay ahead for her. But she was bewitched by him, and so it seemed she'd already forgotten that on the night of her wedding, just as she was falling asleep, a feminine voice had whispered in her ear: "The pain has barely begun, but that's what you've agreed to."

MY WEDDING

For women, a wedding is the pinnacle of girl-ish dreams, the culmination of playing tea-party with her dolls. A wedding is when we're all queens, when we are all respected. They're pure nonsense, simple idiocies. They're capitalist dreams so we'll buy a hypocritically white dress that's miles from our immaculate virginity.

My wedding was a public event, for the people. I was my own wedding. Everyone else—the ones who didn't like it—can go fuck themselves. It was my wedding and I ruled it. The woman should always rule at her own wedding, even if everyone thinks she's a bitch.

MOLE POBLANO

There are a million stories about how mole came to be. As far as I'm concerned, they're all damn lies; even the damned Church wants to take credit. They say it was in Puebla, when a fat bishop son of a bitch asked the Dominican nuns to prepare a quality dish to smooth the way with the Spanish viceroy who was soon to visit. The nuns began to work, when one of them saw another grinding everything together. "Pero, ¡cómo mole!"—"Look at how she grinds!" she said. I like mole because it's the union of our two cultures: the Spanish, through the almonds, clove and cinnamon; and the indigenous people, through the grand variety of chiles and cocoa. It's a dish for celebration.

5 chipotle chiles
12 mulato chiles, deveined and seeded
12 pasilla chiles, deveined and seeded
10 ancho chiles, deveined and seeded
1 pound lard
5 medium-sized garlic cloves
2 medium onions, sliced
4 hard tortillas, cut into quarters
1 golden-fried bread roll
3/4 cup raisins
8 ounces almonds
3/4 cup sesame seeds
1/2 tablespoon anise
1 teaspoon ground cloves or 5 whole cloves
1 or 2 cinnamon sticks
1 teaspoon ground black pepper
3 stone-ground chocolate squares
8 ounces tomatoes, peeled and diced
1 green plantain

1 1/4 cups peanuts
1 teaspoon coriander seeds
Salt
Sugar
15 pieces cooked chicken or a big turkey,
  in pieces, with cooking broth

✳ Soak the chiles in 1 1/4 cups of hot lard,
then place them in a pot of boiling water until
they're soft. Using the same lard, sauté the
garlic and onions, then add the tortillas,
bread, raisins, almonds, chile seeds, half the
sesame seeds, the anise, cloves, cinnamon,
black pepper, chocolate, and tomatoes. Fry
everything together, then strain the chiles
and add them, too. To facilitate matters, the
frying can be done in stages. Then mash
everything else together, using a molcajete
if possible. Once it has a pastelike quality,
use the remaining lard to fry it with the
rest of the ingredients. Add a little broth
from cooking the chicken or turkey, let it boil,
and season with salt and sugar. It should
have a thick consistency. Add the chicken

or turkey pieces and serve, sprinkling it with
the rest of the sesame seeds.

BEAN TAMALES

TAMALES DE FRIJOL

If there's turkey mole, then there should
be bean tamales. They're the perfect marriage, and the accompanying rice can play
the role of mistress, which every respectable
marriage should include

8 ounces black beans
8 ounces ground pumpkin seeds
3 tablespoons sesame seeds
Chiles de árbol
A pinch of ground avocado leaves
Salt
12 ounces lard
2 1/4 pounds mashed corn masa
30 corn husks for tamales

✻Cook the beans, but not all the way,
then strain them. In a dry pan, brown the

ground pumpkin seeds, sesame seeds, and chiles and set aside to mill later. To the beans add the ground avocado leaves, stir, and add salt to taste. Beat the lard with a wooden spoon until it doubles in size. Add the masa and continue beating and stirring until a small ball of it can float in a glass of water. Season with salt and stuff into the corn husks, sealing them so the bean mixture doesn't spill out. Stand the tamales up in a steamer. Cover and let cook for 1 hour.

MEXICAN RICE

ARROZ A LA MEXICANA

1 cup rice

Oil for frying

1 carrot, finely chopped

1 potato, diced

1 cup peas

2 medium tomatoes

1 onion slice

1 garlic clove

Salt

2 cups chicken broth

❋ Boil the rice in water for 10 minutes. Strain and leave in the sun for 15 minutes. Heat the oil in a saucepan until very hot. Fry the rice and carrot, potato, and peas. Mash the tomatoes, onion, and garlic and mix with a little bit of water, then strain. When the rice turns a light brown color, drain the excess oil and add the tomato mixture. Season with salt. As soon as the oil can be seen boiling above the tomato mixture, add the chicken broth and cover until the liquid is absorbed.

CHAPTER IX

Lupe—Frida's rival for Diego—was bold and unpredictable. The kind of woman no one wants as an enemy. She was a genuine warrior: she'd fought for everything she'd ever wanted in life, and she'd continue to do so. When she met Diego's newest love interest, it was like a head-on train crash. What Frida lacked was Lupe's experience. Lupe had led quite a life up until then. She'd studied at a boarding school run by nuns. But knowing she was young and beautiful, she'd make herself fashionable dresses so she could stand near the Guadalajara cathedral, where the wind would blow up her skirts and reveal her shapely legs. This was during the time Diego was self-exiled in Europe as a protest against the direction the Mexican government had taken. He was already a famous painter when he returned and met the enigmatic and beautiful Lupe Marín, who bewitched him like a sorceress. He idolized her to such an extreme that he portrayed her as Eve herself in his mural *The Cre-*

ation, at the Preparatory. There's no doubt Diego's interminable parade of lovers doomed their marriage, though she'd responded to each of them with extraordinary violence. In fact, she tried to bludgeon Diego with a molcajete pestle when she found out he'd slept with Tina Modotti.

Diego left Lupe with two daughters to feed, Guadalupe and Ruth, when he went off to Russia. She warned him: "Go ahead, fuck your Russian sluts, but you won't find me when you come back."

Even when they were separated, Diego continued visiting Lupe's house for meals and to tell her about his lovers. She took great care to hide her jealousy when he told her he was in love with Frida; though by then Lupe was living with the poet Jorge Cuesta, she was convinced Diego was like alcohol and she an alcoholic. One morning in March, Lupe swept into the newlyweds' home like a tempest. Frida was too terrified to ask why she was there.

"I came to cook for Diego because he tells me you're a disaster," she growled while searching for utensils and food in the kitchen.

She rolled up her sleeves, strapped on an apron, and, with the force of an angry Viking, pushed aside Frida, who fell flat on her bottom. Lupe began chopping onions and cursing about the lack of kitchen tools. Frida sat on the floor for a minute, legs splayed, looking up at the whirlwind that had invaded her kitchen. There are some things one woman should never do to another: look inside her purse, covet her boyfriend, or kick her out of her own kitchen. Frida got up with as much dignity as she could muster, fixing her hair so she could be presentable for the battle she was about to initiate with the intruder. She balled up her fists; even though she was small, she was as hot as a habanero. She rushed Lupe, grabbed the knife out of her hand, and threw her against the oven.

"The only one who prepares Diego's meals here is his wife! And you ceased being that a long time ago. So unless you want me to dice you into a Guadalajara girl in chile sauce, it would be best if you got the hell out of my kitchen!" Frida screamed, and with that, she began to cut the onion herself.

Frida had won the first round, but Lupe wasn't done. She set a pot of water to boil and calmly began adding whatever dry and withered vegetables she could find.

"You don't know how to get the fire started with anything or anyone; you either burn it or leave it lukewarm. A woman should know how to move in the kitchen so her man won't want to eat anywhere else," Lupe said, disgusted, tossing a couple of onions at Frida that were already sprouting. Frida snatched the vegetables from Lupe's hands and dumped them into the pot, splashing water on Lupe's clothes.

Frida smiled slyly, satisfied. "Well, perhaps that's precisely why he always went to eat elsewhere when he was with you," Frida said. "Maybe he didn't like having the same old chicken breast every day."

Lupe let loose a war cry. She grabbed a pair of eggs and cracked them with the smoothness of a chef on her rival's head.

"No, little girl, I'm the one with spice here: I can already see that when Diego wants to eat now, he can't even find himself a decent pair of eggs." Lupe took another egg and cracked it against Frida's smaller breasts. Frida felt the egg white running down her body, and she raised her single brow. Coolly, she grabbed a container of flour and dumped it over Lupe, making her look like a Puebla cemita sandwich.

"Diego says he likes the meat close to the bone, because fat is bad for his health and he hates the greasy taste it leaves in his mouth," Frida said.

Lupe smiled malevolently, filling the room with the kind of hate only two such strong women can generate. She searched the cupboard for anything else to throw at Frida, but she found only rancid coffee, stale bread, and a container of sour milk. She used them all.

"Putica, Diego will eventually tire of your flavor and go looking for riper papayas, juicier thighs, delicious pozole, and fresh little hairless tacos."

"You're a flavorless mole de olla!"

"You're a stringy commie jerky!"

"Stale pastry!"

"Used meat sausage!"

There was nothing left to throw into the pot, not even insults, when it finally boiled over onto the stove, putting out the flame. With that, the hate between the two women was suddenly extinguished too. When they surveyed the chaos, they sighed, came to their senses, and burst out laughing in unison. They laughed so long that a neighbor peeked in to make sure everything was okay.

Tears of laughter rolled down their faces and mixed with the flour, coffee, and egg yolks that covered them from head to toe, and they hugged like two kids happy with their mischief. Frida offered Lupe a cigarette and they sat down to smoke together amid the ruins from their battle.

"Your kitchen is a piece of shit," Lupe said.

Frida started to get upset—she'd thought the insults were over—but seeing Lupe pull out a roll of bills to give to her, she realized Lupe was serious.

"Let's go to the Merced market to buy pots, pans, all the things you need to make food the way Diego likes. The moment will come when you'll stop being the reason he comes home at night, no matter how young and beautiful you are. So give him another reason. Go at him through his stomach and you'll hook him like a fish. When he tastes your mole, make it so he'll prefer re-heated leftovers to fucking some gringa."

She never thought she'd hear these words from Lupe, but she knew right away she was being honest and generous. Frida sucked on her cigarette and asked her an infinite number of questions: When will I know that Diego doesn't love me anymore? How much should I forgive? And then she came upon the most important questions of all.

"Do you really think it's possible to trap somebody with food? Do you really think a banquet can be a magic potion?"

"I know that a well-made meal is better than a roll in the hay," Lupe responded in her Guadalajara accent as if this were an article of faith. "I'll teach you so that your table will earn you tributes from everyone."

"What will I give you in return? I have nothing except my paintings."

"That's not a bad idea. . . . Maybe someday you can paint me," Lupe said, then stood up and put her cigarette out with her foot. "Although it wouldn't be bad at all to have a good friend. Someone with whom I could bitch about this fat-bellied frog's stupidities. Let's make a dish that will carry someone to the gates of heaven—but first we really need some decent pots and pans."

Frida became Lupe's student, opening herself to that particular world of alchemy. If she learned to cook, she could bring Diego his lunch while he worked, the way Mexican peasant women would lovingly take their exquisite dishes to their husbands in the fields. It would also give her the chance to befriend this quarrelsome woman and to learn to make delicious offerings for her Godmother on the Day of the Dead. Perhaps that could earn her a few more years of life.

"So, what do you say?"

"Is it true that chiles nogada aren't soaked in batter, just sauce?" Frida asked.

Lupe didn't answer. Their mutual smiles were enough to communicate they had a deal, one consummated with spices, chiles, and stews. They'd come to that magical place, that kitchen where women discuss their pain, their loves, and their recipes.

Before heading out to the market, Frida grabbed a notebook to jot down Lupe's recipes. And maybe because it was fate, she grabbed the first one she found: the beautifully bound black book that Tina had given her before her wedding.

Not only did Frida learn to cook, but she actually surpassed her master. The friendship between the erstwhile rivals became so deep that at one point they lived with their respective husbands and Diego's daughters in adjoining apartments. When Lupe and Frida would cook together, they'd barely fit in the tiny kitchens. Lupe would fill the space with her voluptuous body and Frida with her bulky tehuana folk costumes. As promised, Frida painted Lupe's portrait and gave it to her as a gift, a gift the flamboyant Guadalajaran would destroy years later in a rage. She would come to lament the loss.

The cooking classes started, and Frida began taking meals to Diego at work in a basket decorated with flowers. Her dishes came wrapped in tea towels she lovingly embroidered with the words "I adore you."

LUPE'S CHILES EN NOGADA

There isn't a more Mexican dish than this. It makes you want to sing corridos and listen to mariachis. It sports the colors of the flag, thanks to the very imaginative nuns from Puebla who created it. It's a dish for festive occasions, such as Independence Day. When we used to make it, I'd gather my sisters and their kids to peel the nuts, gossip, and have a drink or two. It's a marvelous experience, just like the flavor.

12 poblano chiles
1 pomegranate (just the seeds)
Parsley for decorating

For the filling:

1 pound pork loin
4 cups water
1/4 onion in one piece
5 garlic cloves, 3 whole and 2 chopped
Oil
Salt
1 candied citron, sliced
1/4 cup finely chopped onion
2 cups tomatoes, peeled and diced
5 cloves
1 teaspoon ground cinnamon

1 apple, peeled and chopped

1 large yellow peach or 3 small ones, cut into pieces

1 pear, peeled and chopped

1 large plantain, peeled and chopped

1/3 cup raisins

1/3 cup almonds, peeled and chopped

For the nogada:

1 cup fresh walnuts, peeled and chopped

1 cup heavy cream

6 1/2 ounces queso fresco

Sugar to taste

Cinnamon may also be added, if desired

Salt

1 cup milk

❋Seed and devein the chiles. Be careful that they don't split. Roast the chiles. To make the filling, place the pork, the water, the 1/4 onion, the whole garlic cloves, and a little bit of salt in a pot over high heat. As soon as it boils, lower the heat and let it simmer for 40 minutes or until the meat is cooked well enough to shred easily. In a separate pan, heat the oil, citron, the chopped onion, and chopped garlic. Add the shredded meat and then the tomatoes. Season with cloves and cinnamon, then, lastly, add the fruits, beginning with the apple, then the peach, pear, and plantain. Add salt to taste. If it's a little dry, add sauce from the pot in which the meat was cooked. Add the raisins and almonds. For the nogada, grind and mix all the ingredients, adding milk until you get the desired consistency. Fill the chiles and place them on a plate to serve. Pour the nogada over the chiles to cover and sprinkle with pomegranate seeds. Decorate with parsley.

CHAPTER X

Frida's first few months as Diego's wife were pleasant and intimate. She found passion in words, in her art, and in her man's body every minute she was with him. Since her wedding day, every dawn would welcome a lustful search through her frilly skirts and the revelation of her breasts at the isthmus of her blouse. They laughed a lot; they played even more. They explored each other's bodies like children discovering an amusement park. A mere graze of their hands, an exchange of glances, or a love letter evoked happiness, shivers, and sparks. Their bedroom at the foot of the majestic volcano Popocatépetl, where they spent their energetic nights, smelled of sex and new love. Over the sounds of the Internacionale and the exotic birdcalls of the valley, they bathed together, only to be covered in sweat later, snacking on fruits that Frida would set out every morning in a large bowl. The naseberries, mangoes, soursops, and capulines only heightened their pleasure. They were a modern Adam and Eve, newlyweds sent to paradise: Cuernavaca.

Diego's art had earned the admiration of Dwight Morrow, the American ambassador. After an avalanche of compliments, he'd commissioned a mural for the ancient Palace of Cortés, where centuries before another tragic love had evolved: that of the conquistador Hernán Cortés and his interpreter and lover, Malintzin. This is how it came to pass that Diego and Frida spent their honeymoon in the city of eternal spring, blessed by an ironic circumstance: the capitalist empire's representative's taste for the work of Mexico's most famous communist painter. The diplomat had convinced Plutarco Elías Calles to change the constitution to favor the American companies exploring for oil, and, to show his gratitude, he paid for a mural decrying imperialism. It was then that Frida realized Diego could be very red, but his eyes twinkled at the sight of green. His hunger for food and women also extended to dollars; for the fat painter, there were no bad dollars, no bad benefactors, even if these were the very opposite of what he preached. To seal the deal, the ambassador gave Diego and Frida his country house to live in while Diego finished the mural. They spent their first wedded days surrounded by birdsong and the fragrance of fruit, looking at the two snow-capped volcanoes, which, according to legend, resembles a warrior yearning for his sleeping lover to awaken.

During those dreamy days, Frida spent most of her time at the foot of the platform where Diego worked, contemplating the mural, which eventually revealed the brutality of the Conquest and the triumph of Emiliano Zapata's Mexican Revolution. In her free time she delighted in the ambassador's house, an architectural wonder deserving of admiration. It had a beautiful garden with fountains, flowers, banana trees, palm trees, and bougainvillea. She also painted, though she kept her work hidden from the eyes of strangers. Now and again, a friend from the capital would visit. They'd take him around, and then have outrageous parties in the evenings. Incredibly, the next morning Diego would bounce right out of bed and go off to paint. Their friends could barely stand, but the couple's energy was infinite.

On one of those early days, they decided to go to Tepozteco, the mountain that boasted a pre-Columbian pyramid at the peak, and the town of Tepoztlán in the valley. Happy because of the day trip, Frida prepared various dishes for the journey. She put them in baskets covered with tablecloths embroidered by local indigenous women.

They had agreed to meet at the Palace of Cortés, where Frida arrived at noon. On hearing about their plans, her husband's assistants asked to join them, eager to participate in the couple's famous discussions. Frida approached the main part of the mural, where a very focused Diego was painting; she was shocked—she couldn't take her eyes off the image of Zapata's horse. She gasped a little and her hands shook. Diego noticed that something was wrong and quickly came down from the scaffold.

"What do you think, Friducha? Isn't the horse magnificent?" he asked in admiration of his own work.

Frida didn't respond. Her gaze was lost in the painting of a mysterious horseman with a thick mustache and a steed that recalled a most terrible memory. She remembered that first afternoon when she'd met the Messenger, and then those moments when she saw him again just before her accident.

"Come on, it can't be that bad," Diego said, turning from her to his creation.

"That can't be him," Frida whispered, staring ahead.

"Not him? Then who the fuck do you think it is?" protested Rivera, scratching his huge butt.

Frida snapped out of her stupor and shook off her fear. She pulled at her braids, ruffled her skirt, and, with the dignity of a hero condemned to death by firing squad, lit a cigarette.

"It's wrong. Everyone knows that Zapata's horse was black, not white. You did it wrong," she said, trying to come off like a critic.

Diego stared at her, surprised. He knew his tiny wife was tough, but this kind of impudence wasn't like her.

"I know, but it looks better white. If I'd painted it black it would have made the whole mural look too dark. Frida, don't embarrass me in front of my assistants!"

"To top it off, it's badly painted. That hoof looks like a cow's, fatty and bony."

Certainly Diego had many faults, some of which he could keep under wraps, but others could be set off like dynamite. Pride was perhaps the worst. Frida's criticism hit a nerve. Furious, he grabbed a brush, climbed up, and painted over the hoof in three strokes. His assistants couldn't hide their surprise. Diego turned, his eyes filled with hate, and faced his wife with the killer brush still in his hand. Frida didn't flinch and continued smoking, daring him. Still in a state herself, Frida thought it was better to stay in character than to explain that she knew the man in the mural. She didn't want him to think she was crazy.

"You're right, Frida. I'll fix it tomorrow. Let's go. I'm starved," Diego said tenderly, and then placed his powerful arm around her delicate neck.

Frida responded with the best reward: a wide and flirty smile and a deep kiss. They strolled together toward the exit, but as they were leaving, she stole a glance back and asked herself how she could possibly think she saw a ghost from her past in that white horse. And when she couldn't find a comforting answer, she did what all wives do in these circumstances: she locked the question away, where it would surely be forgotten.

They drove from Cuernavaca to Tepoztlán with the two assistants, drinking tequila and singing old revolutionary corridos, the kind that fire up the soul and make you want to shout. The old Ford truck jumped over potholes and rocks, dodging wild pigs, chickens, and burros along the way. When they arrived at the mountain, they could see the steeples of the town convent, which rose like Gulliver among the tiny clay tile roofs, the surrounding mountains like proud sentries. The truck snaked through the town's cobblestone streets until it came to a stop under the shadow of an arch near a plaza and the convent's courtyard. The plaza was overflowing with white canvas tents and vendors offering fruits and flowers.

Frida and Diego strolled by the main plaza trailed by kids dressed in regional clothes who shouted out their wares: fruits, wooden toys and snacks. They browsed each tent until the heat forced them under an arch, where they refreshed themselves with naseberry, guava, and cactus ice cream. A boy with a dirty face approached to sell them wooden toys. In his basket he had artisanal marvels carved out of wood: little cars, tightrope walkers, hens that pecked at the ground, racing mice, and airplanes.

"Give me one of your little cars. The red one," Frida said.

The boy gave it to her like an explorer handing gold over to his queen. Frida opened Diego's hands; he was having fun watching her. She placed the little car in his palm, making him look like a giant. Lovingly, she closed each of his fingers around the little red wooden car.

"This is my gift. It's my heart, red like the color of blood. It has wheels, so it can follow you wherever you go, my little Diego."

Like a tender mother, she kissed him on the forehead. Diego closed his froggy eyes, letting himself feel the little toy like a heartbeat. Then he opened them again, put the gift in his bag, and continued eating his fruit-flavored ice cream.

While they tasted their treats, a thin man with a leathery face and a palm-leaf sombrero approached them.

"If you'd like to see the pyramid at Tepozteco, sir, I can take you."

Diego accepted and made a deal with the guide. He and Frida exchanged a knowing look, noting that the man was affectless; his face barely moved when he talked, as if he were a marble statue.

They left the assistants in charge of the food baskets and started up the slope, climbing between rocks and bushes. The incline was steep and challenging. Diego fell behind constantly, his breathing labored from helping Frida drag her long skirt and bum leg. He cursed a mean streak when he almost fell into a ravine.

"Don't bring hatred to Tepoztlán; if you bring ill will, it'll turn on you, sir. Let it out. Before you get there, make your peace with Tepozteco," said the impassive guide.

"Well, that bastard Tepozteco is trying to kill me," the painter said, laughing.

"Then you're simply seeing a reflection. Many people wish you ill."

"Tell us the story of your town," Frida entreated him.

"Well, they say many years ago a maiden used to bathe in the ravine, even though the town elders had warned her not to, and had told her there were spirits there. The maiden ignored them and wound up pregnant. When they found out, her parents disowned her. After the boy was born, the grandfather made various attempts to kill him: he threw him into a ravine, but a fateful wind picked up the baby and carried him to a prairie. The grandfather then abandoned him among the cacti, but the stalks bent to the baby's mouth to give him honeyed water to drink. Then an old couple came by and saw the child. They took him home and adopted him. They named him Tepotécatl, patron of Tepoztlán."

"I like that story. Tell us another one," Frida suggested so they'd keep going. She really wanted to see the pyramid, but Diego was laboring with every step. It was fun to watch them, two city creatures struggling in the wild. The guide began another story, probably learned by rote, and no more special to him than the ones doled out by street performers charging a few coins for the telling.

"This one took place many moons ago, when savage men still ruled our lands and Death came to build temples with blood-soaked crosses. Years passed, and the people lived in large cities in which an eleven o'clock curfew was marked by the ringing of church bells. After eleven, you could hear a woman's laments echoing through the streets. The neighbors grew anguished because the desperate cries didn't let them sleep. They wondered who this woman could be. What was the cause of her pain? Determined to solve the mystery, some looked out the window and discovered a woman dressed in white with a veil over her face. She was kneeling and looking east toward the main plaza. The curious followed her, but she always disappeared into the fog around Lake Texcoco. Because of her grief-stricken voice, the town's women called her La Llorona.

"Some thought she was an indigenous woman who'd once fallen in love with a Spanish gentleman with whom she'd had three children. He didn't love her and wouldn't marry her. He possessed her like a dog, and when he tired of her, he cast her aside. This cruel man later married a rich Spanish woman, and when La Llorona found out, she went crazy with pain and drowned all three of her children in the river. When she realized what she'd done, she killed herself. Ever since, she wails and wails, and you can hear her cry, 'Oh, my children!'

"But others dig a little deeper, to the roots of our Totonac ancestors. They speak of the cihuateteo, women who died in childbirth who were considered goddesses. My uncle Concepción, who was an educated person like yourselves, told me it's Malintzin's shamed soul betraying her children—the Mexican people—by allowing herself to be seduced by that savage man who enslaved us for centuries. Ultimately, it doesn't really matter who the woman is. She will go on crying behind her veil for the loss of her children until the very last of those men leave this land."

When he finished his story, the man took off his enormous sombrero and, using a wet cotton paliacate scarf, wiped his sweaty brow. The sun was going down between the mountains and seemed to wink conspiratorially at the guide. A flock of magpies rushed across the cloudy skies. Frida looked toward the town of Tepoztlán and imagined a little girl playing with all those tiny houses as if they were toys.

"That's a beautiful story," she said, inhaling a cigarette that comforted her as much as her sarape.

Diego scratched his nest of hair and mumbled some profanities as he began to make his way back to town.

"Everything is religion's fault, because of the way it invents phantoms. . . . Fucking Church! The truth is, I don't give a damn about seeing the pyramid anymore. I'm going back: I'm starving."

Whatever else he said was lost, because he'd already started back down the mountain to find a bar that would sell him a bottle of tequila to wet his throat.

Frida finished her smoke as calmly as a woman waiting for her son's tantrum to end. Her eyes were fixed on the horizon.

"The woman wore a veil, right?" she asked the guide, who hadn't moved, waiting for instructions.

"In every story I've ever heard, señora, La Llorona wears a veil."

"Yes. Yes, that's her. She always wears a veil," she said to herself, and flicked the cigarette butt to the wind; the smoke created a perfect arch, like a jump rope.

Frida started after her husband, sure the man in the sombrero had described none other than her Godmother.

Frida dreamt about her that night: she saw her wandering a lonely street, between the doors and elaborate façades of the houses, inviting Frida to come and lament together the anguish that life had in store for them. She reached into Frida's chest and pulled out the little red wooden car, which wouldn't stop moving. The woman in the veil wasn't crying for her children but for Frida.

The very next day, Frida forgot the dream.

MY TRIP TO CUERNAVACA

Why there's snow in Tepoztlán I'll never understand. But its climate invites a refresher, something cool. I think ice cream is a gift to us from the gods who watch over the mountaintop so that we can delight in a taste of paradise. But also so we'll understand that everything can melt in our hands, and that good things are ephemeral.

MANGO TEPOZTECO ICE CREAM

NIEVE DE MANGO DE TEPOZTECO

2 pounds mangoes
2 tablespoons lemon juice
1/2 teaspoon lemon zest
1/2 cup water

3 tablespoons brown sugar
1/4 cup sour cream, lightly whipped
1 egg white, whipped until it's frothy

✸ Peel the mangoes and remove all the pulp from the seed, leaving nothing behind. Chop the pulp and set aside 1/4 cup so the ice cream will have texture. In a blender, mix all the ingredients except the sour cream and egg white. When the mixture is pureed, pour into an ice cream maker. Slowly add the sour cream and egg white. Continue until the mixture gets creamy. Add the reserved mango. Freeze for 12 hours. Remove from the cold 10 minutes before serving.

CHAPTER XI

On a melancholy day, when her black eyes got lost in the morning fog that swallowed the bay, Frida discovered the exact reason for her pain. It had seemed that life was rocking her like a baby, but in fact a storm was gathering, eating away at her happiness. Like many women, she was discovering that there only remained the dream of what she'd wanted her life to be. She got distracted by the seagulls' silly cawing; they seemed to be laughing right at her. She stared them down and cursed them for their audacity until they disappeared into the mist, leaving her all alone, wrapped in her pumpkin-colored rebozo. Her dissatisfaction had many roots: the absence of fidelity in her marriage, her inability to become a mother, and even certain aspects of her own personality. She asked herself: When did Frida cease being a girl in simple clothes and the lightest makeup and turn instead into a bizarre version of Mexican-ness in her long cotton skirts, Oaxaca blouses, and heavy Aztec necklaces? Why did she abandon the vision of herself as a woman that her mother had taught her in order to become Diego's exotic partner, practically a circus sideshow? Was Frida really a tehuana or just a little girl playacting?

These thoughts came to her as she looked out on a beautiful view of the San Francisco Bay, where they'd been living for almost a year. Diego had accepted a commission for a piece at the San Francisco Stock Exchange and another at the San Francisco Art Institute. He'd immediately flirted with the idea of extending the trip and staying longer in the United States; he could make a lot of money now that Mexican painters were so trendy in the art world. In Mexico, President Calles had been persecuting artists with a heavy hand; he'd had murals destroyed and communist artists jailed.

San Francisco offered sanctuary. Frida had arrived hungry for new and unfamiliar things. She'd made new friends and a new world had opened to her that seemed infinite. Everyone treated Diego like royalty. But Frida was left behind, hidden behind her husband's voluminous presence. She was timid, shy, and didn't present herself as an artist, but her sharp comments never missed their mark. With the critical eye of a woman committed to the communist cause, Frida couldn't help but detest the banalities of American society. Half hating, half in pain, Frida spent those days in silence, mourning the loss of what would have been her first child.

Nothing exemplified her recent changes better than the two self-portraits she painted: in the first, she's young and mischievous, with a warm gaze in her bright eyes. In the second, painted a year later, she's melancholic, and, though barely perceptible, the corners of her mouth have begun to drop.

Frida felt hurt. She looked down at her belly, then put her cold hand under the tehuana blouse to pat it. It was warm, as if it couldn't forget it had ever been pregnant. Frida wanted to have Diego's child but her belly was empty: the fetus had been ill positioned and had to be aborted. That was her first marital misfortune, and it was also what broke her relationship with Diego. When she was in the hospital for her abortion, Diego wasn't at her side. He wasn't even working but keeping himself busy with a parade of new lovers.

She remembered how they tore the little Diego from inside her while the other Diego, the big one, sated his lust with his assistant, Ione Robinson, at a fleabag hotel. That made her feel a certain solidarity with the thousands of people who jumped off the Golden Gate Bridge to their deaths each year. Her youthful adversities would soon be overshadowed by those of her adult life, just like the woman in the veil had warned her: the pain would only grow in time.

It would be so simple to end it all, to close her eyes and leap from the bridge. Diego would notice later. Maybe tomorrow. Today he was too busy with a model, the tennis pro Helen Wills. Frida could hear the woman's orgasmic cries from every corner of the hall in which Diego was painting his mural. She didn't dare surprise the lovers frolicking on the floor between the canvases hanging from the scaffold, but she didn't move to keep from hearing them, either. She was absorbed in the image of the woman floating naked on the upper part of the mural. Those were the sportswoman's breasts and curves that she showed off on the courts when Diego visited to get inspiration. As Helen appeared to reach the zenith of excitement, Frida simply left the picnic basket she'd brought and exited the hall.

Back in her apartment, Frida tried to distract herself with cooking and knitting but she couldn't quiet the echoes of the orgasm that kept ricocheting in her head. She looked in the mirror and discovered a stranger, an alien being. It wasn't that her exotic costuming was a mask hiding her personality in order to make her the indigenous lady Diego desired; the costume actually dramatized her own personality. She'd made herself a work of art, and now she didn't know if that was what she wanted. She'd invented herself to be exhibited.

Why go on? she asked herself while strolling past the bay. The pain in her leg was getting worse, as if hundreds of nails were being driven into it. Why smile if everything inside her was empty? She felt like a piñata: beautiful on the outside, empty inside, and so fragile. Diego and life itself conspired to torment her. Frida didn't want to stick around to see what was inside when they broke her open.

She took the path slowly. She'd climb the bridge, which haunted her like a giant beast hungry for her blood, and see if she still had the will to live.

"In your notebook you wrote, 'Have the courage to live, because anyone can die,' " she heard a voice say behind her.

She'd just been thinking about "The Hierba Santa Book" when the words echoed what was in her mind. Frida turned and saw a chocolate-skinned woman with bright, deep eyes like a glass of cognac. She was sitting on a bench, wearing a flimsy silk blouse and a coat. Frida felt an immediate connection to the short-haired woman with prominent cheekbones. She loved her wide smile, as well as the large lemon-yellow balls on her necklace.

"I'm sorry, do I know you?" Frida asked.

"I don't see why you would. I can tell you're not from here, and I grew up in rural Kentucky. There's no reason why a princess like you should turn your face to someone like me," the woman responded. She remained on the bench, feeding stale bread to the seagulls.

"Then there's nothing for us to talk about," said Frida, wrapping her rebozo tighter around herself.

"Oh, of course there is! Women have tons in common. We could talk for hours, regardless of whether we're from Africa, New York, or the Amazon. We all cry, we all love, and we all feed our children with our bodies. We've been doing that since the first day and we'll continue to do so until someone turns out the light, shuts the doors, and throws away the key to this world."

The two women looked at each other. Frida felt fear, though she wasn't uncomfortable with the stranger, who continued to offer her a warm smile. She sat down by her side.

"Do you have a smoke?" she said. "I forgot mine when I left the house. The truth is, I want to forget everything."

The woman pulled out a pack. She plucked two cigarettes, which wound up lit in their mouths. The smoke didn't deter the seagulls, but it did make them stop cawing for more bread crumbs.

"Pleased to meet you, young lady. My name is Eva Frederick, but if you go to the Mission District and ask for Mommy Eve, everyone will know who I am."

They both looked ahead, to the suicide bridge.

"What are you doing around these parts, Eva?" Frida asked, anxiously sucking on her cigarette.

"Feeding the birds. They're like men: their hunger is infinite. If they made love the way they eat, there'd be a lot more happy women and fewer killers on the streets," the woman said as she threw the last of her bread crumbs.

"Amen," said Frida.

Silence. Then a mutual understanding allowed them to laugh aloud together.

"And you, dear, what brings you to San Francisco's great colossus?"

"Well, I'm considering the idea of becoming a corpse. But there's one problem: I get vertigo."

"If you go through with it, you'll be the most beautiful corpse I've ever seen, all wrapped up in that princess gear. You'll certainly look striking at the wake, and you know, there are people who have no class even at their own funeral," the woman said.

It was at that moment that Frida realized what she'd been looking for in that place: understanding.

"Of course, if you're afraid of heights," Eva went on, "then you have a grave problem, my friend, because no one intent on suicide wants to die of a heart attack before jumping. If you're going to do something, you have to do it right, not just attempt it. The world is already full of failed attempts; it's filled its quota of losers and we don't need any more."

"Thanks for the advice. I think maybe it's best to leave it for another day. When I find a less painful way to end my suffering, then I'll do it. I've been in enough pain these days and don't need to pile on more, and there's no doubt it'd be intense when I hit the water."

"Certainly that would hurt, probably as much as getting hit by a train," Eva said in a low voice as she pulled down on her short skirt. Frida spun around to face her, but before she could say anything, the woman's smile overtook her. To calm her, she patted Frida on her bad leg.

"Who are you?" a terrified Frida babbled.

"Eva Frederick."

"Are you . . . my Godmother? Is this your face behind the veil?"

"I'm sorry, I'm confused. I'm just a friend. But I do have many faces, it's true. Here, here, take another cigarette, smoke it. Don't look back to the past. There's something waiting for you at home. It would be a shame if everything ended so quickly. You're a lot tougher than you think."

"You're not Death?" asked an intrigued Frida.

Eva's response was one of the best bursts of laughter Frida had ever heard in her life. And just the mere mention of the rest of her existence was enough to brighten her day. It was her voice, like a church choir, that she had loved instantly about this woman, and now to hear her laugh like this was pure ecstasy.

"You think I could be Death with these curves?" Eva asked, with one hand on her wide hips and the other on her round breast. "I'm a real woman, and we have curves."

"So you're not a dream I'm having."

Eva slapped her head and laughed again. "May God deliver us if this is all a dream! Little girl, there's nothing dreamlike about this life. Every drop of blood that's squeezed out of our hearts is to remind us that we're real," she said, smiling. She abruptly stood up, scaring away the seagulls waiting in vain for more crumbs. "There will always be something waiting for you at home. It won't matter how badly things are going. Look carefully, because it's always worthwhile to go back. And don't forget it, ever."

"Are you leaving, Miss Frederick?" asked Frida, trying to stall.

"The seagulls ate. You, lovely lady, didn't jump. If you can think of something more important to do than making an apple pie, tell me and I'll stay."

"My soul is healed; it's about the only part of me that isn't broken. It's too bad that the soul is such a Christian concept," Frida said a little snidely.

She really didn't like hearing about religious matters. She'd had enough with her mother.

"My dear, food for the soul is not meant to feed politics or credos. I'm sure there's a woman in Russia right now cooking to feed her kids. Praise the Lord our God, who gave us the task of nourishing every soul, whether they're black, yellow, or red. Even a warrior's mother will prepare him a good bowl of soup."

"Women have aspirations other than to spend their lives in the kitchen," protested an annoyed Frida.

"Of course! And that's the kind of talk I expect from women with curves! But no one's going to take away our pleasure in seeing a loved one eating a dish that we've prepared through tears and sweat. Oh, no! That's a divine right!"

Eva stepped away, her hips like a sail on the sea moving from side to side. She didn't say good-bye, but with a beautiful voice right out of a Harlem church she sang a melody that thanked God for the harvest. Then, without turning around to look at Frida, she slyly whistled Jelly Roll Morton's "Dead Man Blues," dancing along on the path that struggled to be lit through the fog. She disappeared until her song was lost in the mist.

At that moment Frida had a great desire to paint that woman. She was filled with it, like a jar that's overflowing. Forgetting about her pain, she rushed to her apartment to begin the piece. Knowing she was entranced, her motherhood frustrated and her leg in pain, each charcoal stroke on the canvas was precise and continuous; they followed the curves that every woman should have, as Eva had said.

Frida had returned to painting, to that universe where she felt free of pressure. Only the paintbrush or the frying pan could calm the cry of desperation in her strangled life.

A few days later Diego noticed the difference in his wife's attitude; she'd stopped being shy Mrs. Rivera and had turned into Frida herself. It happened during a night when various intellectuals, artists, and Diego ass kissers had gathered to fete him at a dinner party. A young woman sitting next to Diego was enchanted by his conversation and shamelessly flirted with him. It wasn't unusual for art neophytes to treat Diego as if he were the most desirable gem from south of the border. There was something about him as authentic as tequila and the pyramids. Sleeping with Rivera was equally folkloric: he was hotter than a chile.

At the dinner party, Frida watched them from a corner of the room, remembering the certainty of Mommy Eve's words. She drank two long bourbons and decided that she was going to be in his life forever. First, the counterattack: she had dressed up. If she was going to go up against all of Diego's sluts, she had to look good. Then she stood up, walked coquettishly among the guests until she came to the musicians, and, with the confidence of a general leading a coup, ordered them to play a Mexican song, something warm and nostalgic that would get everyone's attention: "La Llorona."

She sang it with the same passion with which she cooked and painted. She dared to begin to sing it a cappella, which startled the guests. The musicians then joined in with their instruments. With the bottle of bourbon in hand, she told funny stories between swallows. Finally, she came up to Diego and his admirers.

"Long live the maestro! I'm the one who can tell you all about him, since I'm the one who cooks for him, and artists aren't known by their art but by their hunger— and Diego is very hungry!"

Everyone laughed.

Diego laughed too; he didn't mind being the butt of a joke so long as he remained the center of attention.

"Diego likes beans because he comes from the ranchos, but now he thinks he's the boss: he eats beans and burps ham. Anyway, he's like the beans: as soon as it gets hot, he scrunches up."

She took another swig of liquor. There was applause, more laughter.

"But he married me. And I said to him: 'Now you'll see, puppy dog, who's got your leash.'"

Frida approached the young woman who had flirted with Diego, took her chin in her hand, and gave her a great kiss. She tenderly pulled away and announced to the guests: "I'm going to give you what you've come to see."

She took the drunk and giggly girl's hand. She pulled her to her for an embrace and used her other hand to caress the girl's back and ass. If Diego was going to be an exotic meal, then she'd be the dessert.

"They say it's wrong to steal, which I'd never do, but I'd gladly steal one of her kisses." She kissed the student, who was turned on by then and responded by caressing Frida right back.

Diego smiled uncomfortably. But being the accommodating fellow he could be, he applauded. That was his wife and he loved her just like that. He stood up to pay her tribute.

"Friducha, with you, there are always crops in the fields and a cup of frothy atole."

Frida took his hand to kiss it like a mother greeting her son coming home from school at the end of the day.

"A parrot fell from the sky with a flower in its beak / I only know that I love you and of that love I never speak," she rhymed.

At that, everyone clapped loudly, having fun with the Riveras, who couldn't hear the clamor anymore because they were embroiled in a loving kiss.

Without realizing it, while he was absorbed in his wife's performance, Diego was being hypnotized. In just a short time he'd forgotten about the young woman, who now hid behind the boot-licking artists. Diego positioned himself next to Frida to keep on singing and drinking. Diego's sweet and mischievous look was like the hand that joined Frida's in a portrait she'd painted of the two of them: the enormous artist gazing at his brushes and palette and clinging to his wife-daughter-mother-lover. Frida had won.

The next day Frida grabbed the bag where she kept Diego's little wooden car and, though in a lot of discomfort because of the headache from the hangover she had, took the train to the Mission District, in the heart of San Francisco. She limped around the Mexican migrants who worked in clothing factories and the African Americans carrying boxes of fruit. Caught between the noise and the chaos, she decided to try to talk to a woman selling apples.

"Do you know Mommy Eve? I was told that I could ask anybody how to find her."

"Everybody knows Mommy Eve. What do you want with her?"

"To thank her," Frida explained.

"Well, then, you'll have to go to the Mission Dolores Cemetery, on Dolores and Sixteenth streets. She liked white roses, if you want to take her anything," the vendor said with a smile.

To hide her surprise, Frida quickly bought a bag of apples to make into a pie that she'd serve with malted milk to delight Diego. She walked to the district cemetery, the oldest in the city. With a white rose pressed to her chest, she wandered along the mausoleums and funereal sculptures. Near a great oak, she found a weathered tombstone that read, "Eva Marie Frederick." She'd died five years before. Frida placed the rose on the tombstone, where it stayed until it wilted. It was watered only by Frida's tears.

She'd never tell a soul about her encounter with that woman. It was a secret she kept all her life. Even when she immortalized her in her famous painting, no one knew who it was; no one had any idea who it might be. When Dolores Olmedo bought the painting and asked Frida who it was, Frida wisely responded, "Someone who told truths."

THE FOOD IN GRINGOLAND

I didn't like eating among white people at all. All I wanted was a scrambled egg with a little bit of hot sauce and a basket of tortillas, but there was no way; you have to shut up and swallow whatever insult you might hurl in order to enjoy the modern world.

What I did like were the pastries. They were perfectly constructed. I also liked black-skinned people's restaurants. Everything was colorful there, from the music to the smiles on the waiters.

MOMMY EVE'S APPLE PIE

For the crust:

2 cups flour
1 tablespoon sugar
3/4 teaspoon salt
1 1/4 sticks unsalted butter, cut into pieces
1/4 cup vegetable shortening
6 tablespoons cold water

For the filling:

1/2 cup sugar
1/4 cup brown sugar
2 tablespoons flour
1 tablespoon lemon juice
2 teaspoons lemon zest
The tiniest pinch of nutmeg
4 1/2 pounds Golden Delicious apples, peeled
   and thinly sliced
Milk
A little bit of sugar

✻ First, prepare the crust: Blend the flour, sugar, and salt. Add the butter and the shortening, stirring until it's thick. Add the water to soften it. Add more water if the dough dries out. Split the dough in two and roll it out into two flat circles. Put each on a plate and let them rest for 2 hours or more.

In the meantime, prepare the filling: Mix all the ingredients except the apples, milk, and the little bit of sugar. Cook over low heat until it's a uniform caramel color, then add the sliced apples.

Lift the edge of one of the dough circles to form a kind of dish. Add the apple mixture. Cut the other circle into long strips, which will be laid out along and across the filling, forming a weave. Press the ends of the strips to the edge of the crust to join them. Brush the strips with a bit of milk; sprinkle some sugar on top. Bake the pie at 400°F for 10 minutes. Lower the temperature to 350°F and let it bake for 1 hour or until the filling bubbles and the crust is golden.

CHAPTER XII

Her new attitude made her decide to seek help for the pain in her leg. She may have gotten Diego back, but when she got out of bed every morning and saw the toes on her left leg withering, she began to ask herself if it was worthwhile to live day to day with a pain that was literally killing her. She wondered if it was the price she was paying to live on borrowed time, but the fact that crossing her tiny apartment's living room seemed like walking on thousands of nails made her decide it was time to get help.

That night she dreamt of a port jammed with workers carrying weapons that she had given them so they could go fight in a faraway land called the Republic. There were people of all nationalities, and in the throngs she managed to find Mommy Eve, who hugged her farewell. The hug was tender, as if the woman were giving her the energy with which to deal with her anguished life. Then Eve rushed to board a beautiful sailboat with white masts.

"You're leaving?" Frida asked, running as the boat set sail.

"Girl, I've found the best captain to take me to my death. He knows and admires you. You need a captain to take you to your final rest, someone who knows how to deal with tempests, and yours are spectacular," Eve answered.

Frida turned to the ship. She could see a man dressed as a sea captain on the boat. His manner was gentle but his eyes were metallic, like steel. He used both characteristics as needed. He was chivalrous and correct, like tea in the afternoon, but his hard hands on the steering wheel were as wild as the sea itself. His grand smile promised peace, like at Christmastime. But his cold, enigmatic eyes were always looking somewhere else, saving whoever was available to be saved.

"I know him—that's dear Dr. Leo," exclaimed Frida, standing in front of the ship that was getting ready to go.

After those vivid scenes, though, her dream proceeded the same as all dreams: silly and crazy, all pleasant rambling.

The next day, she sought out Dr. Leo Eloesser, whom she'd met in Mexico in 1926 and who now lived in the city while working at Stanford University.

"So, why were you looking for me, Frida?" asked

the man from her dreams (the real one was shorter).

"Because I know you're the best, and I know you're a communist. I couldn't put my life in the hands of some prude," said a happy Frida.

"And do we communists cure our patients better?" Dr. Leo asked, continuing the game.

Frida enjoyed looking at the Georgia O'Keeffe paintings the doctor had on his walls and was delighted to discover a painting by Diego in the room: *La Tortillera*.

"No, you don't," said Frida, "but at least you don't offer absurd and false hopes about heaven and hell. You cure with science, not with faith."

Dr. Leo would become her best friend, the person to whom she'd write the most naked and plainspoken correspondence. She'd confide in him like no one else. They ended up having a great love for each other and embarked on a most unusual journey: a true friendship between a man and a woman without the slightest sexual attraction.

"My leg is worse by the minute, dear doctor. And my spine pinches every time I put stress on it with Diego's big paunch," she said, explaining her symptoms. "My belly has a hollowness to it that I'll never be able to fill."

"That's all good news."

"Good news?"

"Sure. It'd be bad news if you were dead. In medicine, we cure what can be cured. We can't work miracles; those happen by themselves. And the last miracles the world has seen were Manet and his disciple, Hugo

Clément," Dr. Leo said, grinning. He loved art, music, and sailboats.

Frida let him check her bones as if she were a horse about to run a great race. After a few minutes she thought the doctor was learning about her life through each of her symptoms, in the way a curious man might examine a woman's purse. His face didn't suggest good things, but none of that was news to her. She knew she was in bad shape from head to toe. In fact, she was totally fucked.

"Should I order a coffin made of Mexican rosewood to go with my skirts?"

"It would be even better if you painted it yourself, with those brown landscapes and colorful dresses, little Frida."

"You've figured me out, dear doctor: all my paintings are projects to decorate my tomb."

The confessions she'd make later in her letters were painful. They almost always began: Querido doctorcito; it was a greeting designed to soften her litany of afflictions. Dr. Leo would become so committed to social justice that he became a doctor to the world. He went to China; to Spain for the Civil War to help on the Liberal side; to Mexico to aid the striking workers; to tend to the poor in Tacámbaro, Michoacán; and, of course, to be at his dear Frida's side. And as happens to everyone who sets out to do good, he drew the resentment and jealousy of government suits; eventually, he was even hunted by the CIA.

"That train did a helluva job. It split you in half."

"You have no idea. And then, to make sure my fate was sealed, they sent Diego to kill me again."

"Yes, well, since you've already survived more than a year with Diego, then you'll be able to live the rest of your life with your spine like a broken vessel. You have a congenital deformity in your spine."

"It sounds incurable, dear doctor," said a distressed Frida.

Dr. Leo looked at her, kissed her hands, and caressed her like her own cold father had never done. But he never responded.

Leo Eloesser understood that he was bound to Frida by fate. Years later, he'd write to her with affection from afar: "I kiss your hands, pretty girl, and your short leg. You have no idea how much I miss you, with your folksy skirts and your fleshy lips."

"I want to have a little Diego in my belly," Frida said. "Is that too much to ask of Mother Nature?" She lifted her tehuana blouse and showed him her white belly, as white as hospital linen.

"Your hips are like a building held up by scaffolding. Any pressure and they'll fall apart. That little Diego will finish the job that the train and Diego weren't able to do," the doctor explained as he twisted his mustache in funny shapes.

"If he survived and I didn't, I wouldn't mind taking the risk. In the worst case I'd die, and I kid you not, I died once before," Frida confessed.

"It's very noble of you to offer such a sacrifice to give the great Diego a child, but that child would have less of a chance than you, pretty girl."

"Do I have an option other than to surrender to this half-existence?"

"You have the same option I do, or Diego, or my nurse . . . or the rest of the world. We all make like we're living, but let me remind you that life is simply what's between birth and death."

"It's a shitty option," Frida muttered.

Dr. Leo nodded, but his eyes revealed that he was already making other plans to save a lost community somewhere far away, in some godforsaken corner of the globe.

"No doubt about it, a shitty option," he said.

Dr. Leo would witness Frida and Diego's entire story. Convinced they were both minor gods, and as such could live among the people of the Earth, he delighted in every moment he spent with them. He shared sad times with each, and as the wise man that he was, he learned how to conduct himself with each of them. He found the sweetest of honeys in Frida and her caramel dresses and farmer's-market blouses.

"Diego's mural is finished and now his enormous butt just smiles down on us. So, what are you two going to do now?" the doctor asked mischievously. In his new piece, Diego had half-jokingly included himself naked from the back, sitting on a scaffold, painting the mural.

"Sometimes I think that's his best side. He doesn't talk that way, doesn't complain, and he's as pink as a baby's cheeks. I suppose he did it so his disciples could have a sanctified image to kiss," Frida added slyly. The American art community hadn't liked his joke, but that's how he was: like any other Mexican, fond of puns and a little perverse. "Diego has decided that we should move to a new cage where he can best show off his peacock feathers."

"You're going back to Mexico, Frida?"

"I don't really know. There's a lot of work, but he's spent all our savings on two houses he commissioned Juanito O'Gorman to build. And between helping with the murals, his other buildings, and his personal problems, Juanito's built them. I can't complain. They're pretty and as useless as a Talavera vase, so beautiful and awkward no one knows what to do with them."

The doctor laughed heartily. Frida knew that the adjoined houses Diego had built in the San Ángel district as his "love nest" had little to do with love and a lot with politics. Juan, the young architect who followed Diego around like a puppy and adored his art like a devoted monk, convinced Diego that the houses would be socialist examples of avant-garde architecture. O'Gorman wanted to prove that it was possible to build with maximum efficiency at minimal cost. But neither of them were fools, so Diego managed to get the land to build them on for free, and Juan got an investor. Frida got stuck with a damn electric burner for a kitchen; it was the size of a bean and she couldn't use it to make even a cup of coffee. Nonetheless, the houses were so successful that when Diego showed them off to the secretary of public education, he was so impressed by the low cost to produce them that he immediately contracted Juanito to build twenty-some schools just as bare and uncomfortable. Of course, these were for kids, and no one in those schools would ever need a decent kitchen in which to make mole.

"Diego showed me the blueprints. I like the symbolism. They're two separate houses: his is pink and yours is blue, the two connected by a bridge, like your love."

"Juanito made sure it was a very short bridge."

"Do you like the houses?"

"Let's say that they illustrate perfectly how Diego sees our relationship: he's got the big house and I get the small one."

Dr. Leo sat on the couch next to Frida. With the sensitivity of a surgeon bringing forth a new life, he took her hands and caressed them.

"It's not just my leg and my spine that suffer, dear doctor. I need another opinion from you, but you have to promise you won't laugh at silly me, because I've had enough of mockery from those stupid gringos," Frida said, so softly that only a mouse or a very good friend could have heard.

"I'm right here. . . ."

"Tell me, as a man of science: Is it possible that I'm already dead and continue living only as a favor from Death? Is it possible that all my ills are because I already died and refused to stay dead? Don't laugh, this isn't a game. I think Death is trying to get me to pay for something I owe her."

The doctor straightened the collar of his dress shirt.

He sucked on his mustache, because for questions like that—questions that required mind and heart—he needed a lot of spit in his mouth. He pressed Frida's hands tighter, as if this way he could absorb the impact of her, like a child losing her balance and falling.

"Look, Frida, I'm just a fun-loving doctor who doesn't even play the viola very well, but I think that life is a matter of balance. For every action, there's a re-action. I'm an atheist, because math is the best god and, in my world, everything is taken care of. If you take two from four, you only have two left. Do you understand what I'm saying?"

Frida nodded in agreement. It wasn't that she wholly understood his meaning, but that she knew they were at least on the same page of madness and desperation.

"So, if you're stealing days of living from Death, life has to take away a few things. You can't be deceitful. Maybe your abortion gave you one more year of life. If you take a brick from one side of the scale, you'll have to take one from the other side too. And that's why I'm here: to make sure the equation is in your favor."

"Have you diagnosed me as terminally insane yet, dear doctor?" Frida asked her friend.

"No, but I'll keep you from the madhouse on one condition: prepare me some ribs like the ones I had in Michoacán," he said, offering a smile and remembering Frida's great talent for cooking, "with beans and all, be-cause everything in this country tastes insipid to me."

Frida kept her promise to cook for him. And to thank him for his healing words and comfort, she also painted a picture for him before leaving San Francisco. She drew him like an old portrait: with the innocence of disproportionate features, his neck like a bird's, dressed as a funereal lover with a starched shirt and stiff collar. He looked like a young man who had aged all of a sudden. The sailboat the doctor used to take out on the bay was right behind him. Frida had never painted a boat before, so she asked Diego how to draw the lines for the sails.

"Paint them however you want," he said, without giving the matter much importance, his head already on his next project in Detroit.

Frida painted them flat, with edges tied to the mast with large rings, like curtains.

"That's not what a ship's sail looks like," Diego said one day, taking his revenge for her comments about Zapata's horse.

Frida shrugged. "Well, that's how I saw them in my dream."

RIBS FOR DEAD DR. LEO

When the dear doctor comes to see me, he sends a telegram first that says, "Prepare those ribs for me." And then I know I have to cook that dish he fell in love with when he was still tending to the Indians. I love him; he's my best friend.

1/2 teaspoon ground cumin

1 teaspoon salt

12 garlic cloves, chopped, and 6 whole cloves

2 racks of pork ribs, cut, with the ribs
   separated

2 tablespoons lard

4 cups water

8 serrano chiles

1/4 onion, in pieces

2 pounds green tomatoes (tomatillos), peeled

8 sprigs cilantro, crushed

Salt and pepper

✻ Add the cumin and salt to the chopped garlic, then rub the mixture on the ribs. If at all possible, let the ribs rest overnight so the flavors will be absorbed into the meat. Place the ribs in a large pot, add water until they're covered, then bring to a boil. When the meat can be easily pierced with a fork, remove the ribs from the heat. Fry the ribs for 10 minutes in the lard. Set them aside. In another pot, add the 4 cups of water and whole garlic cloves. Bring to a boil, then add the chiles and the onion; cook for 5 minutes. Add the green tomatoes and cook for another 5 minutes. Remove everything (except the ribs!) and pound on the molcajete until it has the consistency of a puree. Add 2 cups of the broth from when the ribs were boiled and the freshly crushed cilantro. If the sauce is too thick, add water.

In a large pan, reserve 2 tablespoons of lard from when the ribs were previously fried. Add the puree and boil, covered, for 10 minutes. Add the ribs, season with salt and pepper to taste. Stir and let cook over low heat for 20 minutes.

CHAPTER XIII

It wasn't a surprise when Diego decided to stop playing at being the perfect man and got tired of pleasing his wife. The idea of making sure things were okay with Frida became secondary to wanting things to be okay with others. For the painter with fickle heart who was so good at taking risks, there was nothing easier than to attract lovers. And Frida's attitude wasn't helping: she didn't want to be where they were living, she was always depressed, and she had a very short fuse. So Diego simply looked for somewhere to hide, a young body willing to give herself in exchange for the notoriety of being the artist's lover. A straightforward view of this stark scenario would have shown that Diego's weaknesses played out while everything went on as usual in his married life.

For Frida, Detroit was the incarnation of all of Dante's agonies. But for Diego, it was the American heartland, where he'd spark the revolution with his murals. Frida's torture began with the food, which was bland and lifeless, an extension of the gray horizon made cloudy from the factory fumes. A city of bare bricks, tall chimneys, and heavy smoke was not the best place for a baby to be born, but as had been her way her entire life, she hadn't planned what had happened. Frida was pregnant and she was in a daze. She had so many questions about her possible future with a child who would not be welcomed by his famous father; she was so afraid, she hadn't even shared the secret in her belly with Diego.

From her very first days in Detroit, Frida had felt a loneliness that ran like a shiver up her deformed spine. She was alone too much, pacing her hotel room aimlessly, trying to figure out something to do. The room was as negligible as her hopes, and the sign on the hotel door that banned Jews simply reduced the space even more; it seemed built with racist splinters. Detroit was difficult for her, and so was Diego's patron, Mr. Edsel Ford, who was as robotic and cold as one of the perfect machines built by his workers on the assembly line. Frida couldn't find a trace of humanity in his steely gaze and cool bearing.

When they were invited to a party in Diego's honor—where universal man would be joined with machine to create the liberating spirit of a nation that, strangely, didn't want to be liberated—she bit her tongue and, dressed to the nines just like a movie star, allowed herself to be shown off like a beautiful jewel. She was so distressed by the falsity and superficiality of the event that when she heard the automotive millionaire's despotic and racist comments, she couldn't contain herself.

"Are you a Jew, Mr. Ford?" she asked maliciously.

The question caused a sensation among the guests and dismayed the host. Diego was surprised that the rage his infidelities caused in his wife would be directed against the businessman who was underwriting their lodging, meals, and living expenses. Annoyed, he excused himself from a group of professional fawners and dragged her out to one of the Ford mansion's terraces.

"Frida, are you crazy?"

"No, I'm pregnant," she responded, furious.

Rather than announce the news with happiness, Frida had spit it out. But Diego was a much more practical and flexible person than she was, and the first thing that came to his mind were all the problems they'd have with a child. He already had two daughters from his marriage to Lupe and he had no desire to have a new child that would tie him down to a particular place, hurting his ascending career as a muralist, especially now that he'd become a favorite of American impresarios.

"Are you sure, Friducha? We really have to think about what's best."

"What's best will be figured out by a smarter man than you. You can't even fake happiness about this," Frida said.

Diego grabbed her by the shoulders forcefully, and when it looked like he might throw her off the terrace, he brought his head down slowly, carefully, like a train connecting freight cars, and kissed his wife on the lips. He thought they tasted different, like mint. The kiss continued for a while, erasing the other guests from both their minds. If Frida wanted to have a little Diego, that would be her decision. Any discussion would be left for another day; tonight was hers.

The next day Frida stayed in her room to write a letter to her confidant, Dr. Eloesser.

Doctorcito:

I have so much to share with you, though most of it isn't very pleasant. I should tell you my health isn't good. But I want to talk to you about everything except that, because I understand you must be tired of hearing complaints from everyone. I thought that, because of my health, the best thing might be to have an abortion, and so the doctor here gave me a dose of quinine and a very strong laxative. But when he examined me, he said he was completely sure I hadn't miscarried and that, in his opinion, I should continue the pregnancy. He said that in spite of my body's limitations, he thought I could have a child through a cesarean without great difficulty. He says he could take care of me if we stay in Detroit for the next seven months. Please tell me what you think, just tell me honestly, because I don't know what to do.

But Frida didn't wait for her friend's response. She decided not to abort, suddenly hopeful because of the Detroit doctor's words.

* * *

For Frida, there was no way to tell who was an ally and who was an enemy. Any young woman who came near Diego in search of acceptance, recognition, or simply the fun of knowing him could unleash the furious tornado inside her. She seemed unable to remember that that was the way she herself had gotten together with him, while he was still with Lupe. That's why when Lucienne Bloch, the daughter of a Swiss composer, came looking for Diego's guidance with her sculpture, Frida's suspicions grew every which way and with each of Diego's absences. At a meeting of intellectuals one day, Diego enchanted the young blonde with praises for the aesthetic of machines, and he found that the woman could engage intelligently, beyond a doubt. She wasn't just anybody. They went on for more than an hour, the great painter and the young sculptor, talking about their influences and trading opinions on other artists.

When Lucienne got up to get something to eat, she found Frida waiting at the door. As usual, she was dazzling, wearing beautiful jewelry, all gifts because of the new pregnancy. Frida cut Lucienne off like a lioness defending her turf.

"I hate you," Frida said to her face.

Lucienne was stunned and tried to look to Diego for support, but he was already busy with another student whom he'd also entranced like a snake charmer.

"I don't blame you for loving him. If I were in your place, I'd fight for him too," the cool sculptor said. If Frida was going to speak truth to her, she'd answer with truths too.

"Get away from him," Frida said, not moving a muscle.

The two women stared each other down for several minutes, like a duel between old enemies.

"That's a problem. He's asked me to be his assistant on the mural," Lucienne explained.

"He doesn't want you as an assistant, he wants you as a lover. First, he'll entreat you with kind words and a gentle manner. Then, when he gets bored, he'll besmirch you and trade you in for a new lover. If you're smart, you won't take the job," said Frida.

"I know that working with Diego will be good for my career. But he's going to be surprised that I'm not interested in sleeping with him. He's yours in your private life, but I'll be his during the workday. I'll do everything he asks of me except have sex with him. If you can live with those rules, then so can I."

Frida was completely taken aback. It was a bit of a shock to be faced with a response like that after running into so many women who were so eager to seduce her husband. This blond girl with crystalline eyes admired him strictly for his talent and his art.

"Do you like to cook?" Frida asked.

"My hands are made for sculpting. I'm afraid cooking is a subtle art. I'd have to find a cooking teacher as good as Diego is with painting."

"If you come by the apartment tomorrow, we can cook together for that big belly of his," Frida said.

Lucienne accepted immediately. She'd just gotten herself two mentors.

Over time, the relationship between them grew. Once Diego saw that his attempts to seduce her weren't well received, he let himself be guided by his assistant's intelligence and made her his closest collaborator. And in Lucienne, Frida found an ally in a hostile place at a difficult time. In fact, Diego eventually asked Lucienne to come live with them and take care of Frida, which Lucienne immediately agreed to. She was rewarded with wonderful Spanish and Mexican cooking lessons.

Lucienne stayed by Frida's side just as she'd promised Diego. On the Fourth of July, as they were watching fireworks celebrating the independence of the United States, Frida couldn't take being on her feet any longer and retired to her room complaining of pain (part of it was physical but part was also depression). Diego told her to rest and get some sleep.

At dawn, Frida's scream shattered the calm. Lucienne rushed from her room to see what was going on and found a red puddle splattered with blood clots on the bed. Frida wept.

They immediately transported her to Henry Ford Hospital. As they raced her to the emergency room on a stretcher, she noticed the colorfully painted tubing on the hospital ceiling. Her eyes got lost in the labyrinth.

"Look, Diego, look how pretty it is!" she said to her husband, who held her hand.

Then the colors turned black.

Frida found herself naked on a hospital bed, her belly swollen but like an empty calabash. A dark swirl stained her white inner thigh. In fact, the sheets were covered with heart-shaped stains as offerings. The bleeding was slow, like the residue from a snail dragging its shell. Tubes ran from her vagina to feed her broken spine. There was a blue orchid dying on the floor, orthopedic gadgets, and an embryo hovering just above her. When she turned, she saw her unborn child's face. Before he breathed his last, he showed her his eyes and full lips, which were unquestionably Diego's. Frida noticed a small candle at the foot of her bed, its flame about to go out. As soon as it was extinguished, the unborn child disappeared. She screamed in pain. Her child had been torn away from the land of the living. He'd never feel fresh air on his face or taste a meal prepared by his mother. Her Godmother had whisked him away.

"I'm so sorry, my dear," she said as she came to Frida's bedside.

A great hat covered her head, throwing shadows on her veiled face. Her white feathered stole seemed as faded as autumn leaves. Her Godmother was sad behind her veil.

"Why don't you take me and let little Diego live?" Frida asked between sobs, but the lady from the End of Days didn't respond. She took the extinguished candle with both hands and pressed it to her chest, where it melted between her fingers.

"You all belong to me," her Godmother declared. "I was with the first of you who came into existence and I'll be there with the very last. When there are no more of you, I will have finished my work and then we'll cease being bound together."

"Why?"

"Because, for some, death is a sigh of relief, but for others it's a long, long story. Everyone has to tell theirs, whether it's long or short. For little Diego, this was long enough. It was what he needed. Not a minute more, not a minute less. That's how it works," explained the Godmother.

Frida felt only hatred. She didn't want to deal with that cold woman anymore; she didn't understand the pain of being a mother. It wouldn't be until days later that Frida would realize that she was, in fact, mother to all, and that every time she took a life, she suffered in her own way, because there's no greater pain than the loss of a child.

"I don't want to live any longer," Frida told her Godmother.

Death took a step back from her bed. Her stole was disappearing into the horizon, where a factory was churning smoke.

"It'll be as we agreed, not a minute more, not a minute less."

"But when will that moment come? You can't just come and rip everything I love from me whenever you want!"

The woman in the veil took Frida's hand. She extended each of her fingers, exposing her palm to the gray sky. She placed a warm chicken egg inside and folded her fist over it. Amidst the brown speckles on its shell, there was an indisputable mark on the very top: a red stain in the shape of a heart.

"This is what will seal our pact. The creature born from this egg will remind you with its morning song that you'll live as we've agreed. But the morning that dawns without his song, you'll die."

There was no farewell. Frida came to in the hospital surrounded by doctors. Her eyes found Diego. Her lungs took in air and she felt her empty belly.

Five days later, Frida was drawing like a madwoman. She wanted to render the child she'd lost exactly as the doctor had explained: breaking into pieces inside her. Frida asked him to get her a fetus in formaldehyde, but the doctor was terrified of the idea, sure that this was the result of a nervous breakdown because of the loss. But Diego made him understand that Frida was an artist, that she worked out her demons through pencil and paper. Inspired by medical textbooks that showed the stages of gestation, Frida spent hours drawing boy fetuses and self-portraits in which she appeared in bed surrounded by the strange images she'd pulled from her Godmother's visit, her hair now as tentacles, or as roots.

She didn't say a word during her convalescence, she just drew and drew, erased and drew again. Lucienne and Diego would sit in the apartment and just stare at her. Now and then she'd shed tears, but she'd quickly wipe them and go back to her desperate strokes.

She wrote to Dr. Leo the same day she was released from the hospital. It was a long letter in which she thanked him for his care. Writing about her emotions inspired her to impose her will on her pain; it helped her make sense of things. At the end of the letter, she wrote: "There's nothing else to do but put up with myself. I'm like a cat with nine lives." She sealed the envelope with a lipstick kiss and gave it to Lucienne to mail.

"Send it to the dear doctor."

"Would you like anything else, Frida?" Lucienne asked a little nervously.

"I just want to paint," she said.

As had happened after the train accident, she began to work with all her might so she could strip the failed pregnancy from her body and mind.

The commotion caused by the miscarriage and the knowledge now that she would never have children provoked her to tell Diego at various times that she wanted to die. And although he was very committed to his mural, Diego left his lovers and began to take care of Frida, to spoil her as if she were a little girl. As soon as Frida got her strength back, she again began to get up early so she could prepare his food and take it to him while he worked on his masterpiece. His assistants got used to the daily ritual of Frida's arrival with a picnic basket trailing the exotic aromas of moles, enchiladas, and other Mexican dishes. When he saw her come in, Diego would descend from the scaffold to kiss her, talk with her, and show her the new work on the mural. As she set the table, she'd give him feedback on it. It was the closest thing to the relationship she wanted to have with her husband.

Since Lucienne had seen that Frida wasn't very good with schedules, she tried to organize her life so she'd have time for each of her passions. She arranged for Frida to work on her art in the morning. That way she'd work faster and more efficiently but without losing the detail that only patience brought to her art.

One day at noon, an eclipse enveloped the city in total darkness, and Frida felt an icy current circulating between Diego and his students, who were outside watching the phenomenon from where they'd been working on the mural. For them, that cool draft was normal, but Frida understood it as a sign of transformation. While everyone looked at the sun through smoky lenses, she lowered her head, knowing who would arrive with the icy currents: the Messenger.

She wasn't wrong. In the midst of the parked cars and trucks, a horseman trotted along on a white steed. The Messenger never looked at Frida, just paraded by in silence. The click-clacking of the hooves soon got lost in the din from the nearby factories. When the first ray of sun emerged from under the shadows, the horseman disappeared.

"What did you think of the eclipse, Frida?" Lucienne asked.

"It's not pretty. It's just another cloudy day," she answered, dazed by the appearance of the man who always warned her of fatalities.

Diego laughed, not understanding, because sometimes men just respond with humor when they don't understand profound ideas. Sometimes they prefer to hide behind a joke or a snide comment.

When they returned to the hall where they'd been painting the mural, there was a package of letters waiting to be opened. Many contained proposals for new murals; in fact, there was an invitation from Nelson Rockefeller in New York. But there was also an urgent telegram addressed to Frida. Diego had a presentiment that it was bad news from Mexico. Without saying anything, he read it. Frida became anxious when she saw him go pale.

"Your mother, Matilde, is dying."

The Messenger had announced the tragedy. Frida's desire to return to Mexico was being fulfilled, but in a very macabre manner. It was an ugly play by her Godmother.

Frida and Lucienne left for Mexico the very next day.

These events began to reshape Frida, giving her a kind of ironic complacency about her situation. She might have been passive before, but now she felt like a survivor.

She knew she'd put up with Diego's and Death's misdeeds. The two would take turns trying to make her surrender. But this world offered more than breathing. Before she'd even reached Mexico City, the words from her dream were already echoing in her head: "Not a minute more, not a minute less."

* * *

Cristina and Matilde went to get her at the station. They cried as if their mother had already died, but in fact she'd hung on so she could say good-bye to Frida. The cancer was eating her alive. Their father was crazed with the idea of losing this woman who, though he'd never loved her, had bound him with routine and security.

In the house in Coyoacán, her mother waited for her final reward. When Frida came in, she saw that Mamá Matilde was now reduced to a bag of bones propped up on the bed. She couldn't contain her tears. Her mother barely managed to pat her on the head a few times.

"Frida, my child . . ." she whispered.

"I'm here; I've come back."

"You never left. I know you'll never leave this house again," her mother responded.

She closed her eyes. Knowing these were her last days on Earth, her daughters prayed a rosary for her soul.

She died a week later. The sisters wore black dresses and reddened eyes for the wake. Between Hail Marys and Our Fathers they buried Mamá Matilde. At her tomb, they placed yellow flowers and candles that would light her way to the hereafter. They all came back to the house in Coyoacán to be with Guillermo. Frida asked Lucienne for some private time and went to walk in the gardens. A few chickens ran after her black skirt, hoping to be fed. Frida discovered an egg in the coop that had a heart-shaped mark at its very top. She tried to touch it, but to her surprise it moved on its own. The shell cracked like desert thunder. The strange miracle of life wrung itself out before her very eyes: first a tiny beak emerged, then a head, wet and featherless. Finally she saw all of him: a wee chick, yellow and black. He opened and closed his eyes, trying to focus his sight. The first thing he gazed upon wasn't his mother, which was any one of the anonymous hens running around the house, but Frida, who couldn't stop crying.

"Good morning, Mr. Cock-A-Doodle-Do," she said to the chick, who was trying to stand up.

She took him in her hands and brought him to her room to take care of him. She made a nest from old clothes in a box and put a lamp light on it for heat. The chick didn't seem bothered by her efforts to care for him. They both seemed to feel good about it. During the two months she stayed with her family, the chick followed her everywhere. Frida understood that the little chick was the manifestation of the agreement with her Godmother and that, when he grew, his song would announce the arrival of every new day she borrowed. She knew it would be that way until he stopped and she ceased to exist.

Before she left with Lucienne for Detroit to live with Diego again, she asked her sister Cristina to take care of the little chick, which was already looking thin and weak. With her suitcases and memories, Frida set off on her long trip.

After several days of tiring travel, she arrived at their place in Detroit and found a man in a suit waiting for her. Frida didn't recognize him. He was thin and had short hair. He came closer. "It's me," he said. Frida realized this was her husband, Diego, who'd been put on a diet because of gastrointestinal distress and was now incredibly thin. In fact, he'd had to borrow the suit because nothing of his fit. There were no words between them. Frida rushed to his arms and he snuggled her like a pigeon. They remained like that, wrapped in each other for several minutes, crying.

BASKETS FOR BIG BELLIES

I don't like Detroit. As a city, it more closely resembles a poor old town. But I'm happy that Diego is enjoying his work here and has found inspiration for his frescoes. It's the capital of modern industry, a monster made of machinery and towers puffing fumes. I can only fight that with my petticoats, my blouses with their low necklines, and the Mexican dishes my husband likes in his big belly. All you have to do is give him a bowl of mole and he's happy.

MOLE GUADALAJARA STYLE

MOLE TAPATÍO

2 1/4 pounds pork loin, cut into small pieces
Salt
4 ancho chiles, roasted and seeded
4 pasilla chiles, roasted and seeded
1 roasted onion
2 roasted garlic cloves
1 cup roasted peanuts, unsalted
1 teaspoon chile seeds
4 allspice berries
2 cloves
1 cinnamon stick
Lard

❋ Cook the meat in enough water to cover and a dash of salt. When it's tender, remove from the pot and set it aside. Reserve the broth. Soak the roasted chiles in hot water for 5 minutes until they get soft. Then mash with the onion, garlic, and a bit of the broth. Separately, crush the peanuts, chile seeds, allspice berries, cloves, and cinnamon, adding a bit of broth as well. Heat 3 or 4 spoonfuls of lard in a pot and fry the peanut mixture. Remove from the heat and add to the chile mix. As the two mixes blend, add a little broth so the mole won't be too thick. Let it boil for 30 minutes over low heat. Season with salt, add the meat, and let it boil for 5 to 10 more minutes. Serve with rice, tortillas, and refried beans. You can add a pinch of crushed peanuts to each plate after it's served.

CHAPTER XIV

Frida looked up, like a vain macaw, as she arranged her dress of crazy colors and found a pair of cold eyes fixed on her body like a tiny piece of ice. This gave her an intense pleasure but also made her as nervous as a virgin. The two women's gazes came together in an unusual way, synchronizing their breathing and their desire. Those cold eyes undid the Oaxaca blouse that hid Frida's breasts. Frida straightened up, like a peacock extending its feathers in courtship. Those eyes stripped her of her skirt, blouse, and heavy jewelry, making her as jittery as if she were walking on fire.

"You're flirting with Georgia O'Keeffe?" Diego asked when he discovered the scene between the two painters.

Frida lowered her eyes and giggled like a kid. Diego grinned. That made him look a lot better, because the suit he was wearing really didn't fit him. Even though he was gaining weight, the thinness gave him an interesting look. Frida, as always, was an impeccable pre-Columbian princess, a muse turned into art. After all they'd been through in Detroit and Mexico, she'd concentrated on being a wife again, with all that implied, including feeling the envy of others. There's no such thing as good envy, and if it comes from a woman, it's always bad.

"You know I don't care. I think women are more civilized and sensitive than men. We're pretty straightforward when it comes to sex. Our pleasure center is in one place, whereas you have yours distributed all over your body," Diego said as he gave her a little kiss on the forehead, a kiss filled with all the love he felt for his wife.

But Frida wasn't totally convinced by Diego; she figured the kiss was a way of marking his territory, a subtle way of letting everyone know: *You can flirt with her, but remember that in the end she's mine.* That wasn't easy to ignore, since Diego was the man of the hour. And not just tonight but for months now. His charms were talked about all over New York. A modern version of the Pied Piper of Hamelin, adored almost to the point of reverence as the world waited for his magic brushes to showcase prosperity at the most important business, cultural, and political complex in Manhattan: Rockefeller Center. Now that he was a guest of the powerful Rockefeller family, which had so much influence it didn't need the presidency to manipulate the strings of power in the United States, Diego knew he was having his prime moment. If the Rockefellers wanted to make Diego a deity, then all of Manhattan would pay tribute.

"I don't need your permission. You didn't ask for mine to have a roll in the hay with your assistant Louise. And even though I wouldn't have given it, you would have done it anyway," Frida said.

Her tone wasn't as acidic as a lemon, but it had a familiar sarcasm to it.

Diego continued to smoke his smelly Cuban cigar, sucking on it continuously like a scolded child sucks on a pacifier.

"Diego, come meet my wife, Georgia!" the gallery owner Alfred Stieglitz said, his arm around Diego's back.

The gallerist/photographer seemed disproportionately small next to the muralist. They seemed like different species, like an elephant and a parakeet. With his free hand, Alfred signaled to the woman with the glacial eyes. She slowly made her way through the guests, who parted before her thin features, white skin, and dark hair. Georgia O'Keeffe wore black pants and a transparent silk blouse, which made her seem like an Amazon in the city. Her freckles, toasted by the New Mexico sun, shone brightly on her body.

Her warrior walk, with a masculine swagger and the fragility of glass, made Frida die of desire.

"Georgia, I think you know Diego and his wife," Alfred said as he embraced his wife, who remained ramrod straight, with the bearing of a monarch.

Frida ate her up as if she were a juicy apple.

"It's my pleasure," Georgia said, not letting go of Frida's hand. In her role as Mayan queen, Frida was letting those cold eyes eat her up right back.

While Diego and Alfred discussed the Rockefeller project, the two women just stared at each other.

"I'd like to take a picture of Mrs. Rivera," an intruder said.

He was a short little photographer with a wide hat who carried a camera as big as a manufacturing plant.

Frida let go of Georgia, surprised by the interruption. She smoothly placed herself next to one of the pieces on exhibit and gave the camera a profound look. By the time the flash exploded, Georgia was lost in a crowd of people laughing all around her. Frida tried to follow but the photographer attacked again.

"You should have some fun while Maestro Rivera works on his murals. There's a lot to do in this city. What does Mr. Rivera do in his leisure time?"

"He makes love," Frida said, smiling as she moved away.

She might have wanted to add "but not with me," but she was determined to hook up with Georgia.

Unfortunately, it became impossible. The party was raucous and they ended up at a bar in Harlem. The fire that Georgia lit would not be put out that night. Frida held on to the memory of those eyes undressing her. No one had ever looked at her like that. She'd never felt so wanted, or wanted anyone like that in return. To cap her frustration, she drank a cognac in that Harlem bar, which smelled of worker's sweat, while Diego slept through his drunkenness and the band played "Dead Man Blues."

New York was a city of dreams: dreams of success, of reigning immortal over dogmatic art critics, but also more banal dreams, like a wedded bliss that seemed perfect in spite of the cracks in their marriage.

Diego, that consummate communist and self-proclaimed revolutionary painter who would break the chains of capitalism with his brushes, loved being where he was: in the temple of money, in the mausoleum of impresarios, in the divine pantheon of millionaires. He proclaimed himself red but inside he was as white as the cinched tuxedo shirt he wore with false modesty to innumerable elegant events.

Frida loved being the center of attention, but she couldn't quiet her yearnings for motherhood, for her family, and for spicy food eaten with tortillas. While Diego worked, she sighed and lay in a hot tub for hours, waiting for transformation like a butterfly emerging from a cocoon; or maybe it was a miracle she was waiting for. But it was in vain. Everything remained the same. Diego came and went with women on his arm like shopping bags after a sale. Reporters followed her as if she were the main attraction at a circus. The bohemian get-togethers where liquor ran like a river had become daily events because every intellectual and socialite wanted to hang out with the Riveras.

Soaking in the tub, Frida realized her agreement with her Godmother was not insignificant. There are only so many humans who get a second chance, and if she was the chosen one in the crowd of people who were on this life's journey with her, then she should try to have a good time in the process. As her fingers splashed in the water, she began to laugh like a madwoman. Her memories floated out of order in front of her, tickling the soles of her feet. There were those painfully lived moments, like psychotic paraphernalia, which she now understood as supremely sane instances. Her mind started to wander. The water offered images from her past and present, of life and death, of comfort and loss. She fell asleep in the tub, sealing the image of herself like a photographic negative to use in one of her future paintings.

"Are you going to stay like that all day? I think you want to become a fish," Lucienne said when she woke her a couple of hours later. With an amused look on her face, Lucienne handed her a towel. Frida opened her eyes and shivered all over. Her fingers had begun to turn blue from the cold.

"That's not a bad idea. They say fish lead fun lives. Just imagine the orgies on the shoals!" Frida joked as she wrapped herself in the towel.

"I don't think I'd like it. It'd be very wet, very slippery," Lucienne said, making a face. She began to comb Frida's long hair, which spilled over her naked body like tar.

"Well, you don't have to be a fish to be wet and slippery," Frida said, spicing up their chat. She pressed her hand to the towel.

Lucienne didn't respond; she let both their smiling

faces reflect back from the mirror. The only sound was of the comb sifting through Frida's hair.

"We're still talking about fish, right?" Lucienne, confused, finally asked.

As a response, Frida's laughing eyes shone just below her thick brow. Her mischievousness always played out with her friends.

"Let's go out tonight," she declared.

"What about Diego?"

"He's fucking some gringa."

"Are you sure?"

"Diego only does four things in life: he paints, he eats, he sleeps, and he fucks. He's not working and I didn't make any Guadalajara-style pulled pork for him to gorge on. If you look in the bed, you'll see there's no fat man sleeping there, so there's only one option left. And since Detroit I'm not included in that one."

The comb stopped going up and down. Lucienne's hand dropped to her side, like that of a little girl who's just discovered her parents are separating. Frida shrugged as if it were no big deal, like something akin to forgetting a birthday. Once Lucienne realized Frida was fine, she continued combing her hair.

"What would you like to do?"

"We could go to the movies. Maybe there's a Tarzan movie with lots of gorillas."

"You're so weird! Why do you like movies with apes?"

"They remind me of Diego. But I like them better. They're funnier and they don't talk."

Letting the combing continue, Frida began to arrange her hair in cute little buns and intricate braids.

"I want this to be *our* night. Tomorrow we have to have dinner with the big-shit Rockefellers and I always find their parties so boring."

Lucienne repeated Frida's bad words. She and Frida were always joking around, teaching each other profanities in various languages. Frida's Spanish repertoire was vast.

"We went to the movies two days ago. Let's go to Chinatown. Then we can go to the Village and have drinks. Shall we invite the *Vanity Fair* delegates?"

"Do you think Georgia O'Keeffe would come?"

"I think she's already gone back to live with the coyotes in New Mexico. She's a strange bird. She takes refuge in the desert whenever she can."

"That's too bad. I wanted to sleep with her." Frida shrugged her shoulders.

For Lucienne, Frida's homosexuality was new. She'd found out about it from Diego.

"Of course, you know Frida's homosexual," he'd said, joking around. "You should have seen her flirting with Georgia O'Keeffe at her husband's gallery."

Frida couldn't have imagined that the Rockefellers' party would be her farewell to their elite world. A young Nelson Rockefeller, vice president of the family's eponymous commercial center, had commissioned Diego. Nelson was a great admirer of his work, and perhaps because of his innocence and the rebelliousness that comes with youth, he thought it'd be a fine idea for a famous capitalist such as himself to employ an important communist to paint his financial temple. They'd first met years before, at Diego's house in Mexico, when Frida was an advanced apprentice in the kitchen. From the moment the finely dressed young man arrived, sticking his nose in the Yucatán stew Frida was making to celebrate their meeting, she understood Lupe Marin's words: "A well-served meal can be the most powerful of spells." The young man made arrangements to fly Diego to New York and peppered Frida with questions about Mexican food, to which she responded coolly. After their banquet, Nelson was hooked on the couple's style, on Diego's magnificent brushes, and on the culinary subtleties that Frida had to offer.

Introduced to their magic world, Nelson became an expert of sorts on pre-Columbian and popular Mexican art. Totally drunk on Diego's charisma, Nelson proposed he paint a mural in New York. Diego immediately christened what he was sure would be the high point of his career: *Man at the Crossroads, Looking with Hope and High Vision to the Choosing of a New and Better Future.* Rockefeller approved the idea immediately.

But criticism of the mural at Rockefeller Center came right away. When the mural was almost finished, Diego astutely changed the figure of a simple worker to that of Vladimir Lenin. This sent the newspapers into a frenzy about the communist character of the work. Young Nelson took charge of the situation and came a few days before the opening to check out what would be adorning his building. He was a thin man with intelligent eyes and a sharp nose like a hood ornament. He dressed soberly and always had his hands in his pockets, effecting a casual and disinterested look; it was the same look Death might have after an eternity of stealing souls.

"Maestro Diego, Mrs. Rivera, I've come to invite you to a small party at my house," he said at the foot of the scaffold, his gaze never leaving Lenin, who seemed to be giving him a snide look.

"What's the occasion?" mumbled Diego as he climbed down.

"To talk about that," he said. His hand flew out of his pocket and gestured toward Lenin's head. "Your worker looks very bald, very goateed, and very red. Perhaps there's been a mistake. He didn't look like that in the original sketch."

Diego murmured something indecipherable, as if he were chewing on his own words.

"If I take him out, it will alter the concept of the mural. If what you want is something patriotic that will exalt the Stars and Stripes, I can put President Lincoln next to him," Diego offered, as if he were negotiating at a market.

"This will be a building where important impresarios come and go, and I fear that some of my clients might be offended. It's a small change," insisted young Rockefeller.

Diego, annoyed, scratched his butt.

"I can't. . . . It's impossible."

Slowly, Nelson Rockefeller shrugged, like a feudal lord who can move marionette strings to get workers to do as he pleases. He smiled at Frida and bade her farewell.

"Mrs. Rivera, I'll see you tonight at my house. I can also work wonders with cocktails. They may not be as magical as your dishes, but they'll comfort the soul just the same," he said. And he left with the same ease with which he'd entered.

To tell the truth, the party was very pleasant: a small get-together with friends, artists, and intellectuals from high society, all gathered in young Nelson's apartment, which was much like a museum with all its paintings and sculptures by big-name artists.

"When my family asked for a mural that would make people stop and think, I initially recommended Picasso or Matisse. Modern art is an art of liberation," he explained to Frida, who looked gorgeous, and to Diego, who sat as proudly as a lion, ruler of the jungle. When they'd arrived at the party, they were surrounded by photographers hoping to get the next *Life* magazine cover.

"Then I remembered that my mother's a great admirer of Diego's, and after my visit to your house, where I ate that delicious Guadalajara pulled pork, I felt compelled to commission him."

"The young man is very smart," Diego said, affirming him.

Frida lowered her head as if she were grateful for the compliment to her food.

"I hope our disagreement will be understood as

a matter of ideology," he explained to Diego as he led Frida by the arm to the bar. "And now I'll have to steal away your wife to show her that I have culinary magic in my hands as well."

Nelson and Frida strolled among the guests, greeting and waving to them as if they were the prom king and queen on their star night. They settled in a room where his wife, Tod, was talking to some friends from church. When she saw Frida, she gave her a fake smile, as if she were looking at an exotic reptile at the zoo.

"What a pleasure, Mrs. Rivera. Nelson tells me you paint and cook marvelously."

"She's a better painter than me!" Diego yelled from the other room. He was drinking from a large glass and already surrounded by admirers.

Frida smiled and lowered her eyes.

"My mother was indigenous. She taught me a few recipes before she died," said Frida, showing a little racial pride.

"It's a pity about her death. I hope she found a good guide from the Crossroad Club," Nelson said in condolence. He asked the barman to let him make the drinks.

Frida looked at him questioningly.

"Surely, you've heard the story of the Crossroad Club," Nelson said as he expertly mixed some gin and vermouth for a dry martini.

"The Crossroad Club? It sounds interesting," Frida said, arching her thick brow with curiosity.

"It's just a story, the stuff of washerwomen," murmured his wife, as if they'd been transported to a poor neighborhood.

Nelson finished pouring the drinks and placed Frida's in her hands with an exaggerated chivalrousness.

"Tell me the story; it sounds very interesting to me," she said as her cherry-red lips touched the cold martini. It wasn't Frida who jumped when she smelled the fragrance of gin and vermouth but rather the drink itself, which shivered from Frida's warm caramel kiss.

"I should tell you it's really an urban legend, the kind you tell kids to scare them just before bedtime. I heard it from an old man who used to work in one of my father's buildings. He had white hair and would boast that he was descended from the first African slave in the Americas. He was quite a talker. I would get hypnotized by his stories. Everyone called him Old Pickles. He loved to whistle songs he'd learned in the brothels in Chicago."

"Sometimes he can be so trivial that I think I'd rather die of boredom hearing how Diego kisses the behinds of the communists," whispered Mrs. Rockefeller to a friend. It was meant as a secret but Frida heard her poison talk.

Tod Rockefeller got up from the sofa with an English stiffness and walked off to where Diego was talking about politics and false conquests.

". . . One day I decided to eat the leftover Thanksgiving turkey up on the roof, where I found Old Pickles, eating his lunch of sardines and a red apple. As soon as I got up there, he asked me to sit by him, without really caring that I was the boss's son. He found things like class and people's positions a bother at lunchtime. Ultimately, we all eat lunch sitting down," said Nelson, happy to have an audience interested in his story.

"A woman in San Francisco told me something similar," Frida said, remembering the scent of Mommy Eve's apple pie.

"He started telling me everything there was to know about everybody in the company. Who slept with whom, who hated my father. But when he mentioned an old Polish accountant who'd died, he crossed himself and said, 'I hope he found a good guide at the Crossroad Club.'"

Rockefeller paused to wet his mouth with the martini. The gin lit up his eyes. "I asked him, 'What's the Crossroad Club?' and Old Pickles explained it to me without ever stopping his chewing on those smelly sardines. He said that once we die, we all have to journey to find our destiny, and the Crossroad Club was founded to help lead us down that dark path. It's a group of souls who work to guide each person to their destiny. It was almost like he was describing a business. He said that, in life, those souls had been much admired, well-known, and much loved by many others. That's why they're chosen: because people recognize them when they meet them. When it's our time, we all want to see a familiar face on the other side."

Frida was spellbound by the story. It explained her complicated situation very simply. The images of the revolutionary horseman kept coming back like a flood.

"Like who? Who are those guides?" asked Frida excitedly.

"I don't know. Maybe George Washington, or Dante, or Matisse. I suppose each person has a different guide."

"If I die, I'd like to be guided by a naked Mary Pickford," a guest who'd been eavesdropping chimed in.

Nelson smiled and nodded over at Diego, who was still charming everyone with his talk, glass in hand.

"I'm sure it'd be Lenin for your husband. From what I can tell, he's obsessed with him. I'd normally be surprised that a man should want that Communist to be his guide, but there's no question that everyone's different," Nelson said almost to himself. He was pensive for a moment. Then he turned to Frida as if he'd awoken from a dream.

"Who would you pick from the Crossroad Club, Mrs. Rivera?" he asked abruptly. "Who'd be your guide to Death?"

Frida gave him a dumb smile to avoid responding. It would certainly be problematic to let on that she already knew the answer to that mystery: that the person had already appeared at key moments in her life, always wearing a broad sombrero and on horseback, and that she'd known him since she was a child when the revolutionaries came to her house.

"I'm an atheist," Frida said coldly, putting an end to the discussion.

Nelson Rockefeller took her hand, which was covered in rings.

"You can deny the Christian god; that's your right. And if you knew the Fifth Avenue pastor like I do, he'd say you're right. But you can't deny the existence of

Death. There it is, behind every corner, waiting in silence to come and offer us his hand. And that's not a matter of believing or not believing, but of simply ceasing to exist," he whispered.

Frida remained quiet. But she met Nelson's icy stare, carrying the weight of dollars and power, and saw his lips slowly part to offer her a frightening smile. Sometimes absolute power is considerably more terrifying than Death.

Nelson got up from the sofa with an empty glass. He stuck his hand in his pants pocket and winked at Frida.

"I think the day you die, you'll become a member of the Crossroad Club. You're someone chosen by Death. It's been such a pleasure to meet you. I hope someday you'll forgive me for what's about to happen."

He took a slight turn and disappeared among the guests. For a moment, Frida thought he'd told the story just to scare her, to let her know she shouldn't trust a man with so much money, because they're the result not of dreams but of hard realities. She decided to forget everything and just have fun at the party.

But she'd been right in not wanting to trust young Rockefeller: the very next day he showed up while Diego was putting the finishing touches on the mural. He brought guards, who quickly positioned themselves around Diego's assistants. Nelson didn't seem angry; in fact, he was wearing the same chivalrous smile from the party the night before. And with that same God-stomps-ants-and-humans smile, he extended an envelope toward

Diego containing the rest of the agreed-upon payment for the mural.

"You can't do this to me," Diego muttered. Enraged, he broke his brushes.

"You know very well I can do anything. The solution regarding the image on the mural that I've asked you to remove is very simple: if Lenin is on the wall, then there's no wall."

And having said that, he tossed them out of the building, with an elegant nod of the head to Frida. Diego's services as an artist were no longer needed. There was no going back.

Diego, furious over this dirty trick, frothed with rage like a rabid dog. It wasn't the armed guards that dissuaded them from opposing Rockefeller's decision but rather his smile and that pose with his hands in his pockets, like a man calmly surveying the construction of his empire. That very afternoon, hammers and chisels began their work. The grand mural that would have consecrated Diego as the artist who would save the people through his work came down in pieces. Diego had never understood the Mexican saying "You don't pee in your own crib."

Three months later, and after more than four years of living in the United States, Frida's dream of going home came true.

THE BIG CITY AND ME

Our stay in New York was paid for by a really big shit. He had dollars to spare, but deep down I admit I liked him. Rockefeller spent his daddy's money collecting pre-Columbian idols like Diego. Even after the crap he pulled on us, he still came to see us at our home in Mexico. He always asked for my pulled pork and for blue tortillas. He said there were three stages in life: youth, middle age, and "You're looking well today."

GUADALAJARA-STYLE PULLED PORK
COCHINITA PIBIL

According to the rumor mill, it was in Yucatán that the Indians first tasted pork after the conquest of America. That's why they came up with dishes such as Cochinita Pibil. Preparing this dish requires the greatest care, giving each phase the time it needs to make sure it turns out the way it should. Most people like to use pork loin, but Eulalia prepares it with the shoulder blade, which is juicier.

4 plantain leaves
7 ounces achiote
1 cup sour orange juice
1/4 teaspoon ground cumin
1 teaspoon dried oregano
1 teaspoon ground white pepper
1/2 teaspoon ground black pepper
1/2 teaspoon ground cinnamon
5 allspice berries, roughly ground
4 bay leaves
3 crushed garlic cloves
1/2 teaspoon pequín chile
4 ounces lard
3 1/3 pounds pork loin or shoulder blade
8 ounces pork loin with ribs

✳ Warm the plantain leaves over the heat to soften them without splitting them. Line the pot with the leaves so that they stick out and can be folded to cover the meat.

Dissolve the achiote in the sour orange juice. Add the spices, garlic, and chile, and pour over the meat. Let marinate for at least 8 hours, but overnight is preferable. Melt the lard and pour over the meat. Put the meat in the pot, wrapping it with the plantain leaves. Wet the leaves a little with water, so they won't burn. Preheat the oven to 350°F, then roast for 1 1/2 hours or until the meat falls apart. Shred the meat and serve in the pot with the leaves. Accompany with tortillas.

COCHINITA SAUCE

LA SALSA DE LA COCHINITA

3 red onions, chopped
4 habanero chiles, chopped
1/2 cup chopped cilantro
1 cup sour orange juice or vinegar

✳ Mix all the ingredients together and let rest for 3 hours. Serve as a condiment when using the pork in tacos.

CHAPTER XV

The day Frida discovered her husband had done her wrong, she decided that belly of his was dead to her. Her blood was boiling. She felt guilty for having played a part in such a terrible act, but there were other reasons for her anger too. This is what she got for being such a dummy. There's no greater anger than to discover betrayal right under your nose. She felt like such a fool that it was all she could do to not smash all the dishes.

Since the Riveras returned from their exile in the U.S., Frida had felt a little alienated from her country. People had forgotten Diego; after so much time away, he was a stranger. The newspapers didn't write about him anymore. Everything had changed. Even the rural mariachi music on the radio had been replaced with boleros by Guty Cárdenas and Agustín Lara's murmured melodies. It was still true that General Cárdenas's government sympathized with revolutionary movements and communists, but it was also true that the great golden age of muralists had passed, now that there was the possibility of war in Europe.

Diego had also changed. He was a shadow of the big fat glutton she'd fallen in love with. The diet he'd been prescribed in the United States—which prohibited all the wonderful delicacies that Frida made—had turned him grumpy, temperamental, wrinkled, and tired. For the phlegmatic painter, everything was wrong. The canvases stayed white weeks at a time, while the liquor bottles paraded before him.

Desperate, Frida wrote the dear doctor in hopes of comfort from a friend: "Diego doesn't feel well, so he hasn't started painting yet. That's made me sadder than ever. If I don't see that he's happy, I can't relax, and I'm more worried about his health than mine."

Frida wasn't dumb. She knew Diego blamed her for his current situation, as if she'd influenced the decisions that brought him tumbling from his pedestal. But there was no way Frida was going to accept membership into that club of women who took on their husbands' disgrace at work simply for suggesting they could do better. If what he wanted was to hide in his den like an injured coyote out of fear of failure, that was his cowardice and nothing more.

So while Diego mourned his losses, they tried living in their new homes. The square blue and pink houses in the San Ángel district welcomed each day with the noise of dogs and parrots and the morning song of the little plucked rooster Frida still called Mr. Cock-A-Doodle-Do. The new houses reflected the state of the relationship: beautiful but cold. Frida decided she wouldn't be brought down. She'd make those bare brick walls her own. She'd cover them with pots and pans, piñatas, plants, cardboard Judases, and paintings, all in an attempt to overwhelm the home's modern cool with a more folkloric and fiery touch.

The only thing she couldn't do was cook, and that was grave. Whenever she went into that tiny kitchen, her tehuana skirts were so big, they covered cabinet doors and obscured windows. One day she decided to raise Diego's spirits and prepare him a pipián mole sauce but discovered that in the kitchen there was barely room to heat an egg. Annoyed, she took the burner up to the ample roof where she had more room to make the pipián—quite a feat, considering the struggle against the modern architecture. Irritated because of the ridiculous kitchen in her home, which was more appropriate to a dollhouse, she invited the house's architect over to dinner. Juanito had already heard that Frida was an excellent cook, so he came over ready for a feast. Instead, Frida served him two beans, one chicken wing, and one tortilla, all beautifully arranged on a plate.

"This is the only thing your kitchen is good for— enjoy it!" said Frida. Then she placed the fragrant and delicious pipián mole sauce on the table for Diego.

O'Gorman's architectural theories found strong opposition in the Mexican woman represented by Frida: she believed the kitchen was the heart of any home. That day Diego laughed at the expense of his friend and disciple. Of course, he never confessed to Frida that he'd had quite a bit of say about the space and arrangement of each room.

Frida was happy that her witticism had cheered Diego up a little bit. Her glutton of a husband ate up the first plate of pipián without sharing. It wasn't until the second that he took pity on Juanito and offered him some. At the end of the meal, they talked about Trotsky, the Revolution, art, and the damn capitalists on the other side of the Río Bravo. Later, Diego smoked a cigar as smelly as a sugar refinery and as big as a rolling pin. He drank a bottle of tequila and concluded the visit with O'Gorman by shutting himself up again in his studio.

"He looks thin," Juanito said before leaving.

"No, he looks fucked," Frida corrected him.

And at that very moment, she decided that Diego needed someone to help him get his papers in order, to straighten up his studio, and even to pose for him for the new mural that had been commissioned. And that person had to be her best friend: her sister Cristina. Cristi was her sure thing, her refuge, her comfort. Since they were kids, they'd always had a very strong emotional bond, even though they were very different. Frida was the intellectual, the artist, the woman of the world, and married to the famous painter; Cristina was the opposite: submissive, beaten, a little bit dim and simple, mother to two children, with a marriage so disastrous that just talking about it hurt. She didn't bother with books, except when she needed to check a recipe. She'd lost her good sense somewhere along the way.

When her husband, who normally treated her like

a punching bag, left her after the birth of their second child, Cristi went to live with her parents. She was the one who took care of their mother and was now taking care of their father, Guillermo, who would spend hours shut up in his studio staring at the family photos to see if he could capture some of the happiness he'd never had. Frida and Cristina complemented each other in every way; they were the pillars of their family's life. That's why Frida immediately took her by the hand, adopted her two kids as her favorite niece and nephew, showered her with gifts and money, and brought her to live in the two houses in San Ángel. The joyful noise of the children terrified Mr. Cock-A-Doodle-Do, and curvy Cristina's gay laughter filled all the empty spaces that had emerged between Frida and Diego. At that time Frida's only physical contact with Diego was an occasional gentle pat. Since the miscarriage in Detroit, sex was like an illusion, like with the pyramids at Teotihuacán, said Frida: you know they're there but you never go see them.

Frida would bring her niece and nephew to the studio to liven things up.

Good and grouchy, Diego would sit in a corner smoking and reading the paper while the sisters prepared a meal on the portable stoves that hung from the ceiling. They never stopped their chatter. And his canvases remained white, waiting for a brushstroke.

"You should work," Frida said. "I know those people out there are the stupidest in the world, so forget about those bastards. You're better than them."

"I don't like it."

"Like what, painting in general or specifically your painting?"

"Both," muttered Diego, burying himself in the paper so he could hide from the kids and his sister-in-law.

Frida served the meal while singing a corrido. Cristina followed along, smiling her sweet smile. And Diego just smiled back, perhaps a little warmer at Cristina.

"I'm going to take the boys with me so you'll get to work on that canvas, which is in a sad state because you haven't even wet your brushes. Cristi can help you organize your receipts and your papers, okay?"

"Of course, Friducha, I'll take care of little Diego for you," her sister said.

"And if you're a good boy, Diego, maybe we can go party in Xochimilco on Sunday," Frida proposed.

That was her mistake. Not the part about Xochimilco, because since she'd gotten back from the U.S., she'd been wanting to go back to that enchanting corner of paradise where canoes float like lazy clouds between lilies and goldfinches. But everything else.

Everything.

It was, in fact, in Xochimilco, where her niece and nephew served as witnesses, that Frida blew up like a volcano.

The day had begun cheery and full of hope. Frida had opened her eyes at the first note from Mr. Cock-A-Doodle-Do. She thought it was wonderful to be there, alive and in the world. That rooster's daily cry was magical; it reminded her she was toying with fate and that, in spite of her pains, she was winning.

She dressed, wearing a coquettish black blouse with a low-cut neckline, with green and red embroidery. She also wore a long, heavy skirt with frills, which hid the corpse-like green her leg had taken on after they'd cut off a pair of toes. When she'd first seen her leg after the surgery, she couldn't help but feel that she was literally dying off, piece by piece, but she calmed herself and thought: *It's better that my Godmother take my leg than my heart*. Having convinced herself of that, she made some complicated braids that crisscrossed her head like an orgy of snakes. She dressed up with an amethyst and jade necklace, some earrings from Oaxaca that were just a little smaller than the candelabra in the cathedral, and a pair of silver rings. She was ready to go to Xochimilco.

Frida raced across the bridge to her husband's house but the door was locked. She began to knock, beating out a rhythm and singing like a morning dove. She could hear Diego cursing. She'd left him the night before with a bottle of tequila and a guest, talking about socialist art. Not really caring if the chat had ended just a few hours earlier, she insisted they go out as planned that day.

"Goddamn it, Frida, cut it out! There are only dead people sleeping in here!"

She could hear noises—a lot of noises. Diego was coming and going, looking for the keys. He opened the door. But he didn't wait for Frida to come in before rushing back to bed to bury himself in the sheets, which Frida yanked from him like a mischievous child.

"It's dark in here. I'm going to open the blinds."

"What an asshole you are, Frida. Have pity on this

half-dead man," Diego protested, nude, rolling himself in the sheets like a taco. When he saw he was losing the game, he sat up and began to kiss Frida.

"You stink!"

"Yes, I stink like a free laborer. Pure tobacco, sweat, and tequila."

"Get dressed. We're going to Xochimilco with Cristina and the kids."

Diego dove back into the sheets. He muttered something incomprehensible. Frida surveyed the room. The canvas that had for so long been blank was on the easel, its emptiness replaced by bold strokes. A female nude, back turned and kneeling, embraced a giant bouquet of arum that filled the piece. The image was beautiful, as crushing as a passionate kiss, or a morning fuck, or a prohibited caress. It was Diego, just like Frida liked him.

"Cristi didn't say anything about that," Diego said.

"She should have. She probably forgot. You know she's a little bit scatterbrained. We agreed a week ago. I even cooked an Aztec pudding for you."

With the dishes already prepared and in baskets, ready to be eaten, accompanied by a couple of bottles of tequila, there was no way to get out of the day trip. Diego got up, throwing the sheets aside. The wind made a few sketches fly as he went to get dressed. But a strong scent slapped Frida as soon as the bed was uncovered. It was the sweet smell of spilled semen, of sex mixed with sweat. For a minute she wanted to run very far away from that place, to rush to Coyoacán and fall into her sister's arms and forget everything, but a cool voice calmed her, reminding her that there had only been family and friends at the house yesterday—no one for Diego to seduce.

She thought that madness and jealousy were not a particularly good combination and forgot about it.

Cristina and the children showed up about a half hour later. She looked tired and in a bad way.

"What happened?" Frida asked.

"Nothing. After helping Diego, I went home and ran into Carlos. Then I couldn't sleep."

Frida's response was a hard squeeze and a kiss on her forehead. Cristina was as cool as an ice sculpture but Frida didn't notice.

The basket with the culinary magic was set in the trunk of the car with the same care as a coffin in the ground. Then the entire family climbed in. The young Covarrubias and his wife Rosita (who was also an excellent cook) joined them, as did Diego's assistants and two journalists.

In the little town of Xochimilco, they rented two large rafts. Each raft had a name: sometimes a woman's name, sometimes something trendy. But their vessels, with bright colors and little roofs adorned with flowers, had names that Frida would never forget: *Traitor* and *La Llorona*.

It was precisely with that song that they were welcomed by mariachis. Frida and the kids sat up front so they could play with the water. Once arranged in the raft, with the mariachi band in an accompanying raft, the group put their fate in the hands of the rowers, who used their giant wooden paddles to push them forward and make their way between the lilies, jumping frogs, and dragonflies. On the banks, they could see flower beds, cypresses, and ahuehuete trees. Above them, the sky was so blue it hurt to look at it. The mariachis played a Zacateca march and then a sad waltz. A few swallows danced in the sky, provoking laughter below. Frida was happy, drinking, embracing her friends, and joking around about her life, about Diego's weight, about the Rockefellers' bad ways, and about Mexico's misfortunes. There was no room for her own misfortune.

The food appeared as if by magic: tacos, quesadillas, pambazos, and snacks were passed around for everyone. They bought beer and sweets from vendors who came paddling up.

Frida finished singing a corrido with the mariachis and blew out a big cloud of smoke. She arranged her poblano rebozo around her waist and cinched her skirt. She felt raindrops on her face. The sky thundered somewhere far away, already threatening to jealously spoil the happy day. When she turned, she saw her nephew on the edge of the raft with a little red wooden car: it was the one she'd given Diego. The boy played innocently, never knowing she was watching. Surprised, she looked around, shaking her head and trying not to scream. At first she thought the boy must have taken it from Diego's house but something instinctual immediately awakened her suspicions.

With two strides across the raft, she reached Cristina's son playing with the wooden car and grabbed him by the shoulders. Surprised, the boy dropped the toy, which fell in the water. Frida screamed in terror and bit her hand. The palpitating little red car sank into the deep waters and was lost.

"Where did you get that toy, Toñito? It was your Uncle Diego's!" she exclaimed, irritated.

The boy was still frightened. Used to his father's beatings, he brought his hand to his face for protection.

"I'm sorry, Auntie. You frightened me and I dropped it."

It was now impossible for Frida to get it back. But it looked like no one had noticed what had happened. The party went on and the raft continued on its lazy way.

"You shouldn't take things without permission!" Frida said, angrier by the minute.

The boy lowered his gaze, increasingly more frightened. But he found the courage to speak.

"I didn't take it," he said. "Diego gave it to me to play with so I wouldn't bother him while he worked with my mother."

Frida felt her bad leg go cold as ice. Then the cold went up her spine and froze her completely.

She nailed her eyes on Diego, who was sitting next to Cristina, laughing sweetly next to him, holding on to him the whole time. Diego would give her his glass to drink from and Cristi would act reluctant with affectionate little slaps. Frida took note that when her sister's fingers grazed his, they weren't unfamiliar. There was no doubt in her mind that those fingers had already traveled over Diego's body. Diego rooted like a little pig asking for his corn, clearly already familiar with Cristina's lips. Her sister whispered something in the painter's ear and Frida felt as if her body were going under the very same waters as the little toy on which she'd staked her love for Diego. She didn't need to see Cristina frolicking that morning with him; she didn't need to see her posing for the painting of the arum; she didn't need to see them sleeping together until dawn.

She didn't need evidence: Diego had betrayed her.

Nobody understood why Frida suddenly started beating on Diego. Young Covarrubias and his wife separated them, though she continued kicking and screaming profanities at him. In spite of their efforts, Frida still managed to land a slap on Cristina's face. "You're a whore," she said.

Cristina cried but she didn't touch where she'd been hit. She tried to apologize, to explain that Diego had seduced her . . . but Frida had already rented another boat to take her back. Diego didn't say a word. Instead he lowered his eyes and stared at the deep waters that, with its algae and fish, now guarded his love for Frida.

THE SAN ÁNGEL HOUSE

We set up our first altar for the dead today in our new home. We were joined by Isolda and Antonio, Cristi's kids, in a corner of the studio. I put up a beautiful photo of Mamá Matilde and another of Lenin. We set out a pot of green mole, which we made up on the roof because the kitchen Juanito built is good for nothing.

GREEN MOLE

MOLE VERDE

2 serrano chiles
2 cuaresmeño (jalapeño) chiles
1 poblano chile
1 cup peanuts
5 ounces peeled pumpkin seeds
1/2 cup sesame seeds
1 teaspoon coriander seeds
15 green tomatoes (tomatillos)
2 garlic cloves
2 cloves
3 allspice berries
1 cup chopped cilantro

1 teaspoon sugar

1/2 cup chopped epazote

3 romaine lettuce leaves, chopped

1 avocado leaf

1/2 cup lard

8 pieces chicken, cooked, plus reserved broth

✳ Roast the chiles, peanuts, pumpkin seeds, sesame seeds, coriander seeds, tomatoes, garlic, cloves, and allspice. Pound them and the remaining ingredients together in a molcajete, with the exception of the chicken and the lard. Heat the lard in a pot and add everything from the molcajete, cooking over medium heat, stirring constantly until it's thick. Reserve some of the paste for serving. The paste should be thinned a bit by adding broth from cooking the chicken. Add the pieces of chicken and heat until it boils. Serve with tortillas.

CHAPTER XVI

When she looked out the window, Frida realized that one of the new demons terrorizing her was laughing right in her face. She looked out, amazed at her sister Cristina, who was at the gas station right in front of her apartment. Frida could have just stayed there, letting Cristina taunt her, but the rabid dog inside her got the better of her. Frida put down her cup of coffee and brought her cigarette to her mouth, where her lips held it in a hateful grimace. Without a word, she left her ex-boyfriend, Alejandro, sitting by himself, his mouth agape, and raced down the stairs with little hops as her bad leg would allow, and went up to her sister like a bull rushing a red cape. Frida grabbed her through the car window and shook her as if she were a saltshaker as she screamed a string of obscenities.

"You fucking whore! C'mere! Did you see me, you slut? You know I live here now. Why do you come here? I never want to see you again! Get the hell out of here, you good-for-nothing!"

Alejandro had hurried down and by now had separated the two sisters, who were fighting like children over sweets spilled from a piñata. Once restrained, Frida upped her kicking and insults. Cristina, terrified but with a bit more control, decided to get out of there as fast as she could. Frida ran after her for a few yards, spouting all sorts of horrible things. In spite of all this, both sisters had the same tears in their eyes, exactly the same in shape, color, and hurt. They loved each other, but the betrayal had cut off all possibility of forgiveness.

Alejandro understood that pain was making Frida crazy. He understood she was different now from when they'd known each other. She'd cut her hair in a rage, as a vendetta, leaving behind those elaborate braids her husband had loved so much. She no longer wore her tehuana dresses, either, or jewelry. Now she sported European clothing, tight skirts, and sober jackets from the latest issue of *Vogue*.

Frida and Alejandro returned in silence to the apartment. She let herself drop into a large leather chair as if someone had just beaten her. She put out her cigarette, which was all ashes anyway, and quickly lit another one. She was smoking with desperation.

"This is a very nice living room, Frida. Your little house is quite charming," Alex said to break the tension.

Frida curled her lips and stroked the leather chair as if it were the skin of one of her lovers.

"You like these? Diego bought them. I chose the blue

because he'd already bought red ones for Cristi," she explained. Then she put out her new cigarette with a long sigh.

That strange declaration reminded Alejandro that what might be bizarre in the outside world could be quotidian in Frida's. Even though Frida had decided to live alone, she continued to see Diego. It's what made Alejandro decide to leave her complicated life once more and avoid these uncomfortable circumstances. Before he left, he gave her some advice.

"Frida, leave here. You don't need to hurt yourself even more with these things."

It was a tempting suggestion for Frida. Alejandro knew her well. At the door they said good-bye with a kiss on the mouth. And when Alejandro left, she realized she was alone with her paintings. She surveyed them nostalgically. And then she cursed Death, who kept her alive while her heart bled. She could see the hurt that haunted her in each of her works: every brushstroke carried the tears she'd shed as punishment. She wiped her eyes now and decided to take her friend's advice. She spoke with a lawyer to arrange her divorce papers and make sure she got as far away as she could, to New York. She packed her bags and left.

"I've done everything I can on my end to forget everything that happened between Diego and me," she wrote to Dr. Eloesser on the flight. "I don't think I've been completely successful, because there are things that are stronger than sheer will, but I couldn't go on in such a sad state anymore. I was taking giant steps toward becoming one of those really shocking hysterics who act like idiots and nobody likes. I feel good that, at the very least, I was able to control this state of idiocy somewhat. . . ."

In Manhattan, she went back to the carefree life she'd had years before in the same city. She met up with Lucienne and Ella Wolfe and went back to Harlem to see silly movies with gorillas and to marathon parties and outings in the Village.

In the evenings, she'd step out on the terrace and watch the sun disappear behind the skyscrapers while cursing the agreement with her Godmother, especially now that Diego's absence made her heart bleed. One day she felt an impulse to connect with Georgia O'Keeffe. Luckily, Georgia was in the city. When she called her, they talked for hours, like a pair of old friends who hadn't seen each other in a long time. Art and unfaithful husbands were common themes for these two hurt wives. Feeling confident, Frida invited her to dinner at her place and they agreed to meet the next night.

Frida got up early to go to upper Manhattan, to the Latino neighborhood, where she managed to get what she needed to make dinner. Dressed in an elegantly tailored suit, she strolled through the Puerto Rican groceries looking for chiles, tortillas, and spices. She could hear boleros and danzones coming from the open windows and it made her feel at home. Inspired and pleased, she prepared the meal to a soundtrack of jazz.

Georgia arrived at dusk wearing a simple cotton blouse and black slacks. But Frida had decided to take on her exotic character again and was wearing a heavy jade necklace, a long raspberry-colored skirt, and a lace blouse. The women drank together, allowing the brandy's alcoholic powers to loosen the tension in their bodies as well as their tongues. Frida served various dishes, which Georgia devoured ecstatically. It had been a very well-thought-out menu, designed to relight the fire they'd felt the day they first met. And it was unquestionably responsible for allowing the sexual tension to emerge anew.

"You have a strange look in your eyes," Georgia said, once they were in the living room, each with a glass.

"How's that?" Frida asked, meeting her gaze and curving her mouth into a questioning half smile.

Georgia took her hands delicately, like a groom receiving his betrothed at the altar.

"You look deeply, as if you were drowning in my eyes, but when you laugh, your eyes turn into a beam of light."

"Maybe I want to hypnotize you," Frida said a little sarcastically to cover up her nerves.

Georgia laughed so hard that it became contagious, and as they both laughed they finally relaxed.

Frida took her friend's hand and sweetly kissed it. With her free hand Georgia played with Frida's short hair and let her eyes dive into hers and pirouette like an underwater dancer. Then they began a game to get to know each other's bodies: Frida kissed Georgia's face while Georgia caressed her firm breasts through the flowery blouse.

"I like your breasts."

"Really?"

"Yes . . . I like them."

"They're very small . . . like a couple of peaches."

"They're the right size to fit in my hands," said Georgia, using both hands now to caress them.

Frida sighed, letting her breasts—useless to Diego's unborn child—feel desired and tingly under Georgia's hands. When Georgia lifted her colorful blouse, Frida raised her arms to be undressed. They kissed again, slowly, as their fingers ran up and down each other's backs. When their lips parted, Frida had already unbuttoned her friend, who shamelessly showed off her milky skin; freckles swirled around her breasts, which were cupped by a simple white bra. Frida looked for a space on Georgia's neck to kiss, then started down her chest, following the soft curve of her breasts. Then she kissed her belly, where she found her belly button. She explored it with the tip of her tongue. Later Georgia licked around Frida's erect nipples, increasing her excitement.

She came up to her ear and whispered: "I want you."

In response, Frida unbuttoned her new lover's pants, letting her hand find her way to her sex. She rubbed it slowly until she felt they were both moving with the same rhythm.

"I want you too," Frida finally said as she got rid of her heavy cotton skirt, her shoes, and her white underwear.

Frida had a small sex, with very tight labia and very

fine hair. Georgia's delicate hands soon found her clitoris and proceeded to softly rub it, making Frida wet. She began to rock her hips, hoping for greater pressure, all the while sucking on Georgia's breasts with contained passion. She was tormented by desire and finally tried to penetrate her friend with her hand.

"Go on," Georgia whispered, and sighed loudly.

Frida began to satisfy Georgia using a faster rhythm. Georgia's movements suggested she was close to orgasm and Frida didn't want to ruin the moment by being clumsy. Her instincts were on the mark, and a little later she heard Georgia's moans and felt her intense and wild contractions with her fingers. They continued until Georgia lay back on the couch, quiet and sweaty. Frida snuggled up to her lover's chest and they kissed tenderly.

"Thank you," Frida said.

"For what?" Georgia asked.

"For reminding me I can change."

"You've always been able to change, Frida," the pale artist told her. She turned to look at her and pulled her closer. "From the moment I met you, you reminded me of a Navajo story that I heard in New Mexico. It's called 'The Ever-Changing Woman.'"

"'The Ever-Changing Woman'?" Frida asked with a grin. She was hoping the night would last, that there would be lots of intimate chatter between the two; she'd always thought that it wasn't just sex that was enjoyable but especially the words that hover above nude bodies afterward.

"In the summer, when I get away from my husband by going to my house in the desert, I get together with my Indian brothers and sisters to hear their stories, because they contain a lot of truths. I heard about the Ever-Changing Woman, or Asdzaa Nadleehe, from them. She's Mother Earth, which is why they believe that she's a changeable creature, like the seasons: she is born in spring, matures in the summer, grows old in autumn, and dies in winter. But her existence doesn't end there. For them the universe is made up of many worlds. They believe the point of origin for the first man and woman was kernels of white corn. At first they were brought up together, but neither one appreciated the contributions of the other, so they were separated, which brought people misery. That's why every time you go from one world to another, you change. Some things are left behind and some are brought along to help you rebuild in the new world. But Death never ceases to exist in any of those worlds. It's tied to us. The gods gave us ceremonies to remind us of that."

"And who am I?"

"The woman who changes with each season, who struggles to have a child so she can cheat Death . . . but you won't succeed, because she's already inside you," Georgia explained.

When she heard those words, Frida just stared at her own nakedness and at her body deprived of the gift of procreation. She understood that pain was part of the deal she had with the woman in the veil, but better than that, she understood her true nature as a truly singular woman.

After the silence, she and Georgia began to touch and kiss again until they reached a new climax. From the couch they moved to the bed, and at midnight they were again silent, embracing, resting in the nude, just listening to each other's breathing and the traffic on the streets.

"Are you happy?" Georgia asked shyly, as if she'd broken a piece of porcelain.

"Right now I am. Tomorrow I'll go back to my version of Calvary. It's my destiny. I have to go back to Mexico, I have to see Diego. He's written to ask me a favor."

She didn't know what else to tell her, though in certain ways she felt that she was understood better by Georgia than any of her other lovers. She knew these were stolen moments, that in the morning they'd wake up and put on their masks, pretending to be professional colleagues, and talk about brushstrokes and colors and textures. She didn't care, though: that night they both thought they'd created a work of art. They slept in peace until Frida dreamt of Mr. Cock-A-Doodle-Do's song; in some ways he was helping her see a new day through her dreams.

Resigned to having to return to her life, she wrote to Diego: "Now I know that all those letters, all those adventures with all those other women, were only flirtations. Deep down, you and I love each other very much, which is why we put up with so many affairs, knocks on the doors, profanities, insults, and international reclamations. We will always love each other."

When she returned to Mexico, she took her sister Cristina a basket full of flowers and desserts as a sign of forgiveness. Cristina hugged her and they cried together all afternoon. The love between them was much greater than the slip with Diego. Even though Frida told her sister that she'd forgiven Diego, too, Cristina didn't believe her.

GEORGIA'S DELIGHTS

Georgia made me laugh when she said she painted flowers because they were cheaper than models and didn't move. Plus, I told her, they'd never sleep with her husband. She agreed. I love to prepare dishes for people I love. I love to think of a menu as a series of tributes, of caresses, so that they'll feel captivated.

MOLE DE OLLA

1 pound shredded beef
2 1/4 pounds beef shank

2 garlic cloves, chopped

1 1/4 onions, chopped

5 guajillo chiles, seeded

2 ancho chiles

4 Roma tomatoes

Salt

1 ear of corn, husked and cut into chunks

2 carrots, peeled and sliced

2 squash, sliced

1 sprig epazote

1 xoconostle (prickly pear) cactus, peeled
    and cut into small squares

14 ounces premixed masa, rolled into small
    balls

Cilantro leaves

Lemons

Chopped onion for serving

❋ Sauté the meat with 1 garlic clove and 1 onion. Then puree and strain the chiles, tomatoes, and the remaining garlic clove and 1/4 onion. Pour the mixture into the pan where the meat was cooked. Add salt, the corn, and carrots. Cover and cook for 45 minutes over low heat. Add the squash, epazote, xoconostle, and the masa balls. Cook for 10 more minutes. Serve accompanied by cilantro, lemon, and onion.

CHAPTER XVII

When Frida first met him, she thought he was archaic, old, old-fashioned, tedious, boring, and solemn— one of those pieces of furniture you inherit from your grandmother and then relegate to the corner of the room. Nonetheless, he was a revolutionary hero. Every communist in the world admired him, though none of them offered him asylum. Being Stalin's enemy was no joke. To be hated by the leader of the Russian party was a mortal sin. Still, President Cárdenas decided to let Trotsky into Mexico in spite of the fact that it would make him a target for critics on the far left and the far right, and put him in a bad position with both God and the devil.

It wasn't a good situation, but Diego embraced it without hesitation because of his political beliefs. He was the one who'd interceded in favor of the revolutionary, well aware of the fact that assassins could be hiding anywhere, ready to blow the head off the only person in the way of Stalin's crowning himself as his country's only master. That's why he asked Frida to host this man, one of the principal architects of the Soviet communist revolution. Anyway, that's what he tried to tell her while she was still in New York. Frida agreed to do him the favor without complaint.

"Women are humanity's wheels of progress. We could say that you're an absolute force in and of yourselves, but that would be lying. You're more like a state of harmony and balance that religion, government, and we husbands have turned into a comfortable pillow on which to rest," said Trotsky, whom Frida referred to as the Goateed Man. (Frida called him various names behind his back.)

Trotsky was making a toast, lifting his glass of tequila. Diego said nothing and sat down next to him so he could hear. Frida poured tequila for everyone, enjoying tending to her guests. She was offering a great dinner for Trotsky's entourage, family, and friends. André Breton, the surrealist, had traveled with his wife from Paris to meet the communist thinker.

"In our imperfect society, women have been capable of sewing together skins that over time became textiles with beautiful embroidery; they have raised children who became workers, soldiers, and doctors who fought for liberty; they have sowed fields with the seeds of the future; they have taught and educated the people. Yet their time is embarrassingly consumed before a pot in the kitchen. They've spent half their lives like that." Trotsky turned to look at Frida. His eyes shone on her, slaves to his glasses.

He licked his lips like someone who likes his dessert on the side. "Women have cooked so much that, if that time had been spent trying to liberate humanity, we'd have been living in freedom a long time ago. Nonetheless, I have a very hard time imagining a free world without the pleasure of food, which is why I praise this table and, even more, the hands that created everything on it. Thank you, Mrs. Rivera: each bite is a battle won for the people," Trotsky said in closing as he drank his tequila.

Everyone present did the same. Frida knew her cooking was affecting the refugee's body like an elixir, rejuvenating him and relieving the pain of his exile.

Frida smiled at him, letting the guests' applause engulf her. She'd made every dish as a tribute to Trotsky. Each plate had been prepared keeping in mind what Lupe had told her: "At your table, everyone will honor you." Perhaps because she was competing with Diego, or because she wanted to be noticed, or maybe just because she could, she'd decided to win the admiration of the man her husband most admired. Frida wanted Trotsky to surrender to her and allow her to exact her immature vengeance on Diego.

She wasn't surprised when she felt Trotsky's hand under the table caressing her thigh. That clandestine attempt at seduction caused her to make a face at Diego, who couldn't even begin to imagine its source.

With the war in Spain and the political storms all over the world threatening human destiny at the end of the

1930s, Frida had become completely committed to the communist movement. Once she had accepted that she was bound to Diego for life, she'd returned to Mexico to help him with Leon Trotsky's exile.

She went to Tampico herself to welcome the Russian exiles, as if she were an Aztec ambassador, a red version of Malintzin. Her first impression of Trotsky wasn't very good. He was wearing baggy wool pants and a plaid cap and walked with a cane. He was also carrying a huge portfolio and looked much shorter than he actually was. His heavy coat seemed like it was waiting for a new ice age to cover the Earth. And though he walked ramrod straight, with his goatee up in the air like a retired general, his age detracted from his vigor. Never mind Natalia, his wife, who Frida always thought of as a bitter bureaucrat. But these were her guests. Because of them, she'd fixed up her parents' house on Londres Street in Coyoacán, sending Cristi to live in another house a few blocks away and her father to live with her older sister. When Guillermo found out that his Coyoacán castle would be lent to an important Russian, he gave Frida some advice.

"If you hold this man in esteem, tell him not to get mixed up in politics. It's very bad."

Being host to the revolutionary made Frida proud and gave her a reason to live. She served as translator, given that no one in the Russian group spoke Spanish and Natalia didn't speak English. Then she decided to use an international language: food. She certainly knew about that. Her culinary delights could be enjoyed in any language. The Russian couple loved them, especially because they were accustomed to austere meals of cold herring, insipid vegetables, and plain flavors. It was at Frida's that they discovered the sensation of mole on their palate: that perfect consecration of chile, chocolate, fruit, and bread.

"Every bite of this dish makes me think that food in Mexico has completely rejected European canons. Fight for its authenticity! Insurrection is an art, however, and like all arts, it has its rules," said Trotsky one morning when he got up and ran into Frida and Eulalia, the cook, preparing a meal.

To help him wake up, they made him a cup of coffee with cinnamon and brown sugar. When Frida saw him standing in the doorway, recharged and smiling, she shot him a sensual look meant to attract. But she continued with her work in the kitchen, leaving Trotsky with his awakened desire.

"What are the rules of the kitchen, Frida?" he asked.

Frida washed her hands and showed Eulalia the recipe they were working from in "The Hierba Santa Book" so she could follow it correctly to get its magical flavors. Frida picked up a cigar and put it in her mouth like a hummingbird sucking honey from a flower. She performed the gesture with the necessary calm to let a poisonous lust extend over every part of the old man's body. She lit the cigar. She took a deep breath and then slowly exhaled smoke that danced around Trotsky's white beard and nose. The Russian could smell mint, vanilla, and lemon. He had to sit down, surprised by how his pants were bulging.

"The rules are simpler than what you might think. The first is that no one goes into a woman's kitchen without her permission. That's as big a sin as sleeping with her husband. Maybe even worse," said Frida, now sitting by Trotsky's side. "In the kitchen, you can be ignorant, mean, or careless. But you can't be all three at once. Otherwise, you end up shaking the rice while it's cooking, or not adding an ingredient because you forgot to buy it, cooking pasta and salsa together, cooking the meat with more oil than all of Lake Chapala, or serving burnt beans."

A smile emerged on Trotsky's face that extended to a laugh so robust that he unintentionally scared away Mr. Cock-A-Doodle-Do, who had been pecking at some leftovers.

"What will you delight us with today when we have guests?" asked Trotsky.

"Fish soup, Veracruz style; fish with cilantro, Costa Chica style; and a couple of cream buns, all family recipes. Tequila and pulque, to brighten the day. Everybody needs something to sip and something to smoke for fun."

"Pulque?" asked the Russian.

Frida signaled Eulalia to pour some of the juice they'd bought at the corner store. They'd added guava, giving the liquid a pink and creamy color.

"Long ago, the pre-Columbian native people drank this during religious ceremonies. The priests used it to communicate with the gods."

The old man didn't dare try the beverage. It looked slimy, like a bodily fluid.

"What is it?" he asked, unable to hide his disgust.

"It's fermented maguey juice," said Frida as she pulled the glass away from him. "It's important not to insist that people try things against their will. The palate is for pleasure, not for obligations."

"There's something witchlike about you that delights and surprises me. Maybe you're poisoning me with your food, because since I got to Mexico, I see everything differently."

Frida leaned back as she exhaled the smoke from her cigar. Somewhere in the kitchen, Agustín Lara was singing "Sólo tú" on the radio.

"Does the green of the pasture now remind you of melons? Does blood recall cherries? Does the sticky happiness of an afternoon conjure nougat?" Frida asked.

"Yes, yes . . . something like that," Trotsky responded. He nodded affirmatively to each interrogative in a gesture that was very his: very professorial, very much a word lover.

"Then maybe something of me is coming through in the salt. To live life, you have to season it. You can see that because I'm not in good health, I have to put up with a lot. Of course, sometimes you're just a bitch your whole life. If you don't suffer, you don't learn. So I use a little bit of thyme, chile, clove, and cinnamon to sweeten the taste of things."

Frida took his hands, the tips of her fingers rubbing the skin on his old-man knuckles. "Look at us: you without a country and me without a leg."

Eulalia turned away to hide her giggles. Trotsky

hadn't understood a word, since Frida had chosen to speak in Spanish. But once Eulalia laughed, Frida translated it into English, and then they all laughed heartily.

To accompany the coffee, Frida offered him a cream bun, which they ended up sharing. When there were only crumbs, she picked them up with her fingers and slowly ate them as if she were kissing the air. Trotsky could have contemplated her for hours, but Diego came into the kitchen like a hurricane landing and uprooting palms and boats.

It was, in fact, that very day that Trotsky would make the toast about women and top it off by touching her thigh, echoing the morning's flirtation.

After the great banquet that evening, Diego took Trotsky to see Frida's paintings. She stayed in a corner, between shadows, waiting to see what he'd say.

"This is marvelous! It's as if all that is this country could be concentrated in the soul of one woman!"

"They're just self-portraits," said Frida, shaking off the compliment.

"Fuck, Frida, they're better than mine!" roared Diego.

"There's a lot of power in your hands. Anybody who can use brushes like this—and also cook meals like those we enjoy every day—must be a great artist," Trotsky said, squeezing her hands.

He raised his finger as if he'd just remembered something and, running off like a gnome, went back to his room to get a book to give to Frida as if he were a servant and she was his empress. Frida read the title: *Con-*

cerning the Spiritual in Art. It was by Kandinsky, the Russian artist. Trotsky stepped away and Diego began to get ready for another meeting or some such thing.

Frida opened the book and found a marked page. Someone had underlined a passage in pencil: "Color, in general, is a way of exerting direct influence on the soul. The eye is the tempering hammer. The soul is a piano with many keys. The artist is the hand that, through a specific chord, makes the human soul sing."

Between the pages of the old book, Trotsky had left her a note. "Tomorrow at ten, at Cristina's house." Frida had to bat down her smile to avoid giving away her crush on the leader of the Russian Revolution.

When Diego had asked her to help him with Trotsky, she'd agreed without too many conditions, knowing that the relationship with her husband would be like the waves that come and go on the shore: sometimes he'd be home, sometimes not. They were still husband and wife, and divorce was not talked about anymore. On some drunken nights Diego would take her, and Frida would let herself be loved.

There was nothing in the way of her having an amorous adventure with the Russian. Cristina and the kids would be out of the house for most of the day; her sister had set things up to accommodate the affair. And the two lovers arrived on time for their date.

After Trotsky had possessed her, Frida looked out the window to the street; she was wrapped in an old colorful sarape that had been a gift to her father a long time ago in Saltillo. Her head was spinning after the slow and tender sex she'd had with the Goateed Man. Her cheeks were still pink, the embers from the fire still burning.

"Frida, your brush is a marvel. Every time it battles the canvas, there's a war. When we talk about revolutionary art, I can only think of two artistic phenomena: works that reflect the revolution, and works that, while not thematically linked to the revolution, are imbued with a new consciousness derived from the revolution. That's where your work falls," said Trotsky. He couldn't take his eyes off one of the self-portraits Cristina had hanging in her bedroom.

Trotsky seemed less old when he talked; when Frida looked at him, she thought he could take on the entire Russian army with the force of his words. Even though his body couldn't hide his years, he was vigorous and sure of himself, like a young troublemaker who can't find a rival to challenge him. He was wearing just his briefs, an undershirt, and his glasses. His thin legs, like white branches, held up his hairless trunk, a barricade against any hurricane.

"Do you believe in Death?" she asked him.

"Death is a reality. It's not an article of faith, Frida," he said, thinking and adjusting his glasses.

"It's useless to talk about this. Forget I said anything," muttered Frida.

Trotsky didn't give up that easily. He came close to Frida to see what had caught her attention outside the window. He was surprised when he saw a newborn baby chick, bald and dead on the ground. Up above, on the branch of a fig tree, its mother called it from the nest without response. He supposed the little bird had tried to fly, or perhaps it had been startled and lost its balance, falling from its cozy nest to its death.

"My father used to tell me a story from ancient Russia about a soldier who returns home with only three pieces of bread and gives them to three beggars along the way. The three, who are fairies in disguise, grant him three wishes that he uses to defeat demons. His greatest treasure is a magic bag in which he can keep everything, even Death. And so that's what he does: he traps Death, saves his kingdom, and lives forever. It's just a story to scare kids, though—a shadow of medieval times, when emperors ruled over everything. The only way to defy Death now is through science."

"Death isn't afraid of microscopes, of that I'm sure."

Trotsky was playing with her hair. Frida was letting him please her, purring with pleasure.

"You defy Death with your art, Frida. I don't know what fate lies before us as far as art is concerned, but I do know that if humanity can reach the heights you do, then we'll be incomparably stronger, wiser, and more subtle. We will be more harmonious, our movements more rhythmic, our voices more melodious. Our existence will take on a more dramatic dynamic. The average man will be like Aristotle, like Goethe, like Marx. And even above those heights, new peaks will emerge."

"Have you considered that we could have sex again while you talk?" Frida asked. She put her cigarette out, a little tired of the the Goateed Man's bombast.

Trotsky considered it, and then he smiled.

* * *

Diego loved to take up his guests' free time. Just like Trotsky, he was obsessed with his work, but that didn't keep him from taking the old man around every week to tour places near the capital. Always the professor, Trotsky merely nodded at whatever Diego showed him, whether it was pyramids, colonial towns, or some forest. During those day trips he began to collect cacti, which he then repotted and set in rows in the courtyard at La Casa Azul.

Diego tried to control himself around Trotsky, because his admiration exceeded even the wildest fawning that made reporters in attendance want to throw up. He always let the revolutionary explain his point of view and then he'd immediately agree with him, happy to be a simple fan to his political leader. But it was ironic that in spite of all the compliments, honors, and shameless bootlicking that Diego did before Trotsky, the revolutionary's attention was focused solely on Frida. He wrote her ardent love letters that he'd hide in books that he'd give her every night before going to bed. For her part, Frida communicated through the exquisite language of food.

The affair between them didn't last very long. Frida still felt hurt from Diego's betrayal and she was sure she was only doing it to get even with him. She was hoping for a different kind of lover, and it was clear the Goateed Man would never satisfy her appetite for men and women. The affair reach a crisis when the two couples, escorted by various members of the entourage, decided to make a trip to Hidalgo, just east of the city. The convoy of cars stopped at the beautiful paradise that is the hacienda San Miguel Regla, with the idea of visiting the pyramids the next day. Trotsky and Natalia enjoyed a cup of coffee in the shade of a willow tree, thrilled with the surrounding views. The hacienda was set in a privileged place, encircled by leafy trees. The magnificent estate had once been the property of Pedro Romero de Terreros, the first Duke of Regla, who'd gotten rich from the mines at Real del Monte during the eighteenth century.

Diego and Frida had gone on a leisurely romantic stroll on a rock bridge to feed the ducks in the pond. Their conversation was trivial, limited to their doings that day, but it was cut short when one of the guards came up to Frida with a book.

"It's from Mr. Trotsky," he said.

Frida opened it and discovered a fat letter tucked into its pages, which she immediately tried to hide.

"What the fuck is that?" Diego asked, curious.

"Some notes about Kandinsky's concepts of art."

"You're such a motherfucker! You don't give a royal shit about any of this but you're leading on the old man. You should be ashamed of yourself!" Diego exclaimed.

"Oh, is it more objectionable to lead on a man than a woman? How many gringas have you led on with your blather so you could have a roll with them, huh, Diego?" Frida responded, on the defensive.

"That's unnecessary. If you want to argue because you got caught, go fight with someone else. I'm not going to be your punching bag." Diego spat angrily. In his eyes, treason couldn't be defended.

He walked away, leaving Frida with her letter from Trotsky. It was nine pages long, and in it he begged her like a little boy not to leave him and to please live with him.

Frida was disgusted. If she'd had any hesitation about ending the affair, that letter gave her all the reason in the world to do it. She would tell him the very next day.

But that night Frida couldn't sleep. It was impossible to drift off while consumed with her ridiculous guilt over Trotsky's desperation. She took a walk on the terrace where they were staying, watching the glowworms dance to bring on the rain. She was surprised to hear the neighing of a horse, and then, a few minutes later, she saw the Messenger in the shadows by the willow tree. His white eyes shone just like the horse's.

"What brings you around now? Is my time up? That wasn't the agreement, and you know it. So long as my little rooster, Mr. Cock-A-Doodle-Do, sings each morning, I'll still be here," Frida said in defiance.

The man just stood there. She wasn't the reason for the visit; it was someone else. The Messenger was her Godmother's herald. The glowworms began to curl up in strange ways, swiftly forming a kaleidoscope, which shone brightly in the dark. Frida could hear insect wings. She was stunned by the wonder of what she was seeing. A little Seurat-like, each glowworm became part of a new image, which Frida's eyes slowly began to make out: First, she could see Trotsky reading, sitting quietly, looking up from his book and out the window. Outside, a car; men with luminous eyes climbed out of it. Sparks, without a doubt from gunshots aimed at the revolutionary. Trotsky falling to the floor, riddled with bullets. His time on Earth finished. Frida gasped, filled with pity and gratitude for the image her Godmother had just allowed her to see.

"You can't kill him after all he's done to get away. Maybe he can cut a deal like I did. Give him more time," she pleaded. "Tell her to take part of my life."

The Messenger turned into the night, briefly illuminated by the glowworms.

The pyramids at Teotihuacán rose magnificently in Trotsky's eyes. He nodded his head with pleasure, in his typical gesture of approbation. Diego told him strange tales about cannibalism among the pre-Columbian indigenous people while Frida remained quiet, trying to figure out the best way to let Trotsky know that he was about to be shot dead. When they arrived at the Calzada de los Muertos between the pyramids of the sun and the moon, the visitors felt an intense heat, as if a magnifying glass were being held above them.

"I should drink something," said Natalia, taking a seat on a step as she fanned herself with a handkerchief.

Diego sat with her and did the same. But Trotsky insisted on climbing to the very top of the majestic Pyramid of the Sun.

"Why we don't we stop and drink something?" Frida asked.

They all turned, but no one had a response. Then a pulque vendor appeared, as if the question had been an evocation. The indigenous man carried two large containers with local pulque.

"Now perhaps you'll try the pulque?" Diego asked with a smile as he stood up to get the vendor.

"It's a good day for it," said Trotsky, offering Frida his hand. Followed by the two guards who escorted the old man, they walked toward the vendor, leaving Diego behind like a chastised child.

"Have you read my letter?" Trotsky whispered in her ear.

Frida tried not to make a move that would give anything away to their respective partners. She continued walking with her regal gait.

"Yes, and you know my answer. However much you insist otherwise, I've decided it's over. However, I need to tell you something very important, which has nothing to do with your youthful caprice." Very seriously, she turned to him. "Leon, they're going to kill you. They're going to shoot you. Several men are coming. You'll hear a car in the night."

"How do you know? Is there a spy in our group?"

"No. It's something you'll never understand. That's why I've asked that you get another chance, like they gave me. You just need to cut a deal with her so she won't take your life so violently," Frida explained.

One of the guards had already caught up to the vendor and come back with two glasses of pulque. Frida looked down at the thick liquid with its mucousy strings and knew it was a sign.

"Like I explained to you the other day, this is the drink of the gods. This will be our ceremony. Drink it and ask to live one more day; she'll hear you."

"No, I won't do it, Frida. What good is life to me without you by my side?"

"That life is called marriage. And there's Natalia waiting for you," Frida said.

Trotsky stared at Frida. He didn't understand what she was talking about, but he thought it was perhaps some kind of ritual to end their affair. He brought the drink to his lips. He found the thickness of it distasteful and his stomach turned as if he were going to throw up. But he drank it all. In the end he thought its sharp taste was comforting and fresh. The pulque's alcohol went through his body, reactivating dead cells. His tired eyes acquired a new light and his pains vanished. Trotsky thought something had changed.

"Now you also have an agreement with her," Frida said, kissing his hands. She turned around and returned to the group, which had been watching them the whole time.

Trotsky nodded in approval. He tried to get his wife to try the pulque but she refused, nauseated by it.

* * *

There had been barely perceptible details that Trotsky's wife had begun to notice. She couldn't explain it, but she was bothered by something. The fear that she'd be abandoned as a useless wife had depressed her so much, she'd begun to lose weight, to forget things, to say silly things, and to be sick all the time in an attempt to get the attention of the man she'd been married to for thirty-five years.

Trotsky's security detail also noticed the change, and since they weren't fools, they soon figured out what was affecting him so dramatically. As practical men, they confronted Trotsky and asked him to stop following Frida around like a puppy. They told him a scandal would discredit him and undermine his role on the world stage. They "suggested" he move. The old man chose a place on Viena Street, very close to La Casa Azul. It also had a large courtyard, where he could write and watch his wife get old, accepting not only his exile from Russia but also from Frida's heart. Diego was the only one who didn't take things well. He screamed that it was rude to leave like that, that it was disrespectful to him, his host.

"Shut up, Diego," Frida said in his ear before he could continue with his tirade.

Diego was surprised at her attitude. "Don't you understand, Frida?" he asked after they'd stepped into another room to talk.

Frida didn't want to make the problem worse. She lit a cigarette and hit him with the truth head-on.

"The one who doesn't understand is you. Let him go. He'll be better without me in his life. I've already done much more than I wanted to."

Diego suddenly understood everything that had been going on right under his nose. Frida had had her revenge, but what she didn't know yet was that it would not be sweet, that it would leave a disagreeable taste in her mouth, like a stale and sour orange.

The day Trotsky moved out of La Casa Azul, he wrote: "Natalia comes to the window and opens it to the courtyard so that my room gets some fresh air. I can see the shiny strip of lawn that grows along the wall, the blue skies above and the sun shining everywhere. Life is beautiful. I hope that future generations will liberate life from every ill, from oppression and violence, and that they'll enjoy it in its plenitude."

Those last words could be interpreted as an ode to his wife and to life, but only Frida understood that they were words of gratitude to her for having shared with him some of those months that Death had granted her in exchange for her offerings. Frida thought she'd saved Trotsky from the machine-gun attempt on his life, but months later an ice pick in the revolutionary's head finished what Death had only postponed.

She wondered if Leon had received only a few months of grace or if there was ever anything granted to him at all. The answer never came, because Death is always a mystery.

Frida had exacted her revenge on Diego. She turned the page, grabbed the reins of her destiny, and continued with her life as a free woman.

DINNER FOR TROTSKY AND BRETON

The Goateed Man liked to be surprised. There wasn't much to say because Diego would interrupt me or whoever was anywhere near Trotsky; that's why I just cooked. I could say much more to him about my vision for a better world through my flavors than with words. That's what we both wanted: a better world. Who doesn't want that?

SNAPPER WITH CILANTRO

HUACHINANGO AL CILANTRO

1 snapper, weighing about 4 1/2 lbs., cleaned and washed

8 cups finely chopped cilantro

5 pickled chiles, cut into thick slices

2 large onions, sliced

4 cups olive oil

Salt and pepper

✳Make three cuts across the snapper's back so that it will be well seasoned. In a large pot, prepare a bed using half the cilantro, half the chiles, and half the onion. Pour half the oil over it. Season with salt and pepper. Place the fish on this bed and then repeat, making another layer with the remaining cilantro, chiles, onion, and oil. Preheat the oven to 400°F and bake for 40 minutes, occasionally basting with the sauce so it won't dry out. Serve in the pot.

CHAPTER XVIII

As soon as the wrapping paper hit the floor, a scream rang out, echoing through every corner of the building on Fifth Avenue. In the hallways of the elegant Condé Nast publishing offices, the terrified scream kept ringing like the bells of the Apocalypse.

A few frightened secretaries dropped *Vogue* covers and drawings by Covarrubias for the *New Yorker* to the floor. Alarmed, they went looking for the source of the cry. A security guard, pistol in hand, had leapt up, fearing an assault. The workers whispered with doubt and anguish, afraid to open the door to the room from which the scream had come. Finally, an executive secretary got up her courage and opened the door to her boss's suite. And there was Clare Boothe Luce, editor of the very cosmopolitan *Vanity Fair*.

Her office was large enough to hold a circus. And on her ostentatious black desk surrounded by leather chairs there was a pile of wrapping paper and a partially opened package. Madame Clare had taken refuge in a corner, next to the huge windows that looked out on an autumnal Central Park. She appeared to be in pain, her hands to her mouth, trying to keep down another scream.

Her eyes were popping out of her head, and tears ran down her cheeks, smearing her expensive makeup. She was clearly hysterical, as if living a nightmare. This wasn't the same woman who could be such a despot about fashion, food, and cocktails. There wasn't a trace of the vanity that her staff was so used to—just terror. She raised her trembling hand and pointed to the package. The secretary and the guard took a step toward it. It had arrived that morning from Europe. They both gasped when they saw the inconceivably sick image. If it was a joke, it was really tasteless. Nobody in their right mind would do such a thing. Yet, the artist behind the spine-chilling image had just been on the cover of *Vogue*, and various articles inside had lauded her recent exhibition.

The painting detailed the suicide of Clare's best friend, Dorothy Hale, with excellent technique. Dorothy had hurled herself off a New York skyscraper. In the painting, the suicide had three stages: Dorothy's tiny figure leaping from a window, a closer look at the model as she falls, and then, finally, the inert and bloody body on a platform of sorts where she's just landed on her journey to the afterlife. Her eyes are open, staring ahead, as if crying for help. Beneath the image, a banner explained the tragic event in bloodred letters: "In New York City, on the 21st of October 1938, at six in the morning, Dorothy Hale committed suicide by throwing herself from a very high window of the Hampshire House. In her memory . . . this retablo was executed by Frida Kahlo." An angel flew in the sky on the upper part of the piece, among the clouds and skyscrapers. Apparently, Frida didn't think the painting itself was bloody enough and she'd added stains to the frame, as if Dorothy herself had splattered it on the way down.

"Destroy it!" Madame Clare ordered her secretary, but neither she nor the guard moved, both hypnotized by the disturbing painting.

Frida never knew about the scene her work caused in Madame Clare's office. She was far from it all, totally submerged in the temporary ether that makes fools of even the most clever women. That sleepy toxin had only one name: love. And it wasn't Diego who was causing her sighs but a slender man with dreamy eyes, fine features, and the manners of a delicate bird, like a swallow. Nickolas Muray was Hungarian descended, which was easily noted in his noble bearing and icy eyes. Although he came from a poor family, at twenty-one he was already one of the most famous photographers in the United States, sought after by magazines like *Harper's Bazaar* and *Vanity Fair*. He was the perfect prince: an airplane pilot, a fencing champion, a devoted father to his two daughters, a generous patron of the arts, and a lover of modern art.

In spite of all that, he was simple and tender in intimacy and reminded Frida of her father, Guillermo; it was probably for that reason that she fell for him completely.

She'd met him sometime before in Mexico because of his friend and party buddy the young Covarrubias; they both also worked for the same magazine. From the beginning, the photographer had been enchanted with Frida's scents, colors, textures, and flavors. Just setting foot in La Casa Azul in Coyoacán was a journey of the senses for him, further stimulated by the paintings, the cardboard Judas, the Talavera tableware, the hairless dogs frolicking around Frida's skirt, the parakeets chattering, and the featherless Mr. Cock-A-Doodle-Do fleeing from the guests. Add to all that her exquisite dishes and fragrant desserts and any palate would be absolutely on fire.

After Trotsky left her house, Frida went on with her life, bragging to friends and acquaintances that she'd finally divorced Diego, even though she fully understood that their relationship was like a drug addiction. She couldn't stop herself from saying all sorts of contradictory things. "I was sick of that giant belly and I'm finally happy living my own life!" she exclaimed to a table of artists. "That fat old man would do anything for me, but I can't imagine asking for anything," she'd say. But minutes later, nostalgia would hit her and she'd murmur, "He's so tender. I miss him so much."

Among the guests at that dinner during which Frida

had so many contradictory feelings was Julien Levy, who had been completely taken with Frida and her work and was hoping that she'd exhibit with him in New York.

"You shouldn't pass up the opportunity, sweetheart," a flirty Nickolas said. Frida responded with a sexy smile, the kind that lights up lovers who really know how to enjoy each other.

"Why are you interested in my work? It's nothing special," she told Levy. She shrugged her shoulders and drank a shot of tequila to drown the embarrassment, chaos, and precision of being right on the verge of success but perhaps about to dive into the abyss.

The divorce from Diego had given her the energy with which to try to remake her life with Nickolas as a lover. And, just recently, a famous actor known best for his gangster roles had paid a generous sum for several of her paintings. So even with her misfortunes, she was now a painter in her own right. If her life continued after Diego, it was because of her art. She wouldn't give her Godmother any reason to take away her promise to let her live.

"I'll help you with the exhibition," Nickolas promised.

And he did—not just as a lover, but also as a friend: he helped her with the packing and shipping of the pieces, as well as with the catalogue. When Frida left for New York with her lover, she said farewell only to Mr. Cock-A-Doodle-Do, who just stared at her with his big buggy eyes.

"I'm leaving you with a task, so don't fuck it up. You

have to welcome every day with a song. Every day from here on is very important to me," she said, and left for her show.

Nickolas was proud to be Frida's partner, and was deeply in love with her. But he never quite got that she was more fireworks than girlfriend. He didn't suspect that she was still seeing Diego and that it was Diego who insisted she visit the *Vanity Fair* offices to see about work.

"Clare's a very pleasant woman. Ask her to pose for you and you'll be able to sell her the painting," he assured Frida as he kissed her good-bye on the forehead.

Frida knew Diego was happy because of her exhibition and that he treasured the moment like a proud father sure of his offspring's success.

Once in New York, her stay with Nickolas was a hazy dream. Not only did she enjoy her lover's charms, but the air of freedom around her allowed her to seduce anyone she deemed worthy of taking to bed, from Levy the gallerist to an old man who bought some of her paintings.

Opening night was grand. Frida looked radiant. She was finally respected as an artist and it was happening in the very city where Diego had had his biggest failure. The critics treated her very well and everyone she knew came to see her at the gallery.

"Beautiful," whispered Georgia O'Keeffe as she stole a kiss from her in the bathroom.

"The show?" asked Frida coyly, knowing full well she was the queen of the night.

"The artist," she said, and they exchanged the knowing look of longtime lovers.

After they recalled their lustful nights together, they went back out to circulate among the guests. They saw Nickolas, who was chatting with Madame Clare Boothe Luce.

"Do you like him? Is he good to you?" asked Georgia.

"I don't deserve him. I treat him badly because I'm so used to the way Diego treated me."

"Be happy, Frida. You're the woman who changes, the one who walks with Death," Georgia said in farewell.

Frida winked at her and went to take her new lover's strong arm.

"Frida, Madame Clare loves your work. She'd like you to paint something for her," said a smiling Nickolas; it was with his smile that Nickolas conquered everyone.

"It'll be a pleasure to paint for you."

"I'd like to give the painting as a gift to Dorothy Hale's mother. Dorothy was my best friend," she said, moving her wineglass from one hand to the other. "She was beautiful. It would be a shame if her face were lost forever. You could immortalize her."

"Is that the girl who committed suicide? I could do it as an altarpiece," explained Frida, full of emotion. But she was talking in Spanish and never saw in Madame Clare's smiling face that she was not understanding a word.

It's certainly true that Madame Clare had no concept of those small laminated pictures, always painted very simply, in which the artist paints accidents from which the virgin has saved the victims. They're very popular in churches all over Mexico, where they're treated as offerings.

"Whatever you see fit. Your painting has the kind of female power that will do her justice."

And so the deal was made.

Dorothy Hale's name wasn't mentioned again until later, after she and Nickolas made love to celebrate her opening. Exhausted, they were resting in the nude in an unmade bed, embracing, gazing at the first signs of light at dawn, now turning red as it hit the buildings. Nickolas was on the verge of falling asleep, whispering sweet nothings innocently while she touched him with her breast. Frida pulled the sheet up to cover her deformed leg.

"Don't cover it up. Everything about you is beautiful, your defects and your greatness."

"Only a loony could say my leg is beautiful. It should be banned from all of my lovers' sights. That's why I wear long skirts."

"I like it. I'm a loony. In fact, I also like that ritual that you Mexicans have of giving food to the dead. It's kind of sick, but I like it."

Frida opened her eyes wide and shot up out of bed, looking out at the first rays of light, which seemed to embrace her like a giant. She realized that, due to the hoopla around the opening and her rupture with Diego, she'd forgotten the date: her show had opened the night before the Day of the Dead.

"Today is the Day of the Dead! I need to make an offering! What happened to my stupid head? How could I forget?" she exclaimed, panicked.

Nickolas stayed in bed, just watching her pace like a maniac. She was nude and jumping around the room, grabbing clothes and jade necklaces.

"Forget about that, Frida. Come to bed. We'll figure that out tomorrow."

"No, there won't *be* a tomorrow!" she screamed with all her might. "Can't you help me? It's a matter of life and death!"

But Nickolas thought maybe she was drunk and just turned over and covered himself with the sheet. "You drank too much. Come to sleep and we'll talk tomorrow."

There was no discussion, just screaming and punching and curses. Frida finished dressing and left, hurling obscenities at Nickolas, who never understood the hysterics. Frida was terrified of faltering on her promise. If her Godmother got angry, she could cancel their deal outright. Out on the streets, which were beginning to stir from their slumber into full-blown urban life, she felt aimless, lost in a huge metropolis, dressed as a Mexican folk figure and about to die. She thought of going to a temple to render tribute, or to a church, but nothing seemed up to the dignity or the majesty of Death. She cursed, thinking that if she had her Hierba Santa Book, she'd cook up a banquet; but the notebook was on her desk, back at La Casa Azul.

When her tears rolled down her cheeks and dropped into the steam from the Chinese laundries and the morning dew, she saw the Messenger in the middle of the street, between yellow taxis and fire engine lights. The white horse breathed a blue cloud to show her he was real. The Messenger pulled on the reins and lightly spurred the horse in Frida's direction. He adjusted his sombrero and crossed paths with a couple of rabbis, a baker folding his receipts, and a pair of workers in overalls arguing about the fight from the night before. None of them saw him, for the simple reason that he wasn't there for any of them. The white horse reached Frida, who lifted her anguished eyes.

"You came for me, right? She sent you, I know. I just want to explain that everything's a mistake. I've never not paid my respects but I should have made an offering. I'm very sorry." Her voice trembled.

The Messenger stared at her hungrily and offered her his hand.

"You want me to go with you?" Frida asked. Of course, there was no response. His hand remained outstretched toward her. It was a hand made rough from life behind a plow, life on a hacienda. Frida took it, bidding farewell to the world. She felt the dryness of his calluses, the cuts like leather, the roughness of the countryside. In one quick move, she was sitting on the horse. But before she had a chance to get comfortable, she felt a sharp wind on her face and closed her eyes.

When she opened them, she was surprised to find herself in a New York apartment. The Messenger had vanished. She felt dizzy, but the feeling passed quickly. She could hear her own breathing, so she assumed she was still living. She was taken aback by the sight of a woman combing her hair. She was a beautiful and distinguished woman, with a bearing that comes only from expensive caprices. She was dressed in an elegant black satin gown, and her nipples were erect under the fabric. She was singing "Dead Man Blues," the same song she'd heard Eva Frederick whistling. When she saw the woman's light eyes looking back from the mirror, Frida realized they were the eyes of the dead.

"I was a fool to think things would get better," said a voice at her side.

Frida turned and found the same refined woman: the same dress, the same hairdo, but now wearing a shiny brooch of yellow flowers. There was no doubt: it was Dorothy Hale.

"Things never get better. I knew it when I lost my son. You should have learned that long ago, my dear," said a slightly surprised Frida, returning the gaze of the reflected Dorothy.

"How can you stand it? Doesn't your soul ache?"

"Every day."

The Dorothy in the mirror arranged a series of farewell notes that she'd written beforehand. Her singsongy humming filled the empty apartment, where the loneliness was overwhelming.

"I was offered everything to seal the deal, but I couldn't accept it. The very idea that there would be more pain was so terrifying to me, I couldn't take her word for it," explained Dorothy as she tried to deal with her wet hair.

Blood began to spill from her neck, drenching her dress, which stuck to her skin. Frida noticed that her skull now looked like a split watermelon. She understood that Dorothy was talking about her Godmother and about a deal not too different from what she'd been offered years before: to continue living in exchange for a sacrifice per year. Anything from her love to her health.

"To extend your life in exchange for suffering? Life for pain? If that's what she offered, that's not too bad. In the end, we're all born to suffer," Frida whispered.

The Dorothy in the mirror put the yellow brooch that was now stained with red on her other self. Frida turned to the bloody Dorothy and offered her a girlish smile, complimenting her the way women do at the salon.

"It's a beautiful brooch."

"You like it? Thank you. It was given to me by a lover, Isamu Noguchi."

"Really? I can't believe it! He was my lover too!" said a surprised Frida.

They stood there looking at each other. There were two of them, but the reflection in the mirror remained singular.

"One of the best," said the bloody Dorothy in a mischievous tone.

Frida bit her lip. The Dorothy in the mirror left a red lipstick kiss on the farewell note for Noguchi.

"Who would have thought? Diego hated him. I told him Noguchi made me scream more than he did."

The bloody Dorothy made a little squirrel noise. They both liked it. Frida stopped talking, because the Dorothy in the mirror was walking very elegantly toward one of the apartment windows. When she opened it, a gust blew in, scattering all the papers.

"I had a party, I invited all my friends, I drank and had fun. Then they went to the theater to see a Wilde play. I told them I was going on a long journey," the bloody Dorothy explained to Frida while her double climbed onto the windowsill. "That's how I killed myself. I didn't have any money. I'd lost my beauty and my charms. What did I have left?"

The Dorothy in the mirror paused on the windowsill. The wind was whistling through the apartment. Her fingers let go of the window and she launched herself off the sixteenth floor. No one heard a scream.

"Should I have accepted the deal?" the ensanguined Dorothy asked in desperation. Her mouth had begun to fill with blood.

"I don't know. I ask myself all the time if it was the best decision. Life has an awfully high price," Frida said.

Dorothy couldn't do anything but offer her the smile Frida would later capture in her painting: her eyes aimless, lost not because of Death but because of life.

Frida closed her eyes to wait for her death; she'd stopped hearing her heart beat. When she opened them, she realized she was right back on the street where the Messenger had picked her up. Her heart resumed its normal beating. In the distance, like an echo, she could hear a rooster crowing. It was Mr. Cock-A-Doodle-Do announcing the new day. She remembered she'd asked Cristina to set up an altar for the Day of the Dead in La Casa Azul. The woman who had betrayed her had just saved her. Her lungs filled with fresh air.

She sighed and decided to go back to the apartment, where Nickolas was surely worried. He was too beautiful, too correct. You can't marry the person who steals your heart. That's the stuff of romance novels or tele-novelas; in life, you get who you get and that's that. That's how she knew she couldn't stay with Nickolas and that she'd always be bound to Diego, even if she continued to hate him because of his betrayal. It was all part of the deal her Godmother had made with her. Her future wasn't especially pretty: alone, without a partner. But her paintings would be there, and now she had an offer to show in Paris. Her brushes, her oils, and her fruit-bowl colors would be her only true loves.

She opened the door quietly so as not to wake Nickolas, her perfect love, who was sleeping like a child. She undressed, got in bed, and embraced him. Comforted on hearing his rhythmic breathing, she decided to enjoy her time with him as long as it lasted. In a little bit, she fell asleep.

Madame Clare was horrified by the painting. Her initial reaction was to destroy it but her friend Nickolas Muray convinced her otherwise. Nonetheless, she contracted another artist to get rid of the wording on the banner that said, "Commissioned by Clare Boothe Luce, for Dorothy's mother." Strangely, she also got rid of the angel in the sky.

Since she detested the piece, the famous editor gave it to her friend Frank Crowninshield, a fan of Frida's art. The painting wasn't seen for several decades. One day it mysteriously appeared at the front door of the Phoenix Art Museum, where it's on display.

RECIPE FOR NICK

Nick came to Mexico because Miguelito Covarrubias invited him to visit. He liked to eat well and always liked to have the right wine with each dish. One day I was brought a bag of chiles and a bottle of tequila, so I made him pork loin. He loved it, although he suffered because of the chiles.

TEQUILA PORK LOIN

LOMO AL TEQUILA

2 1/4 pounds pork loin

15 pitted olives

Cuaresmeño (jalapeño) chile strips

Sweet red pepper strips

4 garlic cloves, crushed

Salt and pepper

1 cup tequila reposado

1 tablespoon butter

1 tablespoon wheat flour

✳ Stuff the loin with the olives and the chile and red pepper strips. Rub it with the garlic, salt, and pepper. Place it in a pot with 1 cup of water. Cover and roast for 1 1/2 hours at 350°F. A bit before it's done, pour the tequila over it, then continue cooking. Mix the butter, flour, and juices from the pot to make a gravy to serve with the pork loin.

CHAPTER XIX

She first ran into him in an out-of-the-way café in Montparnasse. It was a little hovel that reeked of dust, old leather, and rancid wine, that particular fragrance that becomes infused in the texture and is so much a part of restaurants in the Old World, as if each new cup of coffee were another brick in the wall of a history going back as far as Roman times. Frida was sitting, in pain because of a kidney infection, and tired of her leg's handicap. The eccentric came in behind her. She felt how the air parted when he walked, distancing itself from him, leaving him to his madness and his genius. She felt the shiver rise up her injured spine. She turned slowly to meet the man's eyes, jumpy like a pair of nervous insects, and lacking all good sense. Only his mustache seemed madder than his crazy eyes: long and thin and extended, it flew through the air like a trailing plant. That mustache was so powerful that it seemed to lead Dalí, rather than the other way around. His voice wasn't strong; he was a fake about everything. His image was delightful but not so much his personality.

"Obsidian eyes call the shells from the sea, so they can dance together to the macabre symphony of Death," Dalí said with the pompous pose of Puss in Boots trying to talk up his owner to the king.

Frida felt a cool shiver just like when she met up with the Messenger, and like when Dorothy Hale committed suicide. The man's voice came from deep inside his mind, where all his thoughts cohabited with madness.

Frida had kissed a glass of cognac with the delicate sips of a jealous lover. The warmth of the liquor ran through her limbs while Dalí, wearing a cape like a marquis and carrying a cane like an Andalusian knight, settled in a chair as though he were a Catholic king sculpted out of stone for the cathedral at Santiago de Compostela.

"You know something about Death?" asked Frida.

Dalí got comfortable on his make-believe throne.

"She's the one who gives and bestows. The one who doesn't just grant but also takes away. The end of everything, though not the beginning. She exists because *we* exist. The day that everything stops, she'll do her thing, and since she's Death, she'll die," the painter said in recitation.

Frida agreed. No one could have described her Godmother any better.

"Mrs. Rivera is here to show her work. It's a shame that the dead man isn't here to see it," said André Breton, who hadn't acknowledged Dalí when he came in.

Breton stuck a pipe in his mouth, which made him look like a bored English professor, an image far from that of the leader of the surrealist movement, as he preferred to call himself.

"Of course, Dalí would have liked to see Mrs. Rivera's work. It would have been like seeing his own work. . . . What a pity he died," said the poet Paul Éluard.

Since Dalí had applauded Franco's triumph and allowed himself to be seduced by the religion of the dollar, his old surrealist friends referred to him in the past tense, as if he'd really died.

Mary Reynolds, Marcel Duchamp's partner (with whom Frida had stayed in Paris after the scattered and egocentric Breton had offered to arrange a show for her), came up and whispered in Frida's ear: "He's pure theater. Vaudeville personified. He's as innocent as a eunuch. Gala has already cut his balls off."

Frida giggled when she heard that. She laughed again when she turned and saw the ostentatious artist, still in his chair, contemplating the mortal world through his godlike eyes. The taunts had taken him back a bit; he was sweating. Without his wife nearby, he was like a cub who'd lost his mother.

Breton lifted his glass. Marcel Duchamp looked at him like a mischievous boy about to put a thumbtack on his chair. The poet Paul Éluard came up from his newspapers with headlines about upcoming wars, and Max Ernst pointed his nose at Frida. His foxy white hair appealed to Frida, who was enjoying his company and conversation. Besides Marcel Duchamp, Ernst was one of the few in the group whom Frida liked. The rest—and not just the artists but all of Paris—struck her as insufferable, as she wrote dear Dr. Eloesser in a postcard. Everything appeared decadent and the surrealists' views seemed useless and absurd.

"You can't imagine these people," she wrote to the doctor. "They make me sick. They're so intellectual and corrupt that I can't stand them. They're really too much for me. I'd rather be selling tortillas on the floor at the Toluca market than have to deal with these despicable Parisian artists who spend hours on end warming their asses at their 'cafés.'"

In fact, that's precisely what she was doing. Duchamp had insisted she come with him to a get-together in her honor. It was the night before her opening at the Galerie Pierre Colle. The idea for the show had been Breton's after his visit to Mexico. After he'd fallen in love with Frida's work, he'd insisted on exhibiting it in France. He'd signed her up but it had turned out to be a really bad idea: Breton left everything up in the air. He never picked up the paintings Frida had sent, or even bothered with the documentation for importing them. Worse yet, once in France, Frida had to lend him money because he didn't have a penny. She figured part of the surrealist dream must be to live on a dime and go out on the streets like a haughty and decrepit peacock. When she wrote Diego about the situation, he was furious with Breton's audacity. He decided to deal with it simply: the next time

Breton set foot in Mexico, he'd personally shoot a few bullets into him.

There were many reasons Frida had decided to do the show. Knowing she was a prisoner of her fate, she wanted to get away from her reality.

She was leaving Nickolas, the love of her life, in New York, and she didn't have the energy to go back to Mexico, where she knew the chains that bound her to Diego would tighten. She was in a no-man's-land, in an emotional desert. That's why she'd gone to the Old World. And now it was a decision she regretted every day: she missed Nickolas; she missed Diego, her family, and Mexico. Moreover, she fell gravely ill on arrival and spent her first week in Paris convalescing. It was not the best way to enjoy the City of Lights.

"Hey, look—it's the Lunatics Club. Hey, André, will there be a full moon tonight?" shouted a strapping man who burst into the café like a gunman from the Wild West.

He was wearing a tight suit jacket with no tie and a pair of too-short pants. He was thick as a tree and bitter like vinegar. His burly mustache wriggled like a hairy worm when he spoke. He was followed by a man who was as bald as a billiard ball; he wore smart little glasses on his sad face.

"Hemingway and Dos Passos," Mary Reynolds whispered to Frida, who immediately liked the rude gringo's forceful entry. It was as if a herd of longhorn cattle pursued by a posse of cowboys had barged into the café.

"I hear there's a lovely Mexican flower around these

parts," said Hemingway as he bowed and kissed Frida's hand.

She let herself go with the moment, especially when she saw that the rest of the surrealists perceived the American like a bottle of sour milk at a banquet of delights.

"That animal killer, Covarrubias, has talked to me about you," he said to Frida in English. "That guy deserves a good beating after that picture he did of me for *Vanity Fair.*" Then he signaled the waitress for something to drink.

Frida was intrigued by his comment. Apparently he was really angry: young Covarrubias had drawn him like Tarzan, putting tonic on his chest hair to make it grow. A funny but not very subtle sketch. Of course, Hemingway now hated every inch of him. But that was nothing new. He loved getting compliments, but any criticism was met with aggression.

Frida took a sip of her liquor, in spite of the French doctors' warnings about alcohol; she was pretty sick of French doctors. She wanted to finish her trip so she could be treated by more humane physicians.

"Borderless, and free of any particular ideas, we are gathered here today to celebrate this woman, who is freedom itself," said Breton, looking as bored as ever, as if life were so mundane that it was imperative to go crazy and turn surrealist in order to enjoy it. "She's a bomb, gift-wrapped."

The rest of the group lifted their drinks in a toast. But before they could go on, there was a disruption. Someone was clapping in the back of the café. It was as sardonic an applause as a clown's laughter, as sad as a suicide's lament. Everyone turned. There was another group of people, but as strange and different from them as could be: a bald man with almond-shaped eyes and a worn suit. Next to him was an Englishman, too pompous to be rich. And next to him a businessman with very well-combed hair, wearing a very nice suit and a silly tie. There was a tiny woman with them, too, who oozed sexuality.

"What a pity," Breton said with disgust.

The new group pulled up chairs and brought their drinks. The small bald guy with the smart eyes grinned at Frida and winked.

"They seem like stinky cheese but they're just kids playing at being intellectuals. If you spread them on toast, they don't taste that bad," he told Frida in an aside.

There was something in his manner that reminded her of Diego: too much confidence and egocentrism for one man. The woman with the pitch-black hair and comets for eyes extended her porcelain hand toward her, as smooth as imported silk.

"Nin . . . Anaïs," said the beautiful girl.

Frida gazed at her with all the pleasure and desire in the world. Anaïs touched Frida's jade necklace like a four-year-old playing with her mother.

"You're beautiful. Everything about you is beautiful."

"Thank you," Frida said in Spanish.

Anaïs turned and gave her a kiss on the cheek, then blushed and pulled away.

"I love your paintings. I recognized you from the photos in *Vogue*," Anaïs said, responding in Spanish.

They stared at each other. There wasn't much more to say; they understood each other like twin sisters. The woman with the big eyes apologized for the comments her bald companion had made about the surrealists.

"Please forgive Henry. He can be a little rude."

"He's a bastard," Frida said, still in Spanish. And since they understood each other, she added: "But they're the best in bed, aren't they?"

Those who understood burst out laughing, though they were few. Most of those present were much more interested in their own work than in trying to understand Spanish. But even Dalí twisted his mustache in a way that, in some parts of the world, might be considered a smile.

"Dear, we'd like you to begin your talk with something more interesting than a surrealist or socialist manifesto. But we're all interested in sex; we all believe any artistic expression without freedom and love is false," said Jacqueline, Breton's wife, a beautiful blond doll.

Breton had met Jacqueline in that very café. He was drawn to the "scandalously attractive" girl who wrote at the table; he imagined he would be the recipient of whatever she was writing. Of course, things didn't turn out that way. But in the end he married the beauty anyway.

"Is sex false?" asked Mary.

"Sex is. We don't need anything else," said the monumental blonde, who threw Frida a kiss in tribute to the affair they'd had in Mexico.

Frida always felt best surrounded by lovers. The more there were, the more allies she'd have.

"Maternity or sex?" asked Anaïs.

"Which came first, the chicken or the egg?" Jacqueline responded.

"Not everyone can experience the miracle of the chicken. Some of us must be satisfied with other things," said Frida. The party had become a feminine brain trust. "That's why sometimes we must break a few eggs to figure it out."

"Warm eggs for breakfast are delicious," said Anaïs playfully.

"Especially if they're from a neighboring chicken coop."

After that, the women were silent. The men's faces clearly showed a question. Not a one of them understood; they weren't even trying. It was only to satisfy their own curiosity that they wanted to know what the women were talking about.

"Let's play Truth or Dare," said Duchamp, suddenly come to life.

"Whoever doesn't tell the truth shall be punished," explained Breton. He bit his pipe and fired at Hemingway. "Ernest, do you have hair on your chest?"

Everyone laughed uproariously. The angry writer threw open his shirt, popping several buttons.

Frida was annoyed to see he didn't really get the game and, like most Americans, had taken it too seriously.

"You're all a bunch of chickens. All you do is chatter. You've never seen a dead body. You've never fired a pistol!" exclaimed the American writer, irritated. He was so angry that he spit as he talked. "If that German megalomaniac is winning, it's because you're letting him."

With the same dramatic force as when he came in, Hemingway left the café. Frida thought maybe he'd go back to his country in search of the dream the United States lost when the air conditioner was invented. Dos Passos got up calmly. He kissed Frida's cheek as if she were a religious statue and disappeared into the Parisian streets.

"Anaïs, are you cheating on Ian, your husband?" asked Jacqueline, getting back to the game.

Ian Hugo, wearing a bow tie, grimaced, falling apart a little bit. He was naïve, certainly, but he could sense bad news coming.

"Punishment," said the wide-eyed woman.

"Cover your eyes and guess who's kissing you," ordered Breton.

Anaïs covered her face with her hair, arranging it like a Hindu princess. It was a honeyed moment. Jacqueline motioned to Frida, who immediately kissed Anaïs on her cherry-red lips.

"Those lips are spicy, like mint and anise. Only a woman who knows how to cook can taste like that. She reminds me of Cuba, and of Spain, but hers is a wilder place," Anaïs said.

When she removed the hair from her face, she got another kiss, this time on the cheek and from Jacqueline.

The game was a surrealist specialty. They played because the world no longer had time to play. They were sure that the moment the suit and tie came into use, humanity had grown up, that it had lost its childhood when afternoon play ceased. Humanity grows old when there's no play.

"I would have liked to ask the dead man if he was a virgin when he got together with Gala," said Max Ernst with as much bile as he could conjure.

"My body is pure. And I am well beyond pleasure," muttered Dalí without even looking at them. His eyes were aimed beyond them, about two feet from the nearest god.

"I knew it," said Jacqueline.

"How old are you, Frida?" asked Duchamp.

Frida made a face. They'd hit her where it hurt. She'd always lied about her age, saying she was born in 1910, with the Mexican Revolution. She'd always shaved off those three years.

"Punishment," Frida said in defeat.

Breton arched his brow. Then, without expression, as if he were asking for salt at the table, he said, "Then fuck the chair."

Frida's single brow arched, too, as if it were about to leave her face. Breton's punishment was malicious. But she sat on the floor, extending her long skirt as if it was a colorful waterfall. Then she began to caress the chair in a subtle and sly way. Little by little she gathered force and brought herself up to the wood. Then she abruptly took on a sexual pose and screamed as if she'd come to an ecstatic orgasm. When she finished, she got up, brushed the dust off her clothes, and sat back down. There was applause.

"I won't be able to sleep tonight. I'll be thinking about this act of yours, Mrs. Rivera," said Henry Miller, his eyes lit up.

Frida knew he was complimenting her.

"Who said it was an act?" she responded casually.

"Is it possible to create something that isn't art?" Duchamp asked Breton.

"Anything made by a free man is a work of art," said Granell, who wanted in on the game.

He was a consummate Trotskyite, just like Breton, although his declarations were often cries in the dark. Stalin silenced them without moving a finger. And so there was a silence now in the surrealist confab, as if the least desired guest of all had suddenly come in: politics.

"Drink me, I'm a drug! Take me, I'm a hallucinogenic!" Dalí shouted dramatically. He waved his cape like a bullfighter and left.

The gathering was turning ugly. Frida wasn't surprised. She was used to fallings-out between Diego and other painters when both liquor and promises of revolution overflowed.

"We need a new game. This one isn't fun anymore," said Jacqueline, puffing on a cigarette.

Again there was silence. These periods when they just stared at each other were so long that they seemed like tedious operas. Frida was sure they did it on purpose, just to underscore their false dramatics.

"Exquisite Corpse," Breton proposed without putting down his pipe.

There was no immediate response, just the silence again to create tension. Then they took a sheet of paper and folded it several times. The group accepted the signal and began to chat amongst themselves. Max Ernst started: he drew a half face from one end of the page to the other. Then he folded it and passed it on. That way they all got to see only half of what the artist before them drew. At the end of the game, there would be a full figure, drawn in pieces by each one of them: an exquisite corpse. The name of the game was, of course, a game in itself: it had come up when they'd played it with words, in French. They'd ended with *"Le cadavre exquis boira le vin nouveau."* Frida and Diego had played it as their own personal pastime when they were living in the States. Frida loved playing the game on their bohemian escapades, because it touched on her purest childhood instincts. She always infused it with her own natural sexuality: she always drew giant phalluses on the figures or gave them some other fantastic sexual attribute.

"I'm a pornographer," she said amidst the laughter.

For Breton, the game was a way to reveal people's subconscious. He was convinced creativity should be intuitive, spontaneous, recreational, and, whenever possible, automatic. That's why he always supported art making while on large doses of liquor or drugs: the further from rationality, the better the results.

"Your turn," Breton said, passing Frida a sheet. She went to work immediately.

Now that solemnity had been banished, laughter came easily and with gratitude. The wine helped lubricate words and the soirée moved along. Frida turned the sheet over to the next artist in line. Everyone did his part. At the end, Breton slowly unfolded the drawing. For just about everyone there, the image was ridiculous, but not for Frida: it was a woman wearing a large hat with a veil. Someone had drawn great feline eyes on her, capable of devouring whatever was before her. She had on a blouse with a low neckline, just like Frida's, but this woman had a robust bosom. She was wearing a long skirt with a slit down the middle that revealed her sex covered with a mass of pubic hair. Then there were her feet. Frida looked at them calmly and paused. It was like receiving a postcard from wherever those who were no longer present now resided. At least Frida knew she was there, even if she was very far from her sanctuary with Diego.

The name of the gallery exhibition was *Mexique*, because Breton had added a bunch of cheap stuff he'd bought to the show. But none of it could overshadow Frida, who remained by far the principal attraction. The opening had been quite the event, with everyone who was anyone in France on the guest list. The newspapers lauded the exhibition: "Mrs. Rivera's art is an open door to infinity and the continuity of art." The Louvre Museum fell in love with Frida's fruity mix of colors and decided to buy one of her self-portraits.

But in spite of everything, Frida felt alienated, isolated from the group of artists who drowned in their own rhetoric. She felt out of place. During the opening party, dressed as usual like a glamorous Aztec princess, she stayed in a corner and watched people come and go. Holding on to her rebozo and her drink, she found her work's popularity overwhelming and exhausting. It may have been too much for a woman who painted only to ease her pain. These kinds of kudos and congratulations could feed Diego but not her. She would have traded in all her success to go back to her husband and have him be true to her.

"Your work is a dream," said a man who looked tough as an oak tree.

His premature baldness shone like a light, and his penetrating eyes were like two daggers for which his sagging eyebrows served as shields. It was the eyebrows that gave his expression warmth. His gestures were kind; they were triumphant.

"I don't paint dreams or nightmares, just my own reality," Frida said.

Pablo Picasso stared at her as if looking for the secret of the work in the woman. He realized she was a painting herself, painted very carefully, with each year of her life.

"I've always said that a painter's reality depends very much on how much past he carries with him. In you, I see a lot of past."

Frida smiled. Maybe she was trying to flirt with Picasso, or maybe she was just looking for acceptance in a hostile world. She got it.

"Painting is my life. Everything started as a way to allay fear and pain. Now they tell me I'm a surrealist painter."

"Well, you see, beautiful . . . I wanted to be a painter and I became Picasso."

Frida gave him an affectionate look. Her thin lips curved like a half-moon, redder even than her red skirt. Picasso was hypnotized.

"You're sad. Your eyes are even more transparent than your oils."

"When I go back to my country, I have to make some tough decisions. I don't know what's next, and I don't know what to do."

"If you know exactly what you're going to do, then why do it? If there was only one truth, then we couldn't paint a thousand canvases with the same theme," said the painter as he took her hand and escorted her among the people admiring her work. "My mother used to sing me an old Spanish song that says, 'I don't have a mother or father to lessen my pain / an orphan I am . . .' "

Picasso's singing was pleasant. Frida loved his serenade.

"If you teach that to me, I'll sing you Mexican songs. The kind in which pain bubbles up from the soul. And if we're still up at dawn, I'll prepare you a Mexican breakfast. I'll make enchiladas and yellow beans," Frida said, and Picasso agreed with a nod of the head.

The night passed chatting with the surrealists. For Frida, being accepted by Picasso was magnificent. He was known as a harsh critic; he had a reputation for being grumpy about others' work. Yet, he had nothing but compliments for Frida. From the moment they met in the gallery until Frida left for Mexico days later, he was with her, trying to make her feel better and regaling her with gifts. Of these, the one she loved most was a pair of earrings made from tortoiseshell and gold in the shape of hands.

When he gave them to her, Frida tried to tell him that Death surrounded her and that, for a long while now, she had been living on borrowed time. But Picasso didn't give her story much importance.

"Remember," he said, "that all you imagine is real."

A MEXICAN BREAKFAST

What I miss the most when I'm traveling is getting up in the morning to the smell of coffee with cinnamon and something good frying on the stove for breakfast. It's the start of a new day, and a reminder of how marvelous yesterday was.

HUEVOS RANCHEROS

2 cooked tomatoes

A pinch of oregano

1 or 2 chiles de árbol, roasted directly over
the flame

1/2 teaspoon finely minced garlic

Salt to taste

4 tortillas

1/2 cup oil

4 eggs

1 tablespoon sliced onion

✻ Pound the tomatoes with the oregano, chiles, garlic, salt, and a bit of water. Cook the tortillas for a few seconds in the oil so they'll get soft, making sure they don't get golden. Fry the eggs, two by two, in the oil, making sure not to break the yolk. Place the tortillas on the plates on which breakfast will be served. Then place the fried eggs on top. Pour the tomato sauce over the eggs. Lastly, add the sliced onions.

CHAPTER XX

Exactly as Frida had described the events to Trotsky the day they'd separated, on a May night in the 1940s a storm came over Coyoacán. It was not a climatic tempest but a political one. A group of Stalin supporters, including the painter David Alfaro Siqueiros, burst into Trotsky's room with machine guns and fired away. They never knew that the old Communist, at that very moment, had been dreaming of the image described by Frida and that he knew ahead of time he'd die from a gunshot. When he heard the tires coming to a stop in front of his house, the brakes, the men's steps, the doors opening, he knew those were signs and threw himself over Natalia, his wife, so they both fell behind the bed before the hail of bullets. Not a single one touched them. He'd survived the call, and Death had kept her word.

Diego was considered a suspect and had to flee. He was helped by two of his lovers, Charlie Chaplin's ex-wife, Paulette Goddard, and Irene Bohus. He went and stayed in San Francisco, painting a mural, without concerning himself with what was happening in Mexico.

After the attempt on his life, Trotsky thought Frida had been right about everything, that he'd been freed of his condemnation. He got careless and welcomed into his home a man who'd once visited Frida in her home in Coyoacán: Mercader.

The Spaniard asked his opinion about some writings. While Trotsky looked them over, in his peripheral vision he saw the figure of his murderer as he lifted the ice pick that he'd nail in Trotsky's skull. Behind Mercader, Trotsky caught a glimpse of a woman wearing a broad-rimmed hat, a lace dress, and a grin like a skeleton's: this was who owned the end, the taker of lives. He'd been deceived: she'd saved his life mere days ago. If he'd had time, he would have cursed her, but the ice pick made a hole in his head, which split like a melon. Trotsky died in the hospital.

The police knew that Mercader had visited Frida. In fact, he'd seen her in France when she had her show. As far as she was concerned, he was just some stranger who'd asked two or three questions and then vanished. Nonetheless, details pointed to the princess in the tehuana skirt. The uniformed officers entered La Casa Azul like a hurricane, dragging away a sick Frida and forcing Cristina to leave her children behind.

The women were locked up in a dark and humid cell that stank of urine. Frida and Cristi didn't respond to the questioning but instead begged that someone please go look in on the children. But the police didn't budge in spite of their tears and tightened the rope a little more to see if they could make the women break.

After a marathon interrogation with questions that had no relationship to the case, Frida was thrown back in her cell like a dog restricted to the backyard. When the waning moon lit the darkness and the night wind blew, Frida was finally able to get her crying under control. She stared at the floor, thinking that if she could just kill her rooster, at least she wouldn't give them the pleasure of locking her up for life.

The wind whistled through the bars, cooling the already exhausted painter's soul and spirit. With the moon shining in the cell, Frida finally fell asleep. She succumbed to fatigue and despair. Her mind wandered past the desolate walls and fled someplace nearby but no less dark. There were candles lit all over, placed every which way without rhyme or reason. Behind them the sky swirled a wild red amidst pink clouds.

"Welcome home, Frida," said the woman in the veil.

Frida joined her, dusting off her courage and her bones.

"My life stinks. Every time I try to fix something, another rock gets thrown my way. This is no way to live; it's barely a way to die," she complained.

"If I recall correctly, neither pleasure nor happiness was part of our deal," her Godmother pointed out.

"But you should have warned me about this, because a life without life is as useless as a womb that can't procreate—which, I should add, you also saddled me with," Frida said reproachfully.

The woman in the veil touched Frida's dirty face, upset about her suffering.

"You still have a lot more life to live, Frida. Look at this candle: it's your life. That flame will burn for a few more nights still," she said, showing her a candle with a particularly bright flame. Frida understood that it was, indeed, her life and that it wasn't going out anytime soon.

"What do I do now?"

"You've become alienated from your destiny, from the ties that keep you alive. This broken chain will only bring you more misfortune. Look straight ahead, and once you see your situation clearly, a brilliant world will await you," said the empress of the dead.

"What is my destiny?" Frida asked.

"You know where it is," her Godmother answered.

Frida awoke when she heard the screeching of the cell door being opened. They were letting her go after two days. The police had found little with which to charge her and keeping her imprisoned had made public opinion turn against the authorities. In the meantime, Diego had decided to come back to Mexico.

The assassin served his prison sentence, while in the USSR he was hailed as a national hero.

Diego had contracted bodyguards for himself while he was painting a mural in San Francisco. He feared being killed for having interceded on Trotsky's behalf. Perhaps that's why, once he saw which way the wind was blowing, he opted to support Stalin's style of communism. He was hoping that would assuage his enemies. But then he heard about Frida's delicate state of health: because of her stint in jail, she was very sick and on the verge of an operation, according to the recommendations of the Mexican doctors. Could he have been the reason for all that? Could this have been because he'd abandoned her? With help from the only man in which Frida confided, Dr. Eloesser, he determined what he thought was best for his wife. The doctor called her and told her to come to San Francisco. Frida accepted, figuring Diego was cooking up a new plan, especially because the doctor had written: "Diego loves you very much, and you love him. But it's true that he has two big loves apart from you: painting and women in general. He's never been monogamous, and he never will be. If you can accept things as they are, if you can live with him under those conditions and subvert your jealousy into work, painting, or whatever helps you live in peace and keeps you so busy you'll be exhausted every night, then marry him."

Diego went to meet her at the airport with an enormous bouquet of flowers, a sweet smile, and a strong desire to be married to her for a second time. Frida embraced her husband and the decision to be together. There wasn't much else to do.

She knew she was forever tied to her ogre-frog.

Dr. Leo admitted her to the hospital and, after about a month, Frida felt well enough to continue her journey, whatever it might be.

* * *

"Here?" a nervous Diego asked. He really wasn't sure about Frida's common sense; she was limping among the tombstones.

"I don't think there'll be too many offerings here. Let's say that it's a very private Mexican celebration," said Dr. Eloesser, who was carrying a basket of silverware and plates.

Diego, carrying another basket, grunted like an ox, while Frida checked the names on the dirty tombstones.

"I found it, it's right here," she said, pointing to the the old stone covered with moss.

Diego dropped his basket. The doctor placed his on top of a nearby tomb. The sun was starting to set. There were only a few visitors left in the cemetery, especially because it was the night before the Day of the Dead. Hectic American life had erased the memory of those who now rested in the mausoleums.

"Clean it before you place the candles on it, Diego," Frida instructed as she extended a tablecloth over the burial place.

The doctor handed her the dishes she'd cooked with the help of his nurse. Frida took each one and relished its aroma.

"Cochinita pibil, in honor of Mamá Matilde. She liked it with tortillas," she explained as she placed it in the middle, near the candles that Diego lit.

"But these ribs are mine," joked the doctor as he handed her another dish.

Frida set it to the side, as if it were a heart offered to a pre-Columbian god.

"I'm starving, Friducha. Can't I please eat something?" Diego grumbled.

"Stop complaining and pass me the rest," said Frida, pointing to the thermos containing the atole and the basket with the Aztec cakes that she'd made from the things Diego had bought in the Latino neighborhoods.

Frida had asked him to get pulque, but it had been impossible to find. In its stead, she'd brought a bottle of vodka, which she now poured into a glass and added to the altar. In silence she remembered Trotsky, his work left unfinished, and his political faith. She thought he'd died like a political messiah: purely because of his beliefs, which she thought was a terrible shame—such men were increasingly rare.

"It's the first time I've built an altar to the dead in my country. A long time ago, I went to Pátzcuaro to see the offerings for the Day of the Dead, but I never imagined I'd make one here, in my hometown," the doctor told Frida and Diego. The smoke from the incense rose and blended with the smoke from their cigars.

"If your country took life more seriously and Death less seriously, it'd be a lot less bellicose," said a very pleased Frida.

Her life seemed to be remaking itself. Diego nodded, accepting her declaration. To make sure the doctor didn't say anything back, he leaned down and kissed Frida tenderly. She savored it as if it were candy.

"I have something for you," he said sweetly.

He put his hand in his pocket and it emerged with a

little red wooden car. The red was now scratched, worn, and opaque. There was no question it was the very same car that had fallen into the water in Xochimilco the day that Frida discovered the affair between Diego and her sister. The same one she'd bought so many years ago in Tepoztlán. The one that encapsulated all her love for her husband.

She was so surprised. It couldn't really be true, but she was already used to living in a surrealist world.

"The little car? How did you manage? It was lost in the water," she babbled.

"You left that day. In all the comings and goings, your nephew thought you were angry because he'd dropped it into the water. He made sure to get it back and give it to me. Of course, he didn't suspect you were angry about something else," said Diego.

"And you've had it all this time?"

"I couldn't throw it away. It was a part of you. I've treasured it all this time. I think if we're going to get married again, it'd be better if you kept it," he said, and placed it in Frida's hands. He folded her fingers over it and then kissed her again.

The doctor looked on, happy to have encouraged the reunion. "We need to go," he said. "The dead are scary here. When they get up to eat your food, I don't want to be around."

"Dear doctor, be assured that they'll come, without a doubt!" said Frida, who was hanging on Diego's arm.

They went back the same way they'd come, leaving

the candles lit to show the way to the food. The tombstone still wore the fading letters that said "Eva Marie Frederick."

In December, Frida and Diego married for a second time.

It was a brief and austere ceremony; in fact, Diego went back to work on a mural that same day. Then they spent two weeks traveling in California. By the time she returned to Mexico, Frida didn't feel any of the soreness or grind of her illness. She prepared a room for Diego in La Casa Azul. She bought a big bed to accommodate his giant body; she put fine lace sheets on it and a pair of pillows adorned with their names.

A few days later, Diego showed up to take his place, leaving the houses at San Ángel to be used as studios, where he went to work every day. Their day-to-day life became the sure routine that gives comfort to couples, with long breakfasts and dinners with friends and family. Life was starting again. Death could wait.

MY SECOND MARRIAGE

I married Diego a second time. But it wasn't the same the second time around. It wasn't better, it wasn't worse. Diego belongs to every-

one; he'll never be just mine. We simply signed
a paper the way people put a letter in the mail:
full of hope and good wishes. But you know all
along the letter will never reach the recipient.
Diego is mine every now and then. If I can live
with that, I'll be able to live the rest of my life,
even if it's the worst time of my life. If I can
do it, then I'll prepare a dish like the ones I
used to make for him when he was working on his
murals: a manchamanteles. We'll sit down to eat,
smiling, as if nothing bad had ever happened
between us.

MANCHAMANTELES
("TABLECLOTH STAINER")

A little more than 8 ounces pork loin
Salt to taste
Aromatic herbs
1 1/2 chickens, cut into serving pieces
3 ancho chiles, deveined and softened in
    very hot water
3 mulato chiles, deveined and softened in
    very hot water

1 big onion
2 tomatoes, roasted and peeled
Lard
3 peaches, peeled and cut into pieces
1 pear, peeled and cut into pieces
2 apples, peeled and cut into pieces
1 plantain, peeled and cut into pieces
1 tablespoon sugar

✽ Cook the pork loin in water, salt, and aromatic herbs. When the pork is half cooked, add the chicken. When everything is thoroughly cooked, strain the broth and set aside. Then cut the pork into pieces. Grind the chiles with the onions and tomatoes, strain, and fry in the lard. Add the broth from the meats and let it boil. Add the chicken, pork, peaches, pear, apples, and plantain. Add salt and the sugar. Let it boil for a few minutes before serving.

CHAPTER XXI

"The only thing I've learned in life is that you don't marry the love of your life or the person with whom you had the best sex. But even if it happened that a person found both those qualities in a partner—love and sex—I don't know that they'd be happy anyway," Frida told her students.

She figured if she was going to teach, it should be something that mattered, something that would actually be useful in their lives. She'd get to the brushstrokes later.

"Let me think about that for a while, cuz sometimes those kinds of truths need time to sink in," said one of the "Fridos," who was sitting between canvases and buckets of paint while painting the wall.

"Don't worry about it too much. Your best sex partner is a long way from being your spouse. Just keep an open mind," said Frida as she blew out the smoke from her cigar.

She was sitting in her chair, enjoying watching her students work. They weren't in a classroom but at the famous pulquería, La Rosita, just a few blocks from La Casa Azul. The pulquerías were where drunks and unsavory characters hung out. They generally met there in late afternoons, when construction workers brought their puny salaries, to pay for their much dreamed-of end-of-day pulque. For ages, those places were usually decorated with sly images of vice that reflected their clientele. It was a way of being honest, of honoring the people. But given the modernity to which Mexico now aspired—wanting to blot out the peasant and spotlight the suit and tie—the government had ordered that all those images be painted over. When Frida found out the students were interested in continuing mural painting after taking classes with Diego, she got the owner of La Rosita to agree to let the students paint the place for free. Frida and Diego would donate the brushes, paint, and whatever other materials they needed. It was a party, an artistic adventure, a little bit of surrealist revelry stirred up by Frida. If there was a way to put her idea of art for the people into practice, there was no better place to start than the pulquería.

The students were very young and almost all came from humble homes. They'd enrolled in La Esmeralda, a painting and sculpture school named after the street on which it was located. The faculty included great artists who wanted to contribute to the crazy idea of creating an ideal place to help prepare creative young people. It was such a unique project that there were more professors than students, and these were mostly the children of workers or artisans who dreamt of a better life. The professors encouraged them to get out on the streets and give expression to what they saw. Of course, there was a lot of politics, a lot of speeches, and a lot of workers'-movement organizing. It was a dream come true for people like Diego, María Izquierdo, Agustín Lazo, and Francisco Zúñiga, the great artists of the day. When Frida was brought on staff, it caused a sensation, in part because of her dress as a tehuana empress, with her colorful shawls and long skirts. These contrasted with the denim overalls the rest of the teachers wore as they went up and down the hallways on Esmeralda Street. The other teachers were awed, too, by the intricate braids and buns tied with dark ribbons that Frida wore in her hair.

"What do you do in your leisure time, Frida?" asked one of the students as he splattered the wall with ochre shades so it looked as if the paint can had overturned.

Frida rolled the question over as if it were a new taste in her mouth. To season it, she sucked on her cigar a few times.

"¡Hijole! People are going to say I'm rich, because I spend all my time locked up in a mansion trying to forget my many illnesses, which never stop bothering me and are making me broke. My leisure time, my leisure time! Let's see. . . . Well, the house doesn't take care of itself, and I have to take care of the cooking and keeping it in order, because Diego likes everything tidy and his food well served. You can see that if it were up to him, he'd be fed hand to mouth. Anyway, I only see you, and my crazy friends. Some are well-off, others are proletarian. But it's always the same: tequila and food. I find the radio odious; the newspapers are worse. Every now and then a detective novel falls in my hands. I like Carlos Pellicer's poems more all the time, as well as the work of real poets, like Walt Whitman."

The relationship with her students was odd. She felt herself decontextualized as a teacher and even criticized her own work. But she was different and had the gift of charisma. It didn't matter what she said: everyone listened. Her monologues were spiced with humor and a passion for life. She talked in common Spanish, peppered with popular sayings, full of irony and originality. Being with Diego again gave her a comfort and security that let her leave some of her melancholia behind. It was as if she'd been born again and, instead of trying to swallow the world whole, she'd accepted her imperfect reality and enjoyed it one bite at a time.

"How was it in Gringoland?" asked one of her students.

"Well, people are really stupid, but unlike in Mexico you can say things right to their faces, without any backstabbing. Here, we're so two-faced and everybody's screwing everybody over. There they're just hypocrites. Very decent, very proper. . . . Everybody's a goddamn thief. But they get over everything by having cocktails together, whether the issue is the sale of a painting or a declaration of war."

"And that's why you live here. . . ."

"No, I live here because Diego lives here," she said

with a smile. "Of course, being able to eat a couple of those delicious quesadillas they sell next to the church helps too."

Frida's position was that she wasn't so much a teacher to her students as a big sister. She poured all the maternal love that she'd been unable to give her own child on those kids from humble homes. From the moment she stepped into class, dressed as the very image of a colorful garden, she warned that she'd never be a teacher because she was still learning about painting. She told them painting was the biggest thing in her life, but that it was hard for her to do. They needed to learn technique and self-discipline. She added that she was sure there wasn't a teacher alive who could really teach painting, that it was something that came from the heart. And with that, she pushed them out of the nest, like a mother bird nudges her chicks so they'll fly. She gave them brushes and showed them that inspiration waited for them out in the world.

"Hey, you, this face came out a little ugly," she said, pointing out the part that was badly painted. Then, without another word, she let her apprentice fix it.

She'd never pick up a brush to correct anything. She thought that would show a lack of respect toward her Fridos. Everyone had to find their own style through their mistakes. Maybe art would have been more fun if there had been more Fridas as teachers.

"Lookee there! Frida herself with her kids!" shouted a man in a suit and silly tie with big blue polka dots.

He had intelligent eyes and a natural smile. And he

walked with a gleeful swagger. It was Frida's old friend, the young Covarrubias.

"Hey, everyone, the sky is falling! The best caricaturist, writer, ethnologist, and anthropologist in Mexico has decided to come down to earth and hang out with the proletariat and, worse yet, to have a good drink in my honor!" Frida said, grinning at him.

She didn't get up to greet him. On the contrary, it was Miguelito who came down to hug her tenderly. He pulled a chair over and asked the owner—who kept an eye on things by hanging out, cleaning tables—for a strong pulque.

"Diego is in San Ángel. You might find him fucking a journalist or telling some politician a tall tale."

"This time I came to see you," he said, giving her a little punch on the shoulder.

The truth was that age had begun to take its toll on Frida's body. There wasn't a week she wasn't in pain. Perhaps her heart had been renewed by the new nuptials, but the rest of her body was falling apart.

"Tell me the truth, are you here just out of curiosity? I know everybody talks about my painting a pulquería. They all want to send me to the nuthouse."

"I'm here in part out of curiosity, and I can see everything I heard was true," her friend said. He handed her a small box, which she opened as if it were a birthday present.

Frida was constantly surrounded by people; she needed to be around people all the time. That's why she was always hosting dinners and meetings to kill her loneliness. Covarrubias was a frequent guest, and—thanks to his studies, intelligence, and humor—it was a pleasure to hear him talk. She plucked a small piece made of black wood from the box. It was the figure of a woman with very large breasts. The texture was smooth to the touch, like silk.

"It's beautiful!"

"It's from my trip to Bali. The other night when you were talking about Death you reminded me of Hine. I thought you might like it."

The pact she had with her Godmother had given her the courage to tell her stories. She liked to joke about Death. She dared it, taunted it, knowing that somewhere, Death was listening.

The students were then surprised by the sudden appearance of a woman with a beautiful bearing and the grace of a swan. Every step looked like a complex dance. She was carrying a pile of quesadillas in paper wrappers. She trailed a fragrance of grapes amidst the food and sauces. There was nothing more incongruent than watching that elegant woman passing out those greasy quesadillas to Frida's students. Rosita was already a dance celebrity when she married Covarrubias, and it was, curiously enough, because of her that he began to get to know the millionaires he ended up drawing. But Miguel was very much a man of the people, and he loved women and children, the islands of the Pacific, jazz in the afternoon in Harlem, and the indigenous places in his native Mexico. So she immersed herself in his partying and bohemian ways. She was a princess among plebeians and she loved it. Rosita gave Frida a loud kiss and, smiling broadly, placed the quesadillas beside her.

"I knew you were going to give us something to think about, but without something in my belly you'd probably have to kick me out," said Rosita, who also enjoyed Mexican food. "So I brought food for your students, because man cannot live on painting alone."

"You guys are outdoing yourselves, but you read my mind. If we're talking about quesadillas, only in Coyoacán do people really know how to make them," Frida said as she pulled a succulent sample from its wrapper. She opened it carefully and poured the sauce over it. "You should be working and not loitering around here with me. . . . Miguel was telling me about this little gift."

"It's from Maori mythology. She's called Hine-nui-te-pō, great woman of the night," said Covarrubias. "She's the goddess of death. She's married to the god Tāne. But she fled to Earth when she discovered Tāne was also her father."

"What a bastard! But that can happen even in the best of families," joked Frida.

Rosita laughed, showing her white teeth. Covarrubias and his wife knew how to laugh, how to eat, how to dance, and how to enjoy life. *Anybody who laughs is always good company*, thought Frida.

"They say this god needed a wife, and so he began a search. He took some red dirt and shaped a figure and married her. It seems they were happy for a while, but one day, while Tāne was out, she began to ask herself who her father was. When she realized her husband was also her father, she was ashamed and ran away. When Tāne came back, they told him she'd gone. He tried to find her but Hine stopped him: 'Go back, Tāne. I'll find our children. Let me stay on Earth.' Tāne went back to the heavenly plane while Hine remains on Earth to bring Death to everyone. A mortal named Māui tried to make humanity immortal by dragging himself across Hine's body as she slept, but she was awakened by a bird tickling her, and she destroyed Māui with her vagina. Māui was the first mortal man to die."

"She killed him with her vagina because he made her laugh? That woman had a terrible sense of humor!"

"Sweetheart, we can be bitches too. All it takes is for someone to touch the wrong feather to our bodies," said Rosita.

Miguel Covarrubias got up and admired the mural. It was delightful. It was in Rivera's style but with the fresh primitivism that was Frida's speciality. It was really the offspring of two very different styles brought together by the students' youthful spirit.

"I hear the president's wife commissioned a painting from you," said Covarrubias without turning his head.

"Tell me about it; she rejected me. She wanted a big basket with Mexican fruits, but she returned it the next day. It's possible they were too sexual for the refined tastes of such mighty politicians," grumbled Frida.

She did commissions now, some portraits and a few more personal works. The still life she was referring to was an explosion of color and phalluses, too lustful for the modesty of the ruling party.

"You really have to have a dirty mind to see fruit like that," said Rosita with her American accent.

"More like you have to be thinking about sex all day to see those things in the piece. And if that's what the first lady sees, she must be a very excitable woman," Frida said, kidding.

When it got quiet, Frida lowered her eyes and spoke low so only her friends could hear. "Did you see Nick when you were in New York?"

Covarrubias finally turned around but Frida wouldn't look at him. It was he who had introduced her to Nick. It wasn't as if Frida had broken off completely with her former lover; they still maintained a sporadic epistolary relationship. In fact, Frida had recently asked him for money for an operation.

"He's well. He asked about you too," said Covarrubias in a serious tone. "His daughters are very tall. They'll be great athletes."

"Sometimes I wonder how things would have gone if I'd stayed with him. He'd already made plans to live with me. He's a good man," she said in a whisper. And as if she'd gotten a jolt of electricity, her face and body became animated, ready to keep partying. "Are you coming to the opening of the mural?"

"If you invite us, yes."

"You and half of Mexico. We've had some really great posters made," said Frida, and handed them a sheet of paper.

They read it together. It was a flyer for a party, to celebrate Frida's triumph as a teacher, to declare that life should be faced head-on, no matter how often it tries to drag you down.

"This is for the people! Including the gossip of the day! Dear radio listener, Saturday, June 19, 1943, at 11 a.m., there will be a grand opening to celebrate the Painting of La Rosita Pulquería, on the corner of Aguao and Londres streets, in Coyoacán," Miguel called out like the street vendors. He was being playful and several students laughed along. "The paintings are the work of Fanny Rabinovich, Lidia Huerta, María de los Ángeles Ramos, Tomás Cabrera, Arturo Estrada, Ramón Victoria, Erasmo Landechy, and Guillermo Monroy, under the direction of Frida Kahlo, professor at the School of Painting and Sculpture under the sponsorship of the secretary of public education. Also sponsoring the event are Antonio Ruiz and Madame Concha Michel, who offer their distinguished clientele a fine and tasty meal, as would be expected from a grill imported directly from Texcoco, and the finest pulque, our national nectar, as bottled by the very best of our domestic producers. Add to all this mariachis with the best singers from the Bajío, rockets, firecrackers, fireworks, invisible balloons, and parachutes made from the leaves of the maguey! Everyone who aspires to be a bullfighter should come to the ring on Saturday afternoon, where there will be a small bull for the enjoyment of the amateurs!"

And exactly as advertised on the flyer, all of Mexico seemed to come to the celebration. It wasn't just Frida who dressed up as a tehuana this time. Her students and friends did the same, and together they looked like a colorful bouquet of flowers floating among the guests. The streets near the pulquería were decorated with bright paper figures, which flapped in the wind and created a buzz in the air. Confetti flew and photographers from movie newsreels and newspapers captured the folkloric images of the event. Concha Michel sang with the mariachis, then Frida, with her throat lubricated by the tequila, put on quite the show.

Puffed up with pride, Diego tried to get some camera time, too, telling unlikely stories and making biting commentary. But his moment in the spotlight ended when the clog dances began, followed by jaranas yucatecas and danzones. The whole place turned into a great dance floor. Frida forgot about her back pain and managed to have a marvelous time dancing to the mariachis. Later, there were self-important speeches by intellectuals who praised the Mexican Revolution.

Frida approached Diego while the poet Salvador Novo was singing, took his hand, and cuddled up to his great chest. Diego felt his wife's warmth. Without taking his attention from the poet, he leaned down and kissed her on the forehead.

"Hey, girl of mine . . ."

"Hey, guy of mine . . ." responded Frida, giving him a little kiss back.

The wild celebration lasted well into the night. There was laughter and cheer. A review in a national newspaper said, "There's a tendency to resuscitate what's authentically Mexican, and everyone does it in their own style."

* * *

Days before the end of the melancholy month of October, Frida got up with Mr. Cock-A-Doodle-Do's song, true to the task of announcing to the world that the tehuana princess was alive one more day. It was a beautiful morning, with the richness of life, the tedium of the kitchen, and the pleasure of dessert. The old wooden bed creaked. It was wide, like what a princess from a fairy tale might sleep in. The baroque caramel-colored posts framed its owner's nighttime slumber. Frida's naked foot touched the cold tile. Then the other foot, the bad one, the one without toes, tried to find some warmth. When she felt the floor, she tossed the sheet as if it were the mast from a galleon. In pain like every morning, she walked with a cane. She sounded a little bell to let the inhabitants of La Casa Azul know that the empress was up. The hairless dogs, the macaws, and the monkeys in the garden jumped with excitement. A servant came in with an armload of bright clothes to put away in her wardrobe. She helped Frida comb her hair and, especially, to dress it up, as was the daily ritual. It was soon a weave of patriotic ribbons and gay flowers. She chose the perfect combination for her hair to look like a burst of colors from a painting.

She went strolling through her house like a noble, singing "La Paloma" to the rhythm of her skirt dragging on the floor, until she met up with Eulalia, who waited for her smilingly. Together they'd sing the song's chorus while they placed a large basket of delicious pastries on the table for breakfast; a rude bee followed them, wanting to get at the pastries. There were yellow and pink ones, sexy croissants, phallic cones, and gossipy elephant ears. Diego, who joined them in song (off-key) with a voice like a trumpet, liked pastries with nuts. He shook the newspaper with glee and read it with accompanying pride and sarcasm. Before giving his wife a spectacular kiss, he moaned about the party in power, because the gringos had stuck their noses in Korea, and because of all the bad that had happened in the world in the previous twenty-four hours.

Frida whistled between sips of coffee with cinnamon. Every now and then she'd nod at her husband's exclamations. Then the real breakfast would appear: fried eggs bathed in salsa, with beans and tortillas. As soon as they arrived, they disappeared into Diego's mouth. He ate with a soundtrack of opinions, tortillas in hand. He didn't like silverware: he thought of it as bourgeois. He only used it when they shared a meal with politicians or famous people. As long as he could, he would be a man of the people, or at least he tried to pretend he was.

Breakfast was over. Diego wiped his mouth on his shirtsleeve. He chased the monkeys around while Frida laughed so hard, she cried. One of the monkeys had taken Diego's hat, and without it he couldn't go to work at the studio. This was all part of the morning ritual. The monkey, jealous of Diego and madly in love with Frida, had decided the hat was smelly and needed to be thrown out. Diego shook the dirt off of it and wiped it down with spit. He cursed for four steps, then disappeared down the hallway, followed by the young man who served as his driver. They drove down to the houses in San Ángel, where he'd once again attempt to defeat the monster of politics through his paintings—a struggle with no known end.

"I'll see you tonight, little one," he said, blowing Frida a kiss. Frida kept it in her heart, to comfort her when the time came that she hated him and wanted to leave him, which happened about once a month, usually as new lovers cycled in as easily as they cycled out.

Frida went out to the courtyard munching on a pastry, thinking that maybe this year would be sweet too. So far, there hadn't been much vinegar in her days. Life was good and she knew she should be grateful. She strolled through the lemon and orange trees. The branches reached out to her, swinging gently in the breeze, then opened a path for the painter until she reached the far stretch of the garden, where a huge table held her offering for the Day of the Dead. The marigolds guarded the pastries, sugar skulls, photographs, and dishes set out for the arrival of the deceased. There was a great cardboard skeleton in the center of it all, dressed like a very pompous woman. To either side, there were images of her mother and father. Farther back, the wooden sculpture Covarrubias had given her coexisted with two sugar skulls that bore the names "Frida" and "Diego," respectively, on their foreheads.

It was the day before the Day of the Dead, and it had been thirty-four years since her near-fatal accident with the train. She looked to the sky and took a deep breath. As the air entered her lungs, she savored the fact that she was alive. She turned a little in order to make a new offering in tribute to the woman who takes lives: the smoke from a recently lit cigarette.

QUESADILLAS FROM COYOACÁN

2 cups corn masa

1/2 cup wheat flour

3 tablespoons lard

1 1/2 teaspoons baking powder

8 ounces Oaxaca string cheese

Shortening

1 cup crema

✳ Mix the masa, flour, lard, and baking powder until you get a thick paste. Use your hands to shape small tortillas. Place some cheese in the center of each. Fold them and fry in the shortening until they're golden. Serve with crema. They may also be filled with pumpkin flowers, huitlacoche, vegetable slices, brains...

DRUNKEN SALSA

SALSA BORRACHA

8 ounces pasilla chiles
2 garlic cloves
Oil
2 cups pulque
Salt
2 onions
3 1/2 ounces añejo cheese
6 green chiles in vinegar

✳ Roast the pasilla chiles, devein them, then let them soak for 30 minutes. Grind them with the garlic. Add oil and pulque until it thickens. Season with salt. Finely slice the onions and, separately, grate the cheese. To serve, add the chiles in vinegar, the onions, and the cheese. This sauce must be eaten quickly because otherwise it ferments.

CHAPTER XXII

Her tears ran down her cheeks like a river in the desert. Not only did they drop down her contrite face, but they marked her cheeks like a scar. Frida's face was framed by the dark and somber lace that gathered around her like a rising tide that could swallow her whole.

There was pain in the gaze, but also pride and enough energy to take on anyone who might dare to challenge the painting. The tehuana lace was a cry for help, the dress was what a hungry bride might wear to catch a man. For tehuanas, a bride's dress is a morning star. They wear white, adorned with gold earrings and a gold necklace, and a skirt with a few palm leaves that play with flowers made from the same fabric. That face framed by such fine lace was the pride of Tehuantepec, in Oaxaca, known for huipils that show off a naked waist, short sleeves, and gauze skirts tied to the waist with a silk band. Frida turned these elements into a new body. It wasn't just her body, actually, but her skin that gave them a new identity.

"It hurts, doesn't it?" Frida said to her reflection in the painting. The woman on the canvas didn't respond because she was frozen in place, crying as Frida painted her. The tears were on the painting, not on the painter's face, which was dry. She was so sick of so much travel on Deceit Street.

She looked over her *Self Portrait as a Tehuana* from her wheelchair. She realized it was very different from the one she'd painted just before: there were traces of the past, of common places, in the twists and turns of her brushstrokes. The theme was always her, and sometimes she copied her prior work.

In her previous *Self Portrait as a Tehuana*, she'd painted herself as a queen, with Diego on her forehead and a network of tangled lines extending throughout the canvas. She didn't feel the same now, though. The new one was gray, with shadows as heavy as steel. The complicated lace didn't lighten up her face. There were no lies in this one: Frida suffered with her whole being.

She finished the piece with a final touch of white. She put down her brushes and opened her journal, which had now become her best friend, her confidante. There was plenty of truth and madness in it. She began to write:

Death backs off
Lines, forms, nests
Hands create

Eyes wide open
Diego feelings
Whole tears
All very clear
Cosmic truths
Tree of hope
Stay strong

It was the best way to deal with her situation. The sunset of her life was shining rays of light between the mountains before totally vanishing. The candle marking her time on Earth was flickering. The wick was short and the flame tenuous.

Shut up in the hospital, the post-op pain had taken over every cell in her body, like an uncontrollable plague. Her spinal cord was like a vanquished city's main artery, completely truncated. It wasn't a matter of cries and screams: it was a total breakdown, complete with bouts of rage and lunacy. Her hospital room reeked of burnt food, as if a fire had been allowed to burn until everything turned to coal. The doctors and nurses began to avoid the hall by her room because the smell was so strong, it stuck to robes and uniforms. Technicians came and checked to see if there was a problem with the air vents that connected the room and the hospital kitchen, but there was no indication of how the smell could travel like that. When visitors came to see Frida, they turned their heads as if they'd been hit on the nose. But Frida seemed wholly unaware of the situation. Between her agony and the drugs she was taking, her senses were very far away.

"They need to give her something. The poor woman is unconscious because of that intense smell," Cristi pleaded. She and her sister Matilde were clinging to Frida, trying to take care of her the way their mother would have. Mati, at her side, couldn't stop crying. The doctor was equally inconsolable. It was one of those days when hope refused to make an appearance. Diego was slumped in a chair, his legs extended so that his mining boots, firmly planted on the floor, blocked the way to anyone coming down the hall. His hands were deep in his pockets, playing with the little wooden car he carried with him whenever he felt empty. His head was down, in shadows, and not just from the lack of light but from his very existence.

"We could give her some morphine, a strong dose," said one of the doctors.

"Do it."

"But I'm not entirely sure about that. She's already showing signs of addiction. If I give it to her, she may never be able to stop using it again in her life."

Mati and Cristi hugged each other. In a family like theirs—torn apart by the injustices of Mexico's social movements, the lack of love between their parents, and their pretenses out in the world—the one who had kept them together was Frida. The one who, as a child, was a rebel, a tomboy, the one who dressed like a man; she was the anchor for these women. Frustration reigned like an angry cloud.

"Give it to her!" Diego roared, not once glancing at the doctor. "Look at how her eyes are begging for a bit of peace. It won't be her first or her last addiction."

The doctor gave a nurse directions. A huge dose of morphine snaked through Frida's system, lighting fireworks along the way. The morphine screwed with the Lipidol she'd already gotten to relieve her back pain. Together they marched toward her brain. Little by little, Frida was able to forget her agony. And as the pain left her body, there was an apparition in her room.

Like a disheveled and surrealist mise-en-scène, the room was transformed as if by thick brushstrokes: half of it dotted with clouds framing a menstruating red sun, the other half dark. A night of gangrenous swirls trying to eat a fetid cheese moon. And all around: forest, plants whose roots lay naked aboveground. They popped out of the walls all around the room.

"I'm a poor little deer who lives on the range . . . / Since I'm not bad, I don't go down to get water during the day / But then at night, little by little, dear / I go to your arms," sang the sly voice. It was hip, street-smart. Casual and cheery. It had an accent, spicy and Mexican. Then he appeared with a leap, dropping feathers and gnats along the way. He arrived at the foot of the bed and made his way on the sheets with the swagger of a drunken cowboy. Mostly featherless and very excited, Mr. Cock-A-Doodle-Do had come to be with Frida. His wattle was wrinkled, like the chin on an old man, and a dog had bitten off part of his beak. There were only three feathers on his tail, which shook ridiculously. Old

and ill-treated, the rooster was a portrait of Frida her-self, but there was no doubt he was alive, just like Frida.

"Is that you, Mr. Cock-A-Doodle-Do? What are you doing here?" asked an intrigued Frida. The bird stuck out its leg, then nestled into the sheets.

"I'm visiting my Friducha. What else would I be doing here? Listen, pretty girl, in hospitals we feathered types are only seen as possible cures; they say a good chicken broth cures a cold, a bellyache, and a lack of love. You know what I'm saying: chicken soup!"

Frida grimaced in an attempt to wink at him. The rooster pecked at the sheets.

"And you know how to talk?"

"And you, you know how to paint?"

"I learned. My father showed me, and I studied too. I continue studying."

"Me too, mija. Or did you think I'd hang out at your house for twenty years and all I'd learn was to eat corn and drink water? Even we chickens have aspirations. You know what I mean, kid! I make like I don't know anything, like I'm just a sax solo in a jazz band, but hanging out among painters, geniuses, communists, photographers, movie stars, and thieves—I'm sorry, I meant politicians—I was bound to pick something up from those sonsa— . . . sensible thinkers."

"You're not doing too badly. I mean, for a rooster," Frida acknowledged.

"You don't paint too badly either. You know, for an old lady," the rooster said, sniffing around Frida. He nodded in approval. "Or should I say, for a little deer?"

"I'm not a deer," Frida said.

"Well, you already have the horns that say you've been cheated on. Diego adds new ones every night." The rooster didn't need to remind her. It was obvious that Frida was an injured animal, suffering arrows through every muscle, bleeding.

She moved, a little nervous. She wanted to go running through a forest full of owls and radishes. She wanted to be free again, but the arrows had hit their mark and felled her. She began to lick her wounds. She was a little deer, in agony because she lived with Diego.

"So, how are you?" her rooster asked, curious.

"I could say I'm happy, but being completely fucked from my head to my toes really messes with me and makes me go through some very bitter moments."

"I see. And Diego's out there somewhere. That's good, right?"

Frida arched her brow. She didn't care for the insinuation, especially from a plucked rooster. She wasn't ready to give him that kind of leeway, especially while she was hospitalized.

"If you're making fun of me, it'd be better if you left."

"Oh, no! I'm not making fun of you. It's just that it's so obvious that every time you feel Diego getting away from you, you have a new pain. If the fat man is hanging out with some new babe, then a new operation pulls on his leash. Those damn illnesses have really good timing, don't they?"

"In the first place, I should tell you that I'm not even Diego's wife. It would be absurd to think like that," she responded curtly. Vinegar was collecting in her veins. "He always plays at marriage with other women, but Diego is nobody's husband and never will be. He might be more like a son, because that's how I love him. And to be clear, I'm not complaining that that's my role. I don't think the riverbanks are worse for letting the river run, or that the Earth suffers because it rains, or that the atom gets sick because it discharges energy. For me, everything has a very natural composition."

When Frida stopped talking, Mr. Cock-A-Doodle-Do was sobbing. A small puddle had grown around him. Chicken broth with onion and cilantro flowed from his eyes like tears.

"Stop! Stop! I'm melting. This is so, so sad. Not even Salvador Novo, with a dagger in his heart, could have said such idiotic things," he crowed.

He put an end to the dramatics. He spit out a chickpea that had gotten stuck in his throat and strolled toward the night table, where he picked up Frida's diary. He pushed back the last of his feathers, cleared his throat, and began to recite from the journal: "'I love Diego . . . and no one else. Diego, I'm lonely,'" he cried melodramatically. He turned various pages. "'My Diego, I'm not lonely anymore. You're here. You put me to sleep and wake me up. I'm going by myself. One absent moment. I steal you away and I leave, crying. It's a gas.'"

"Go away. No one asked you to come here. If I'd wanted a conscience, I would have asked for a goddamn cricket, not a fucking rooster," said Frida, irritated.

Mr. Cock-A-Doodle-Do came closer and pinched

her cheek. "Don't bitch. This is why we've come to this valley of tears. Remember: 'Tree of hope, stay strong.' I didn't say that; you did—the girl from Coyoacán, the Mexican princess. Oh, yeah!"

Frida's red eyes were boiling blood. She locked them on the rooster, her life's determinant. The day he stopped singing, she'd die. That was the deal. But no one had told her what a pain in the ass the rooster could be.

"Shut up."

"Let's be honest, my Friducha; things look like crap. Life's a bitch. We're on the final chapter. Why don't we just end it all and go rest? Think about it. No more suffering, no more infidelities. Just peace and tranquillity. Maybe a little tequila to kill the boredom," Mr. Cock-A-Doodle-Do proposed. He wasn't so bad after all—and he was right. It wasn't the pain that was killing her but the exhaustion from it.

"My Godmother sent you to tell me that?"

"No way! I don't even know the woman. I'm telling you this as your soul mate. I'm sick of life. I spend my time hanging out at the house, pecking with the hope of finding a worm or some stale bread. My greatest hope is to become mole sauce—now, that would be something!" said the bird.

He was pretty eloquent for a fowl, shrewd and clear, which was quite a contrast to a lot of the men Frida had known in her life.

"No, today more than ever, I'm not alone. I'm a communist. I've read my country's history and that of most of the world. I know about class conflict and economic problems. I understand Marx's dialectic materialism, as well as Engels, Lenin, Stalin, and Mao Tse-tung. There's a court of women around me as if I were a queen," she told him with determination.

"I have news for you: all your friends know you've suffered most of your life. You've dedicated yourself to producing the evidence in your paintings, pretty girl, but not a single friend shares your pain. Not even Diego. He knows how much you suffer, but that's different than suffering with you. They can't identify with you."

Again Frida's eyes boiled blood. Again the hatred. She closed her fists.

"Then what did you come for?"

"Just cook me up. The day after the big feast in which I'm the main dish, you'll rest. Good-bye to everything. Good-bye, my love!"

"No."

The rooster puffed up his chest and began singing the melancholy melody from "La Barca de Oro":

> *I'm leaving now*
> *for the port*
> *where the golden ship waits*
> *that's where I should go*
> *I'm leaving now*
> *I come only to say good-bye*
> *Good-bye, dear lady*
> *Good-bye forever, good-bye*
> *My eyes will not*
> *see you again*

nor will your ears
hear my song
I'm going to overflow
the oceans with my tears
Good-bye, dear lady
Good-bye forever, good-bye

Frida closed her eyes. It was tempting to turn him into mole sauce. But she wouldn't give in. Not today, not while Diego was away. He'd rented the room next to hers at the hospital and would spend the night there, away from his lovers. No tomorrow, no day after tomorrow. She'd hold on; she was stronger than Death. She closed her eyes and turned off her senses.

"What's wrong with her?" Mati asked the doctor when she saw Frida talking to herself.

The doctor took the patient's blood pressure while Cristi tried to comb her crazy hair into braids with rainbow-colored ribbons.

"She's delirious because of the morphine. She has hallucinations," said the doctor. Then he left, leaving Frida to be tended to by her sister and a nurse.

A bowl of tortilla soup steamed on the night table, waiting for Frida. The aroma of the chicken broth slowly but surely erased the stink of burnt food from the room. The vapors traveled down the hall to other patients, comforting them as well and underscoring the soup's healing properties. The smell of the consommé accompanied Frida for more than two days while she slept under sedation. The nurses found that she didn't put up a fight about eating; she drank the soup without complaint.

When she left the hospital, she merely exchanged one room for another. Little by little, she just stayed there, in her bed, nailed like Christ, not able to move. There was craziness in her eyes. She went sour, like a peach left in the fruit bowl. Rage swirled around her like clouds of flies on a corpse. She didn't ask for things, just made demands. She screamed as if she wanted to shut down the whole world, which went on without her and didn't care about her fate. She got impatient because she could no longer be who she'd been, because she was now a shadow of her former self. Her pictures reminded her that she was a caricature of the woman Diego had possessed at the foot of the volcanoes, a parody of the Mayan princess who had conquered the United States, a satire of the woman whose lovers had been leaders, artists, and painters.

She would drink two bottles of cognac a day, always followed by a dose of Demerol to ease her pain. The drugs played with her head, silencing her, dumbing her down. Even so, her hands reached for a brush that might satisfy her desire for art. Her brushstrokes on the canvas were dramatic and heart wrenching, like an open wound. Painting had become her religion, drugs her communion. It was an act of pity in the absence of a higher power. For her, divinity resided in people like Stalin or Mao. They were the ones who would save her from dementia. Her compositions were decrepit, her colors overly bright. She was aware of the darkness at the end of the tunnel, but she insisted on continuing to ride the light her art brought her. Even if it was just a little.

Frida couldn't be alone for long. Help was indispensable now, whether from a friend or a full-time nurse. One day Cristina arrived to take care of her and found her in her studio, painting in her wheelchair. She wasn't even a sliver of the beautiful Frida she remembered. Her hair was uncombed and she was wearing a torn skirt and a stained shirt, probably something Diego had thrown away. Her hands were bleeding because the pricking from her injections never healed anymore. Her fingers mixed blood and oil to smear on the canvas as her aimless eyes looked with resentment at her own face in the painting. Her work had ceased to be precise. Her strokes were now slashes in the air, as if she were trying to cut the canvas.

Cristi could see there was nothing left in her. She was a corpse clinging to the world of the living.

Tears couldn't ease the impotence of seeing her best friend destroying herself. She needed to deal with the despair that seeing her sister in such straits provoked in her. With the help of Manuel, a young man they'd hired as a driver, she got her back in bed. Frida just kept talking and painting ghosts in the air as Cristina combed out her hair. Cristina chose a red skirt for her and one of her famous low-cut blouses, one with green and red bands woven together. But when she saw Frida staring at her, she asked her what dress she wanted to wear.

"Put me in the one you've chosen, because that one's made with love. And there's no love here. You know that love is the only reason for living."

Frida was right. Even though she'd surrounded herself with things she loved, objects that signified love to her, and friends who loved her, there was no love left in her. Love had grown sparse, trickling away until it only lived in her memory.

TORTILLA SOUP

LA SOPA DE TORTILLA

Soup is the most handy meal in the history of humanity.

It's probably the first thing that humans cooked. I can just see those cave dwellers putting water over a fire and adding something to the pot. I'm sure it was an offering to the gods. Maybe they didn't understand fire, a storm, or anything else. But this was a way of becoming gods themselves. Soup allows so much variety, from the simplest broth to the most refined. It can be a meal in itself.

For me, tortilla soup is one of the most exquisite that we make in Mexico. It's like us: complex but simple; spicy but delicious; hot but refreshing. It's the perfect communion to understand what we're made of, why Mexico is what it is.

12 corn tortillas
Oil for frying
4 peeled tomatoes
1/2 onion, finely chopped
1 garlic clove, chopped
8 cups chicken broth
Salt
1 sprig parsley
1 sprig epazote
4 pasilla chiles, seeded and chopped
1 avocado, peeled and cubed
1/2 cup double cream cheese, cut into small
   cubes
Sour cream

✳ Cut the tortillas into long thin strips and fry them in hot oil. In a separate pan, fry the tomatoes in a tablespoon of oil, adding the onion and garlic. Cook for 5 minutes over low heat, then add half the chicken broth. Puree everything together. Return to the pot; add the rest of the broth, and add salt to taste. Add the parsley and epazote and cook for 20 minutes. Add the fried tortilla strips, the chiles, avocado, cheese, and sour cream.

CHAPTER XXIII

And so, on a night when the summer rains were stashed away, Frida received a visit from the Messenger. She offered him tequila and a snack and asked to see her Godmother, sure that she'd finally be rid of that constant pain that's known as life. To make sure that would be her last day, she asked her faithful cook, Eulalia, to kill Mr. Cock-A-Doodle-Do, who was so used to being spoiled and cared for that he never suspected that would also be his last day. For Frida, living longer than she was supposed to hadn't been pleasant. Her spine never stopped hurting, and her broken heart never healed.

"I'm very sorry, Mr. Cock-A-Doodle-Do, but little Frida has given the order," Manuel said before twisting the rooster's neck. Exactly as the recipe called for, they hung him to bleed out, then plucked what few feathers were left until his white skin was completely exposed. Later, Manuel placed him in a clay pot, the kind Frida liked to buy at the markets; it was decorated with a banner held up by two doves that said, "Frida loves Diego." He solemnly placed the pot in the kitchen, which always looked ready for a party with its blue tiles, and left the rooster there for Eulalia to perform one of her magic tricks.

Wiping her tears away with her apron, the cook brought out the spice containers and lined them up in a row. Later she arranged the silverware the way a surgeon does his instruments. She stared at the rooster's cadaver and felt such an emptiness in her chest that not even a hug from Manuel could console her. They were both on the edge of tears. There was something of the devil in that rooster; he'd been running around the patio at La Casa Azul since Mamá Matilde's death, and that was a long time for his species. When her tears were dry, Eulalia began the great culinary spectacle. She followed each step of the recipe in Frida's notebook until she turned Mr. Cock-A-Doodle-Do into a delicacy: a chicken trastamal with hierba santa.

Frida spent the day writing in her journal. The last few pages were covered with strange winged creatures. There were no self-portraits in any of her sketchbooks; she no longer had the looks or the will to conjure that spirit. Instead, she was consumed with trying to capture her Godmother's true face. She painted a black angel rising to the sky, the archangel of death. She didn't receive any friends that day, because she was waiting for a much more important visit. Only Diego came by in the afternoon. He sat down to chat with her.

"What have you been doing, girl of mine?" the

painter asked as his thick fingers stroked her bony hand.

"Sleeping most of the time, then thinking."

"And what are you thinking in that silly head of yours?"

"That we're just dolls, without a goddamn clue to what's really going on. We lie to ourselves with the stupid idea that we can control our own lives, then just play the role of being in love when we see a man, of eating when we're hungry, of sleeping when we're tired. And that's just a bunch of lies, because we don't have control of anything," Frida whispered without emotion.

Diego had no choice but to smile bitterly once he realized how lucid she was, in spite of her battered body.

"I have a gift for you, little Diego," Frida said slowly, slurring her words because of the narcotics.

Without letting go of her hand, Diego kissed her face and caressed her.

Frida handed him a ring she'd had made for his birthday. Silver and stone, as big as he was, excessive even for an ogre like Diego.

"You know I love you, don't you?" she whispered.

"Get some rest," Diego said, his tears about to drop.

His wife was dying. She was falling apart like a sandcastle at high tide. He lay in bed next to her and hugged her. They stayed that way for several hours. Convinced she was finally asleep, he went to work at his studio in San Ángel.

Then the curtains opened so the Messenger's white steed could enter the kingdom of darkness. Flames from innumerable candles placed everywhere leapt with joy and the bones in the tombs rattled to welcome Frida, who was riding on the horse. The Messenger stopped before a table set up like an altar to the dead in the midst of the grand feast. Frida dismounted and stepped away from her guide. The rebel, in a very dry but kind manner, said farewell with a nod of the head.

Before her was the most beautiful offering to the dead that she'd ever seen. The sugar skulls floated merrily, showing their sweet teeth. Their foreheads revealed the names of all the people she'd loved: Nick, Leon, Diego, Guillermo, Georgia . . . There were sugared breads-for-the-dead surrounded by bright and splendorous orange flowers. And there was also a menu consisting of the most delicious dishes from her own repertoire: Lupe's chiles rellenos, the dear doctor's ribs, Tina's tiramisu, ice cream from Tepozteco, Eva's apple pie, Mama Matilde's shortbread, the mole poblano from her wedding, Mati's soups, Covarrubias's pipián, and, in the place of honor, the tamale with hierba santa, steaming as if it were still in the pot.

"You called, and I'm here," said her Godmother, making her presence known amidst all the culinary delights that Frida had once offered her.

As always, a black veil covered her face, but now she wore pompous and elegant attire: a beautiful white European dress with white lace and frills that came to her neck. Her heart visibly beat like a drum. In the middle of the altar, on the clay pedestal with pre-Columbian motifs, a candle drowned in a puddle of multicolored wax.

Its tiny flame struggled against the cool air, proper to the dead, as it killed its agonized owner's last living breath.

Frida took a step, standing to her Godmother's right. She realized she was dressed in her tehuana clothes with their jungle and sky colors. She had a sash across her waist like the sunset in Cuernavaca.

"Am I finally dead?" she asked; upon asking, all her pain disappeared, leaving behind its fragile memory, like an echo of a past life.

"Not yet. You asked for an audience. Your life's pavilion is still lit, though it won't last long, just like your time on Earth. It's a matter of just a few breaths," her Godmother said, pointing to the flickering candle. "Come, sit down and drink with me; it's delightful to see you after all these years."

She poured tequila from a blue bottle that gave off airs of enchantment and perdition.

"Our deal was a disaster. Can you please tell me why you threw this shit at me, and why, if there was relief for my life, I couldn't have had it sooner?" asked Frida, enraged.

There was a lot accumulated from all those years of suffering—words saved up to be uttered at the precise moment of her death—but they'd come rushing out of her soul and she said them without thinking, which meant they were the truest of all. Her Godmother remained still as a queen, maintaining—more out of classiness than solemnity—the seriousness appropriate to all the titles given to her as the Lady of Death.

"You chose, not me."

"It was shitty," Frida said, even angrier.

It was a desperate cry. She didn't need to explain to her how she died every day, if not from illness, then from the pain of love. She had continued breathing each day, clinging to her painting as a balm for her soul, trying to keep her pain at bay; she'd paid a very high price for each day of living. She didn't need to explain it—no; her Godmother already knew.

"If you want to annul our deal, then it's annulled. You don't have to go on if you feel cheated. But don't try to cheat me. No one can cheat me," she warned with a stern voice. "No one can hide from me. Remember: my promise is a part of life itself."

Hearing her speak, Frida felt her chest become lighter, free of guilt; her body was more slender, her legs more agile: she was again Frida in the schoolgirl uniform and kneesocks. Frida in fringes, the girl torn apart by the train, pierced by a tube . . . the girl who died that day. On the altar, her flame had been transformed and sat atop an enormous white wax candle. Though she was young now, the dazzling flame was about to be replaced by a fine thread of black smoke.

"How can our deal be so easily undone? Is it really that simple? Wasn't it written in blood? Death can't be that understanding. I'm sure of that."

"Frida, anything can easily stop existing. I'm telling you this as an expert on the matter. But have no doubt that your actions have consequences, no matter how small. Every decision is part of your destiny."

"Aren't there supposed to be fireworks or firecrackers? This is absurd. You can't tell me that every-thing I've lived for can just disappear into the ether because you say so," said young Frida, but she was much more awed than disillusioned.

To her surprise, the same pair of monkeys who had originally welcomed her now came up. They screamed and made grotesque faces.

"The dancer is back! The dancer is here!"

At their side, the cardboard Judas and the sugar skull jumped with joy, as if she'd never left that weird episode she dreamed up when she got hit by the train.

"Frida, there are no pyrotechnics in death. You just die. It's simpler than you think," her Godmother ex-plained.

Frida kept quiet for a moment, considering the op-tion she was being given of dying in the accident, in her beloved Alex's arms. She had to try to imagine a world without Diego, without her painting, without constant pain. But she couldn't do it; it was all emptiness.

"If nothing I've lived has happened, if I never married Diego, if I was never in and out of hospitals, suffering with constant pain, then what happened to Diego? What hap-pened to my family?" she asked, frightened by the quaking in her own voice.

"People go on with their lives when you die. The clock doesn't stop for any mortal," said Death. "But if you have doubts, then here it is." And she offered her a shot of tequila.

Frida held it in her hands. She was afraid to drink it. Revelations, though fortifying, always hurt. Without another thought, she emptied the glass down her throat. But before the alcohol could reach her mind, the images began to appear.

Diego didn't look too bad. Thinner than usual, his skin toasted. The California sun was good for him, as was the house with long Spanish tile roofs that looked like Chinese hats. It was awe-inspiring in its size and splendor. Cypress trees surrounded the mansion. The woman in glasses wouldn't let go of her husband, the famous painter. She herself was something to behold: she still had the same beautiful body she'd had when she married Charlie Chaplin. Paulette Goddard had taken good care of her beauty so she could fulfill all her wishes. Husband and wife had breakfast out in the garden, letting the photographers capture a moment with the fashionable couple, just back from Europe, where Diego had painted a mural for the Michelin company. Diego spoke fluent English; since he'd begun to work in San Francisco, he'd never gone back to Mexico. The marriage to Paulette was his fourth, and it wouldn't be the last. Goddard treated him like captured prey that she could mount on her chimney—until they both found new lovers: for Diego, an up-and-coming blond starlet, and for Paulette, another impresario with whom to seek success.

Cristina, on the other hand, did not look well. The bruise on her eye didn't do her any favors. She was extremely thin. Her daughter, Isadora, helped her pick up the house, which was full of bourgeois touches. They worked in silence, terrified that Isadora's father would find out they hadn't finished their household chores. Antonio, her brother, hadn't survived his childhood fevers. They'd buried him next to Guillermo, who died two years after hearing about the tragic accident that killed his favorite daughter. Mamá Matilde had done everything to keep the family together, but Cristina hadn't been very smart in her decision making. She was condemned to be a battered wife, fearful of her husband's shadow. Sometimes she wanted to ask for help from her sister Matilde, but she'd have to do it on the sly, because her husband had forbidden that they have contact. They lived through their crises like all Mexican families: in silence. For them, life outside the home was alien. The newspapers talked about people who they'd never met in their lives. Personalities such as the Italian immigrant Tina Modotti, riddled with bullets when she went for a walk with her lover, the Cuban Socialist Julio Antonio Mella; or the famous socialist leader Leon Trotsky, poisoned by a Stalinist agent in Stockholm; or even Nickolas Muray, a photographer whose work always appeared in fashion magazines—he was successful and cosmopolitan. (Sadly, sometimes lives are exactly the same.)

No, all of that was alien to the Kahlo family, as was the case with art, whether bourgeois or elite. In fact, all of that was unknown to most Mexican families, for whom the price of tortillas was more important than the socialist manifesto about painting. In that place, there was no time for great artists, only conspiracies and deals to line up behind the next candidate in the democratic

farce that was the official party. There were no muralists, because all the great painters had decided to develop their careers far from a country that was hostile to
culture, where educational achievement was measured
by the number of speeches given to hungry workers
lorded over by corrupt unions. That's how the Kahlo
family lived from day to day, in the innocent realm of
unimportance and the comforting idea that, to feel nationalism, it wasn't necessary to cover a canvas with
colors like watermelon, mango, lemon, soursop, and
pitaya red.

"It hurts to see this. It must be a curse to be able to
see everything like this," sobbed Frida, a little dizzy from
the slap of reality that she'd just experienced.

"Dear, I'm neither cursed nor blessed. I'm just me
and my work is like anyone's. For some I'm a good thing,
for others an abomination. In the end, I'm the same for
everyone," said her Godmother.

"I can't leave them like that. The emptiness is agoniz-
ing. It's bigger than any physical pain I felt in my life. If I
have to go back and suffer my illnesses, calamities, and
shame one by one to keep things on track, then I have to
go on with our deal."

"You'd live it all again? Even knowing how much
pain you'd suffer? Remember, nothing will be different.
You already know what's to come," said the sovereign.

Frida merely nodded. She looked so childish, so innocent. It wasn't the dry and angry Frida that was being
consumed in La Casa Azul. This was a Frida who wanted
very much to live.

"What will guarantee that all I live isn't just an image like what you just showed me? Could it be that what I lived was just an illusion, just so I wouldn't accept the deal to surrender to Death? Your tricks are hard to figure out."

"Even I can't guarantee that your life wasn't just a figment of your imagination. If that's what it was, and you want to try again, it won't change in any way. You'll simply suffer the same indignities twice. You'll retake the same road. You'll make the same decisions. You'll run up against the same walls," Death said.

Frida understood, though her heart trembled at the idea of enduring the same pain and passion if she lived again, even if the first time had been an illusion offered by her Godmother.

"Why did you choose me? Why me? I'm not anyone for you to offer an opportunity like this. I'm a woman like any other. I don't see anything great in me."

"All women are great. Every one is my goddaughter by her birthright. Just as I have the gift of death, you have the gift of life. The reason it's you is in you. Because you're Frida, and there's only one Frida. There's no reason more powerful than that," said her Godmother, who then asked her to sit by her side. "Are you ready to live again?"

Death extended her hand, which held a surgical pincer ready to open the artery connected to her heart.

Before she took it from her, Frida said, "Before I go and live my destiny again, I want to see your real face."

The woman removed her veil. Frida the tehuana took

the hand of her Godmother, who was Frida the Dead, and connected the artery to her heart so that it would beat again. The flame on the altar candle leapt up, consuming the wax and lighting the entire place by itself. Frida saw it was her own face behind the black veil. It was just as she'd explained: she was the end, but each woman was the beginning. The two gazed at one another. Frida found herself, her heart healed, bleeding for the life she'd have to suffer through again. Just before waking, she contemplated the two Fridas in all their splendor.

"Are you awake now, dear? This is a good sign. Stay calm so you can rest a little," the Red Cross nurse told her. Frida was living through her first accident, on the bus. Before she lost her memory of what had just happened with her Godmother, it occurred to her that she still had to survive her worst accident: Diego.

TAMALE WITH HIERBA SANTA

TAMAL DE CAZUELA EN HIERBA SANTA

1 pound masa harina for tamales
1 cup chicken broth

12 ounces lard

2 sprigs hierba santa

Salt

1 tablespoon baking powder

3 ground chiles (ancho, mulato, or pasilla),
    seeded, roasted, and ground

1 roasted tomato, seeded and ground

8 ounces shredded chicken

❋ Mix the flour with the chicken broth until it's like a thick drink. Melt the lard and add it to the mixture. Add part of the hierba santa and salt. Cook over low heat, stirring continuously, until it's so thick that when a spoon is introduced, it comes out clean. Remove from the heat and beat until the mixture turns white. Add the baking powder, integrating it completely into the masa. Separately, prepare a mole with the chiles, tomato, more hierba santa, and salt. Add the chicken to the mole. In a pot, lay down a layer of masa, then a layer of mole, then another layer of masa, thicker than the first. Bake in the oven at 375°F until it's golden on top.

CHAPTER XXIV

At four in the morning, Frida complained in a sleepy voice; a candle with a short wick went out. The nurse who was taking care of her calmed her with soft caresses on her hand, straightened out the sheets so she could continue sleeping, and stayed at her side, like a mother who watches a newborn's sleep.

The nurse dozed off and was startled awake when she heard the bells ringing. There was a knock on the door of La Casa Azul at six in the morning. She went to see if someone dared open the door. While Manuel got up to answer, she realized Frida's eyes were open, fixed, her gaze aimless. Her hands were on the sheets, like a doll playing at sleep. She touched her hands: they were ice-cold.

Manuel didn't find a living soul on the other side of the door. The street was empty but for a horseman on his white steed, making his way on the cobblestone streets, leaving behind just the echo of the horse's hooves.

When he came back in the house, the nurse gave him the news and he shot out to San Ángel, where Diego had gone to spend the night.

"Señor Diego, our Frida has died."

The coffin with Frida Kahlo's remains was placed in the hall at the Palace of Fine Arts. Friends, artists, politicians, and people who admired her came to the wake. In the madness of the moment and deeply in pain, Diego gave permission for the coffin to be wrapped in a red flag with the hammer and sickle, thinking that Frida would have been proud of that decision. An honor guard watched over her body for one day and one night.

With a procession of more than five hundred people trailing the funeral party, the coffin went up and down the streets of Mexico City, the city Frida so loved. When they arrived at the crematorium, there was one more farewell ceremony; later, Frida's body was incinerated.

That evening, clouds began to appear, darkening the city's skies. Saddened by the death of the Aztec princess, they rained their contents down on the streets, making the mourners' loss even greater. The pain was so profound, it seemed as if she had died twice.

Young Covarrubias, Juanito O'Gorman, Frida's sisters Cristina and Matilde, the Fridos, and her friends and acquaintances were all distressed. Tears were shed even in faraway lands: in a corner of Europe, the dear doctor cried for more than two hours as he steered his boat, sailing without a clue as to how lost he'd gotten; Nicko-las Muray felt an enormous impulse to look at the pho-tographs he'd taken of his former lover; Madame Clare, the editor of *Vanity Fair*, shut herself up in her office and re-created the moment of Dorothy Hale's suicide; Nel-son Rockefeller stopped his philosophizing to campaign for the presidency and, after taking a bite of a mole po-blano in a meeting with a labor leader, began sobbing so intensely, he had to cancel the meeting; and Lucienne, Diego's former assistant who'd helped Frida after the miscarriage, tried to sculpt the Aztec princess that Frida personified.

All of that anguish fell on Diego when he returned to Coyoacán. He silently remembered all the times he'd made her cry. He and Manuel just stared ahead on the way home while tears rolled down his cheeks. The bag with Frida's ashes was at his side, where she would have normally been instead.

When the car arrived at La Casa Azul, Diego was tired and hungry. He went in, only to find the animals screaming because of their master's absence. He headed toward Frida's room. He sat by her bed, carefully plac-ing the bag of ashes on it. He stared at it for a few min-utes until his nose brought him back to reality and his stomach jumped when he sniffed the meal by the side of the bed. It was a huge piece of tamale with hierba santa, served in the clay pot with the banner on the side with a romantic phrase held up by a pair of doves. Fri-da's worn notebook was next to the dish. It smelled of chicken, green chile, and exotic spices all blended together. After he put the notebook away in one of the boxes that would just accumulate dust until somebody discovered it, he took the plate and stuck the fork in the tamale. He ate in silence, savoring each bite, letting the juices excite his palate and the flavor comfort his soul. When he'd filled his belly, he felt an incredible peace that he'd never enjoy again.

Suddenly he dropped the fork and sobbed. His lament drew Eulalia's attention. She went to console him. Diego chewed and whimpered. Eulalia stopped at the door. When Diego saw her, he gave her a sad smile.

"She cooked for me and, like always, it was delicious," he said sadly. He took another piece from the plate and ate it little by little. Then he finished the last bite.

"Frida's gone away," he said, "and I never got a chance to tell her how much I liked hierba santa."

In 1957, Diego Rivera died from cardiac arrest.

He was buried in the Rotonda de los Hombres Ilustres, a memorial park for illustrious men in Mexico City, which actually contradicted his final wishes: to have his ashes mixed with Frida's, which were kept in an urn at La Casa Azul in Coyoacán. His daughters and wife refused to carry out his wishes, convinced it was better for Mexico for him to be buried in the Rotonda, where he remains, very far from his beloved Frida.

In 1958, La Casa Azul opened to the public as the Frida Kahlo Museum. Since its opening, every November 2 there's an altar for the dead featuring all sorts of dishes, arrangements, and photographs in honor of the love shared by Frida and Diego and their friends.

"The Hierba Santa Book" is still missing.

RECIPES

The following recipes from the book were adapted and edited for you to make at home. We hope that you and your book club enjoy these Frida Kahlo–inspired recipes.

Pico de Gallo

(Adapted from the recipe appearing on page 10)

This makes quite a large amount, but you can easily scale the recipe back. If you'd prefer, this can be seasoned with ground dried chiles instead of the fresh green chiles.

　　1 pound prickly pear cactus paddles (nopales)
　　2 cups peeled and finely diced jicama (about 1 pound)
　　4 large juicy oranges, peeled and chopped
　　2 cups finely diced green (unripe) mango (2 large or
　　　　3 small)
　　2 cups peeled, seeded, and finely diced cucumbers
　　　　(2 medium)
　　2 cups finely diced pineapple (½ pineapple)
　　2 bunches scallions, sliced

4 green chiles, minced (leave in the ribs and seeds if
   you like heat)
Juice of 6 limes
1 tablespoon coarse salt

1. With the tip of a small sharp knife, scrape off the
   cactus spines and the little brown nodes they are
   attached to. On the outer edge of the paddle, at
   the top, use a knife or scissors to cut off the cluster
   of spines instead of trying to scrape them off. Cut
   off the end of the paddle where it was attached to
   the cactus. Cut the paddles into ¼-inch dice.

2. In a large deep saucepan, bring 2 quarts of well-
   salted water to a boil. (The reason for the depth of
   the saucepan is that the cactus exudes a sticky gel
   that can cause the pan to boil over.) Add the diced
   cactus and boil until tender, about 20 minutes. Drain
   and rinse under cold water.

3. In a large bowl, toss together the cactus, jicama, oranges, mangoes, cucumbers, pineapple, scallions,
   and chiles. Stir in the lime juice and salt.

❋ *Makes about 12 cups*

Herb-Baked Basket Cheese
Queso panela horneado

(Adapted from the recipe appearing on page 12)

This dish is particularly good as an appetizer, accompanied by tostadas or slices of bread.

>1 large garlic clove, coarsely chopped
>¼ cup coarsely chopped cilantro
>¼ cup coarsely chopped parsley
>¼ cup coarsely chopped basil
>1 tablespoon fresh oregano leaves
>½ cup olive oil
>1 round (12 ounces) queso panela
>   (Mexican "basket" cheese)
>Pepper

1. In a mini chopper, combine the garlic, cilantro, parsley, basil, and oregano and pulse to finely chop. Add the olive oil and process to combine.

2. Season the cheese on both sides with pepper. Pour about ¼ cup of the herb mixture into a glass or ceramic baking dish just a little larger than the cheese. Place the cheese on top of the herb mixture and pour the remaining herb mixture over the cheese. Let marinate at room temperature for 6 hours.

3. Preheat the oven to 350°F. Bake the cheese until it is hot and begins to melt, about 20 minutes. Serve hot (the cheese will harden as it cools).

❋ *Serves 6 to 8*

Pumpkin Tamales
Tamales de calabaza

(Adapted from the recipe appearing on page 24)

Making tamales is labor-intensive, but if you have lots of helping hands available, double or triple this recipe.

4 ounces dried corn husks
Boiling water
2 cups masa harina
1 teaspoon baking soda
1 teaspoon salt
⅓ cup lard
8 ounces pie pumpkin or kabocha squash, peeled, seeded, and finely chopped
4 ounces Oaxaca string cheese or mozzarella, finely chopped
1 small handful epazote leaves (no stems), finely chopped
1 red jalapeño chile, finely chopped

1. Place the corn husks in a heatproof bowl, cover with boiling water, and let soak for at least 30 minutes to make them pliable. In another bowl, stir 2 cups hot water into the masa harina; beat with a wooden spoon until completely blended. Set aside for 30 minutes to cool.

2. Dissolve the baking soda and salt in ¼ cup water. In a bowl, with an electric mixer, beat the lard and baking soda mixture together until well blended and thick (it will look like mayonnaise). With the mixer on, add the masa dough by handfuls until completely blended.

3. In a bowl, combine the pumpkin, cheese, epazote, and chile.

4. Place a corn husk on a work surface with the wide end facing you. Spread 3 tablespoons of the masa mixture over the wide end of the husk, leaving a 1-inch margin at the bottom and at least a ¾-inch margin on the two sides (more than a ¾-inch margin is fine). Place 1 generous tablespoon of the pumpkin mixture down the center of the masa. Bring up the two long sides of the husk to force the masa to enclose the filling, then roll up tightly the long way. Fold down the narrow tip to meet the wide bottom edge. The packet should stay closed on its own, but some cooks choose to tie it closed with a strip of corn husk.

5. In a vegetable steamer or a steamer insert for a spaghetti pot, pack in the tamales open end up. Steam for 1½ hours. The tamales are done when the husk can easily be peeled off. Replenish the boiling water as necessary. (Mexican cooks put a coin in the bottom of the pot to alert them when the steamer has boiled dry; when the clinking stops, the pot has run out of water.) Let the tamales sit for 10 minutes before serving.

✱ *Makes 24 tamales*

Horchata

(Adapted from the recipe appearing on page 38)

This is refreshing served over ice.

 1¾ cups long-grain white rice (about 12 ounces)
 2 cinnamon sticks
 2 cups milk
 Sugar

1. In a bowl, combine the rice and 3 cups water. Let the rice soak for least 2 hours (overnight is fine too).

2. Break up the cinnamon sticks and toast in an ungreased skillet until fragrant; take care not to burn them.

3. Drain the rice and transfer to a blender. Add the toasted cinnamon and milk and set the blender at the highest setting to pulverize the rice.

4. Strain the rice through a fine-mesh sieve into a pitcher, pressing on the solids to extract as much rice milk as possible; discard the rice. Stir in 4 cups water. Sweeten with sugar to taste.

❋ *Makes 7 to 8 cups*

Day of the Dead Bread
Pan de muerto

(Adapted from the recipe appearing on page 62)

½ cup sugar, plus extra for decorating
¼ cup powdered milk
2 envelopes active dry yeast
2 teaspoons grated orange zest
½ teaspoon aniseed, crushed
½ teaspoon salt
7 tablespoons butter, cut into pieces, plus 2 teaspoons
    for decorating

4 large eggs

5½ cups all-purpose flour

Egg wash: 1 large egg yolk beaten with 2 teaspoons
water

1. In a stand mixer, with the paddle attachment, combine the sugar, powdered milk, yeast, orange zest,
aniseed, and salt. Mix together.

2. In a small saucepan, combine the 7 tablespoons butter and ¾ cup water. Heat over medium-low heat
just until the butter has melted (do not let boil).

3. With the mixer running, add the melted butter mixture to the sugar mixture to blend. Add the eggs and
1½ cups of the flour and beat well. Add 3 more cups
flour, bit by bit, until the dough starts to come together. It will be sticky.

4. Turn the dough out onto a floured surface. Knead
in as much of the remaining 1 cup flour as needed
until the dough is smooth and elastic; the dough
should still be a bit sticky. Knead for 1 or 2 minutes more, flouring the board as needed. Place the
dough in a greased bowl, cover, and set aside in a
draft-free place to rise until doubled in bulk, about
1½ hours.

5. Punch the dough down and divide into 2 equal pieces. Cut off one-fourth of each piece of dough and set aside. Roll the larger pieces of dough between yours hands into 2 large balls and place on a baking sheet lined with parchment paper.

6. With the smaller reserved pieces of dough, make the "bones" and "skulls" for the bread. Divide each piece of dough into quarters (a total of 8 pieces). Roll 6 pieces into ropes about 6 inches long for the "bones." Pinch the rope in several places to make it look as if it has knuckles (like a skeleton's finger bone). Roll the remaining 2 pieces of dough into 12 marble-sized balls to represent skulls.

7. Drape 3 bones in a spoke pattern across the top of each loaf. Place a "skull" in the spaces between the bones. Cover with a towel and let rise until almost doubled, about 45 minutes. Meanwhile, position a rack in the center of the oven and preheat to 350°F.

8. Brush the loaves all over with the egg wash and bake until nicely browned on the outside and the loaves sound hollow when thumped on the bottom, 30 to 35 minutes.

9. Meanwhile, melt the remaining 2 teaspoons butter.

10. When the loaves are done, transfer them to racks set over a baking sheet. Brush with the melted butter and sprinkle generously with sugar. Let cool completely.

✳ *Makes 2 loaves*

Mexican Chicken Soup
Caldo de pollo

(Adapted from the recipe appearing on page 73)

The soup is served with whole pieces of bone-in chicken, so cut the chicken into serving sizes that will be manageable; for example, cut the breasts in half.

1 whole chicken (3½ pounds), cut into serving pieces
1 celery stalk, cut crosswise into 8 pieces
1 small onion, quartered
2 garlic cloves, peeled
2 allspice berries
Salt
2 potatoes (unpeeled, about 8 ounces each),
   quartered lengthwise
4 large carrots, cut into 2 or 3 pieces each
½ cup long-grain white rice
Chopped cilantro, chopped onions, and tortilla chips,
   to garnish

2 limes, cut into wedges
1 serrano chile, minced

1. In a large pot, combine the chicken, celery, onion, garlic, and allspice. Add 10 cups water and season well with salt. Bring to a boil.

2. Add the potatoes, carrots, and rice. Reduce to a simmer, cover, and cook until the vegetables are tender and the rice is cooked through, 15 to 20 minutes.

3. Serve topped with cilantro, onions, and tortilla chips. Pass the lime wedges and minced chile on the side.

❋ *Makes 8 servings*

Mole Poblano

(Adapted from the recipe appearing on page 97)

This makes enough for a whole chicken. If you want to make turkey mole, double the ingredients.

1 whole chicken (4 pounds), cut into serving pieces
Salt
1 large plum tomato

3 dried chipotle chiles, stemmed

6 mulato chiles, stemmed, ribbed, and seeded (reserve
   1 teaspoon of the seeds)

6 pasilla chiles, stemmed, ribbed, and seeded (reserve
   1 teaspoon of the seeds)

5 ancho chiles, stemmed, ribbed, and seeded (reserve
   1 teaspoon of the seeds)

¾ teaspoon aniseed

½ teaspoon ground cloves or 5 whole cloves

½ teaspoon coriander seeds

½ teaspoon ground black pepper

1 cinnamon stick, broken up

2 ounces (²⁄₃ cup) sesame seeds

¾ cup lard

4 ounces (generous ¾ cup) almonds

½ cup raisins

1 green plantain, peeled and sliced

2 stale corn tortillas, cut into quarters

1 small dinner roll (about 2 ounces), split

1 onion, sliced

3 garlic cloves, peeled

2 ounces (²⁄₃ cup) peanuts

1½ tablets (3.1 ounces each) Mexican chocolate,
   divided into wedges

Sugar

1. Combine the chicken, 8 cups water, and salt to taste in a large saucepan. Bring to a boil. Reduce to a simmer, cover, and cook until the chicken is cooked through, about 20 minutes. Transfer the

chicken to a platter and cover. Strain and reserve the broth.

2. Meanwhile, cut an X into the skin of the tomato at one end. In a medium pot of boiling water, cook the tomato for 45 seconds to 1 minute to loosen the skin (it should start to peel back from the X). Rinse under cold water, then peel and chop. Set aside.

3. In a small spice grinder, combine the reserved chile seeds, the aniseed, cloves, coriander, pepper, cinnamon, and ⅓ cup of the sesame seeds and grind to a powder.

4. Bring a large saucepan of water to a boil. In a Dutch oven, heat ½ cup of the lard over medium heat. Working in batches, add the chiles and fry on both sides. With tongs, transfer the chiles (shaking off as much fat as possible) to the boiling water. Let them simmer gently to soften while you fry the remaining ingredients.

5. In the same Dutch oven, heat the lard again. Each of the following ingredients should be cooked individually and transferred with a slotted spoon to the same big bowl. Cook the almonds until golden. Cook the raisins until they plump up. Cook the plantain until golden. Cook the tortillas until golden. Cook the roll until golden, then tear into pieces. Cook the onion and garlic until softened.

6. Add the chopped tomato, peanuts, and spice mixture to the bowl and toss to distribute the spices. Drain the chiles and add them to the bowl.

7. Working in small batches, puree the mole mixture in a food processor, using just enough chicken broth to blend the ingredients and get them as smooth as possible, but the mixture should be a thickish paste, not soupy.

8. Heat the remaining ¼ cup lard in the Dutch oven and add the mole paste to it. Heat gently and add the chocolate and 1 cup of broth, stirring until the chocolate is melted. Continue adding chicken broth until the mole is of a coating consistency (it should thickly coat the back of a spoon). Let the sauce simmer for about 20 minutes; thin with more broth if it gets too thick. Season with salt and sugar to taste.

9. Add the cooked chicken and turn to coat. Cook just to heat through. Serve sprinkled with the remaining ⅓ cup sesame seeds.

✳ *Makes 8 to 10 servings*

Mango Tepozteco Ice Cream
Nieve de mango de Tepozteco

(Adapted from the recipe appearing on page 123)

2 pounds Ataulfo (Champagne) mangoes (about 5)
3 tablespoons light brown sugar
½ teaspoon grated lime zest
2 tablespoons lime juice
¼ cup crema mexicana or sour cream, lightly whipped
1 egg white, beaten to soft peaks

1. Peel the mangoes and remove all the pulp from the seed, leaving nothing behind. Chop the pulp. Set aside ¼ cup (to give the ice cream some texture) and transfer the remainder to a blender.

2. Add ½ cup water, the brown sugar, lime zest, and lime juice to the blender and puree. Pour the mixture into the canister of an ice cream maker. Fold in the crema and beaten egg white. Freeze according to the manufacturer's directions.

3. When done churning, remove the dasher and fold in the reserved chopped mango. Cover and freeze for 12 hours. Remove from the freezer 30 minutes before serving.

✳ *Makes 5 cups*

Tequila Pork Loin
Lomo al tequila

(Adapted from the recipe appearing on page 253)

2¼ pounds pork loin
12 pitted manzanilla or other green olives, sliced
½ jalapeño chile, cut into thin strips
½ small red bell pepper, cut into thin strips
4 garlic cloves, minced
Black pepper
1 cup tequila reposado
1 tablespoon cold butter
1 tablespoon all-purpose flour

1. Preheat the oven to 350°F.

2. With a sharp knife, make a lengthwise horizontal cut into the pork loin halfway down from the top, cutting almost to but not through the far side. Open the pork up like a book. Arrange the olives, jalapeño, and bell pepper over one side of the pork. Close the pork back up and secure with toothpicks or tie in several places with kitchen string. Rub the outside with the garlic and season with black pepper to taste.

3. Place the pork in a small roasting pan with 1 cup water. Cover with foil and roast for 45 minutes. Uncover, pour the tequila into the bottom of the pan,

and roast until the pork is cooked through but still juicy, 20 to 30 minutes.

4. Transfer the pork to a cutting board to rest for 10 minutes before slicing.

5. Meanwhile, in a small bowl, blend the butter and flour together with your fingers. Place the roasting pan over medium-low heat and stir to incorporate the meat juices. Add pieces of the butter-flour mixture and stir to melt. Then cook, stirring, at a simmer until the gravy thickens slightly. Pour the gravy into a sauceboat.

❋ *Makes 4 to 6 servings*

Quesadillas from Coyoacán

(Adapted from the recipe appearing on page 298)

2 cups masa harina
½ cup all-purpose flour
1½ teaspoons baking powder
3 tablespoons lard
8 ounces Oaxaca string cheese or mozzarella, shredded
Shortening, for deep-frying
1 cup crema mexicana or crème fraîche

1. In a medium bowl, with an electric mixer, combine the masa harina and 1⅓ cups hot water and beat well.

2. Beat in the all-purpose flour, baking powder, and lard. You should have a nonsticky but very soft dough.

3. Divide the dough into 12 equal portions (about 2 ounces each). Form a portion into a flat oval about 2 inches wide. In a tortilla press or with a rolling pin, press (or roll) the dough between 2 sheets of plastic wrap into a thickish tortilla about 5 inches across. Carefully peel off the plastic wrap and transfer the dough to a work surface. Top one half with about 2 tablespoons of cheese, fold the dough over, and carefully seal the turnover.

4. In a heavy Dutch oven, melt enough shortening to get a depth of 1 inch. Heat the shortening to 375°F. Add 2 or 3 quesadillas at a time (don't crowd) and cook until the dough is cooked through, the cheese has melted, and the outside is golden, about 2 minutes per side. Drain on paper towels.

5. Serve with the crema.

❋ *Makes 12 quesadillas*

Drunken Salsa
Salsa borracha

(Adapted from the recipe appearing on page 299)

The authentic version of this recipe calls for pulque, which is an alcoholic drink made from fermented maguey cactus. If you can find it, use it in place of the beer called for here.

> 7 ounces pasilla chiles (about 25), stemmed, ribbed, and seeded
> Boiling water
> 2 garlic cloves, coarsely chopped
> 2 cups beer
> ¾ cup olive oil
> 6 pickled green chiles, diced
> 2 small onions, diced
> Salt
> 4 ounces cotija cheese (queso añejo), coarsely grated

1. Preheat a large heavy skillet. Place 4 or 5 chiles at a time in the skillet and toast just until the aroma is released, 30 to 60 seconds; take care not to burn them. Place the chiles in a heatproof bowl and cover with boiling water. Set aside to soften for 30 minutes.

2. Drain the softened chiles and transfer to a food processor. Add the garlic and process to a paste. Add the beer and oil and process to a thick sauce.

3. Transfer to a bowl and stir in the chiles and onions. Season with salt to taste. Serve with the cheese sprinkled on top.

❋ *Makes 5½ cups*

The Secret Book of Frida Kahlo

F. G. Haghenbeck

A Readers Club Guide

Introduction

In *The Secret Book of Frida Kahlo*, F. G. Haghenbeck takes readers on a magical journey through Frida Kahlo's life. After nearly dying in a trolley accident at eighteen, Frida makes a deal with Death to live. Her injuries from the accident pain and haunt her for the rest of her life, and to keep up her end of the deal Frida must offer exquisite delicacies to the dead every year on the Mexican holiday the Day of the Dead. Her recipes are kept in a mysterious black notebook, El Libro de Hierba Santa—"The Hierba Santa Book."

Based on known events of her life, this fictional reimagining is an intriguing ride that delves into Frida's mind and follows her from lover to lover while also exploring her painting, complex personality, lust for life, and existential feminism.

QUESTIONS AND TOPICS FOR DISCUSSION

1. The novel begins when Frida is close to the end of her life. Why do you think Haghenbeck chose to order the narrative this way? How does beginning the story with death affect the rest of the novel?

2. Early in her life Frida suffered from polio and endured the consequences of the illness for years to come. Reread the story Guillermo tells Frida while she is ill. At the end Frida asks him, "Do you think Death wants to be my Godmother and save me

from this illness?" (22) How would you respond to Frida? Does the story Guillermo tell Frida as a girl relate to Frida's own story with Death?

3. Immediately before Frida dies "for the first time" in the bus accident, "the rebel from her childhood" appears on his horse and greets Frida "with a slight tip of his hat." (47) Who is this "rebel," or Messenger, and when else does he appear in the novel? What does he represent for Frida, and how do her feelings about him change or develop over time?

4. After the accident Frida must convince her Godmother to allow her to continue living. What is Frida's deal with Death? What would you do if you were offered a similar deal? Discuss what you think about the warning Frida's Godmother gives her before she wakes up: "You will always wish you'd died today. And I will remind you of this every day of your life." (61) At the end of her life, does Frida regret living past this first death?

5. As her injuries from the accident heal, Frida begins a painting for her Godmother. This self-portrait is the first of many paintings in Frida's artistic career. How do Frida's spiritual turmoil and physical affliction affect her art and career?

6. While both Frida and Diego Rivera have fleeting affairs throughout their time together, they have

a bond with each other that persists and reignites even after their divorce. How does their relationship survive?

7. Cooking plays an important role in the story and in Frida's life. She learns to cook from both her mother and Diego's ex-wife, Lupe, and she passes her skills on to others throughout her life. Discuss the significance of cooking and food in Mexican culture. Each chapter ends with a recipe or two that relates to the preceding chapter. What is the significance of the recipes for Frida? What do they add to the story and to your reading experience?

8. On a trip to Tepozteco, a guide tells Frida and Diego stories from his town. A story about the grief-stricken maiden, La Llorona, has a profound effect on Frida. When else in the novel does La Llorona appear? How do you interpret the dream Frida has later that night about the woman in the veil?

9. Frida is in a constant struggle to continue living her painful life. Why does she choose this painful life over an easy death? Think about the words "Have the courage to live, because anyone can die." (7, 95, 129) How do you interpret this maxim?

10. Throughout her life, Frida lives in many different cities, but she is always most at home in Coyoacán, especially in the home where she grew up: "La Casa

Azul was Frida herself." (3) What do you think this line means? How does each city she visits (Mexico City, San Francisco, Detroit, New York City, and Paris) affect Frida?

11. Frida is a strong woman whom many people admire, but her physical ailments torment her constantly. Despite her struggles, eventually she understands "her true nature as a truly singular woman." (212) Who is Frida Kahlo? How is she characterized and portrayed in the novel? How do other people in her life see her? Are their impressions of her different from how she sees herself?

11. As an advocate for the Mexican Communist Party, Frida becomes involved with politics and political people early in her life. How does growing up amidst a revolution affect Frida? How do politics continue to impact Frida throughout her life? Leon Trotsky tells her that he can think of only "two artistic phenomena: works that reflect the revolution and works that, while not thematically linked to the revolution, are imbued with a new consciousness derived from the revolution. That's where your work falls." (226) How does his view compare with Frida's art?

12. Frida is a unique woman who meets many interesting and important people throughout her life. What does she learn or gain from her affairs

and interactions with these larger-than-life characters? Consider Georgia O'Keeffe, Nelson Rockefeller, Ernest Hemingway, Leon Trotsky, Anaïs Nin, Henry Miller, and Salvador Dali.

13. In Paris, Frida plays a game called Exquisite Corpse at a surrealist gathering. (266) When the figure is complete, everyone sees the image as ridiculous except for Frida. Think about Frida's description of the image. Why does she feel it is a postcard from Death?

ENHANCE YOUR BOOK CLUB

1. Look up one of your favorite Frida Kahlo paintings and find a passage in the novel that you feel relates to the painting. Discuss how the aesthetic of the painting aligns with Haghenbeck's reimagining of Frida's life.

2. Host a Day of the Dead celebration! Cook one of the recipes found at the back of the book, and recreate one of Frida's delicious feasts.

3. F. G. Haghenbeck's novel is fiction, but it tells the story of Frida Kahlo's real life. To learn what is fact and what is imagination, compare nonfiction accounts, and share your findings with your book club members.